With Hope, Farewell

With Hope, Farewell

Alexander Baron

Five Leaves Publications

With Hope, Farewell
Alexander Baron

Published in 2019 by Five Leaves Publications
14a Long Row, Nottingham NG1 2DH
www.fiveleaves.co.uk
www.fiveleavesbookshop.co.uk

First published in 1952 by Cape

ISBN: 978-1-910170-65-6

Printed in Great Britain

1928

1928

1

Mark opened his eyes and looked up at a strange ceiling. The paper was puffy and loose, yellowing in patches. He felt frightened. He moved his head cautiously. The wooden bedstead was a strange one, and the mattress hard. He relaxed, contented, as the fog of sleep cleared and memory returned. He sat up, pushing the blankets down about his knees and picking with one finger at the corner of his right eye to get rid of the gritty feeling.

'Mickey.' His voice was hoarse and frightening; he did not recognise it. He called again; not too loudly, for he did not want to wake their parents, who were sleeping in the next room. 'Mickey.'

His brother, in the other bed against the opposite wall, turned over suddenly towards him and flung out an arm dramatically.

'Mickey. Getting up? Coming down the front?' But the movement had been deceptive. Mickey writhed down into the blankets again; he was still asleep.

Mark sighed, loudly, and made a face indicative of resignation. His fright at waking up in a strange room had vanished. The room was full of sunlight. The breeze, bearing a faint and tantalising tang of salt, was stirring the curtains. Excitement stirred in his stomach; at last they were at the seaside.

He swung his legs out of the bed and put his feet down on to the cold linoleum. The sensation was agreeable. He stood up and turned towards his brother's bed. He made his face look mischievous; he was always acting a part, self-consciously, making the appropriate face. Sometimes he practised in front of a mirror. 'Come away,' his mother had said once, pulling him away from the mirror; 'you're too old for your age. A boy of ten behaving like that!' Mark was only half aware of the habit. When he was among people, even his own family, he was always ill-at-ease; he did not know how to look or to behave; therefore the set of ready-made expressions, to be worn protectively for each appropriate occasion. Now he was out for mischief, still self-conscious; to leap on his brother and startle him out of his sleep, to tear the blankets off and buffet him with the pillow; as they did in the two-penny boys' weeklies. But, poised by the side of his brother's bed, he changed his mind; better to wash and dress quietly, then to awaken Mickey and deride him for lying abed.

He tiptoed to the wash-stand and poured cold water into the china bowl. He took off his pyjama jacket and washed quietly. Water-pipes rumbled somewhere inside the walls. He pulled a furious face through the mask of soap, and shook his fist in the direction of the sounds that threatened to defeat his intentions. There were footsteps on the stairs; it sounded like someone very old and fat; the clank of a bucket handle. People were moving about downstairs already. A water-closet flushed noisily. A moment ago he had imagined himself to be the only one afoot, with the whole boarding-house asleep around him. He was disappointed. He wiped his face, tore at his wet hair with a comb and went to the window. The sky was pale blue and filled with sunlight. By leaning far out of the window and craning his head to the right, he could just discern the sea at the end of the street, a ruffled patch of grey dappled with sunlight, between the hard grey of the promenade and the pallor of the sky. The sea breeze was wonderful; he tasted it on his lips, felt it searching gently over his body. He tingled with impatience and threw out his chest as he inhaled exaggeratedly.

'Put some clothes on, Mark. You'll catch a cold.'

He drew back into the room at the sound of his brother's voice. Mickey was sitting up in bed scratching under the waist of his pyjama trousers.

Mark pulled a disgusted face. The air in the room seemed heavy now with the smells of the night. It was sickening to stay in here. The gulls were floating in the pale vastness above the rooftops, mewing invitingly; and somewhere in the sky — his hearing seized on the faint murmur and brought it into the centre of his attention — an aero-engine droned.

'Don't be silly, Mickey.' A feminine intonation always crept into Mark's voice when he lectured his brother. He started on a high note and stressed every alternate word. He spoke very carefully, sometimes affectedly. 'You don't know anything about hygiene.'

'Hygiene,' scoffed Mickey. 'You're always catching cold.' He was afraid of his younger brother's lectures. Mark would frown at him like a little schoolmaster and nag on and on; and his parents, if the occasion called for their intervention, would always side with Mark, on whose precocity they doted.

'We learn hygiene at school.' Mark was in his stride now. 'Mr. Rennie takes us. He draws the human digestion on the board.' Mark was rather proud that, since the first occasion on which it had been explained, he and his classmates had been able to listen to a description of the action of the bowels without sniggering. 'And he says that fresh air never hurt anyone. He says you shouldn't wear anything except your pyjamas when you go to bed.' He was able to divide his attention now, an old accomplishment of his. A part of his mind went on delivering the lecture. Another part was listening to the drone of the aero-engine, wondering if it was the joy-riding 'plane from the field behind the town, or one of the machines from the Air Force field at Manston. He heard the power throbbing in the sound; his body felt it, exulting; an Air Force 'plane. The back of his mind began spawning dreams. 'And you want to keep your mouth shut, because you don't know anything about it, Mickey, and you'll get ill one day sleeping with your vest on. Scratching yourself,' he finished disgustedly. Mickey was still scratching imperturbably.

'Yer,' jeered Mickey. He was out of bed and dipping his face into the dirty water Mark had left. He shook his head, joyfully making blubbering noises in his inflated cheeks, 'You carnt 'alf talk!'

Mark was dressed now. He sat on his bed, took a purse from his pockets and emptied its contents on to the blanket. He began to count, putting the money back into the purse; he had seven shillings. He took a black notebook from another pocket and ruffled the pages. It was full of drawings in pencil and coloured crayon; aeroplanes, battles, funny faces with spectacles and beards, more aeroplanes. Inside the cover, written in his best handwriting: *Mark Strong, 47, Khartoum Road, Hackney, London, E.8. Birthday: March 23rd, 1918.*

'Come on,' he said impatiently. 'The breakfast gong'll be going if you don't hurry.'

'All right, all right,' intoned Mickey nasally. 'An athlete all of a sudden, you are.'

'It does you good,' said Mark sullenly, 'going for a run before breakfast.' He was upset by the mockery in his brother's voice. Mickey did not look after himself, but he could run, and play football. He practised on the track at Victoria Park and went under the shower-baths and never had a cold all the year round. Whenever Mark tried to harden himself in the open air he caught cold. He let the part of his mind that was not occupied with the noise of the aero-engine work up a little flurry of hatred against his elder brother. It was not serious; just a little emotional exercise. But, looking at his brother sideways, it made him feel better to despise his coarse, slack, good-natured face, the huge snout of a nose that made him look like the picture of a tapir which Mark had once discovered delightedly in an illustrated dictionary. He peeped furtively at his own image in the mirror. Yes, he was better-looking. His skin was creamy, his lips were full and red. He was in love with his own lips. His hair was thick and black and lay across his forehead with just the hint of a wave. He studied his nose. It was all right; straight enough. He could not push it about with his finger, as he sometimes did when no one else was in the room. There was just the faintest curl of the nostrils; no one would notice. He listened to his brother's Cockney voice, and the hatred vanished in a surge of affectionate contempt.

They crept past the door of their parents' room and down the stairs. The street door was open, a shaft of sunlight lying across the dusty floor like a golden mat. Mrs. Maddox, the landlady, was standing in the doorway of the dining-room with her back to the hall, talking to someone.

Mark stopped for a moment on the stairs. He was terrified of Mrs. Maddox. She always looked at them so searchingly, as if she were prying out all their secrets. He feared the hard, mechanical pleasantness with which she spoke. The two boys scuttled down the remaining stairs and bolted past her.

She looked over her shoulder, her thin face forbidding under a mobcap. She put on a smile: her eyes were hateful. Mark mumbled, 'Morning, Miss' Maddox.' There was a whiff of dust and carbolic from the housecoat she was wearing. Then they were out in the sunlight. Mark's heart was thumping as if he had been running.

'Down the other pier,' Mickey said. When it came to action, he always gave the orders. They began to trot, together. Mickey bounded along, his legs and arms working as if he were running on a track. Mark toiled to keep up with him. He looked up, in a breathless agony, at the veils of high cloud in the blue sky, and let part of his mind dream again. Mickey, his superiority established, eased the pace and they loped comfortably along the promenade together. Margate Pier was about a mile to the east. They should be able to run there and walk briskly back by breakfast.

On the way back, hot and tingling, Mark spoke to his brother. The hostility had gone from between them.

'Did you see those other two boys yesterday?' The Strongs had arrived early the previous afternoon and had had tea at the boarding-house, while the other visitors took stock of them from the neighbouring tables.

'Yes,' said Mickey. 'Looked snobby to me, they did.'

'They were about the same ages as us,' Mark said hopefully. 'I thought they looked all right. The big one had a shrimping net.'

'Crawling after 'em,' Mickey answered hoarsely, 'for a shrimping net. You can buy one, with the money you've got.'

'But it's nice,' Mark protested, 'to have someone to play with. I bet they know all about this place already, if they've been here a few days.' He wondered if they had been to the field from which, on the previous day, he had seen the red joy-riding 'plane come floating over the house-tops time and again.

'Leave them alone.' Mickey was insistent. 'You know what'll happen. An' it'll only make Mum upset.'

'What?' asked Mark; although he knew the answer. He felt sick and frightened. He always did when his brother reminded him. He always wanted to forget the thing of which his brother reminded him. He resented it, but he could not escape it.

'You know what,' said Mickey. He spoke now with a harsh authority that was far beyond his twelve years. 'Mix with them and you'll only get hurt.'

'Mix with who?' It was ridiculous to ask.

'Them. Those others. Leave 'em alone.'

Mark's throat was choked with self-pity. He wanted to cry, but he could not, for he was not alone. Alone he often forgot this thing in the relief of tears. 'Those others.' He knew what his brother meant.

He began to run, madly, so that Mickey could hardly keep up with him. He fell, and Mickey hastened to help him to his feet. Mark was such a cry-baby. He would howl his head off if his knee was bruised.

Mark's knee was raw and bleeding. A patch of skin had been torn away. But he did not cry. He sat on a public seat, his lips compressed, the breath snoring in his nose, as his brother bound the wound with a handkerchief. He sat with his hands clenched together in his lap, trying to make himself cry. He could not cry. For the first time in his life the tears would not come. His eyes were hot and prickling. He was filled with a burning desolation, too deep for him to fathom.

He stood up and limped stubbornly after his brother. Neither of them spoke on the way back.

2

Clara Strong pushed the tablecloth away from her knees and settled herself in her chair. It was always an ordeal to walk into a room and sit down among strangers, to feel them all looking, and to wonder what they were saying to each other. This was the third time: yesterday at the evening meal; this morning at breakfast; now at lunch. In another day, she knew, she would be used to these people and laugh at her own nervousness; but today it was still in her, making her stomach queasy. She would not enjoy this meal.

'Where are those boys?' she muttered irritably. 'I told them to come straight down when they'd washed.'

'Don't worry about them every minute,' her husband commanded. 'They'll come in when their bellies bring them. Two hungry boys.' She was annoyed by the unnatural loudness of his voice. She knew that he was as self-conscious as she was; but when, among strangers, she shrank and whispered, he would lean back in his chair and talk at the top of his voice. Her behaviour always infuriated him; his only increased her embarrassment.

'Joe!' She expostulated with her eyes and with a gesture of her hand.

People were sitting down at the next table. She returned their greeting. A tall woman, looking like a governess in her plain, grey dress, hesitated in the doorway, nodded to her, called 'Good morning' above the clatter of cutlery, and moved into the other part of the room, followed by a burly man in a blazer jacket and grey flannels and by two young boys.

Clara Strong answered, 'Good morning.' She indicated the woman furtively to her husband. 'That's the one I met shopping this morning. Mrs. Muncey. They're here till tomorrow. She seemed all right. She showed me the shops.'

Joe leaned back and stared across at the front part of the room, where the other family was settling down at a table in the bay window.

'Look, educated people. Professional class.'

'She was well spoken.'

'Think she guessed?'

Clara shrugged her shoulders. 'She talked nice enough. And she nodded just now. Didn't she?'

'Well,' Joe set the salt cellar, the pepper pot and the mustard cruet in a neat row, 'perhaps it's all right. Educated people, sometimes they have more sense. And they've got two nice boys there. Perhaps they want company for them.'

'I'll go and call the boys.' She was sick with suspense; she pretended to herself that it was because the boys were late.

'Sit *down*.' Joe fretted.

The boys came in, noisily, and took their places.

'Mum.' Mark was clamant for her attention. 'Mum, we went all the way along the front today till the houses stopped. It was all country where we went.'

'Country,' grunted Mickey. He had started on the bread. 'All bungalows.'

Clara listened to Mark's voice lecturing on, more shrill and excited every moment. 'There was all seaweed on the beach there. Huge piles of it. We tried to walk on it, didn't we, Mickey, and it was too slippery. There was all that kind that goes pop. It smelt ever so strong. I had to hold my handkerchief to my nose. Mickey didn't mind, though. There were all carts lined up there, and they were taking it away. They make iodine out of seaweed. Mum, did you know they make iodine out of seaweed? Mickey didn't know. I told him.'

They were all subdued for a moment as the maid came with the tureen of vegetables. Clara said 'Thank you,' timidly.

She said, 'They're going down the beach this afternoon.'

Joe looked up. 'Who?'

'The Munceys. We could go down with them.'

'Did she ask you?'

'No, but—'

'Well, wait till she does. You know what they'll say otherwise. Pushing ourselves in.' The boys were listening, over their knives and forks. Joe looked round, 'Wouldn't take much to start this lot talking.'

Clara followed her husband's gaze round the room. She studied the people at the nearby tables. It was always hard to tell what they were thinking. When you were suspicious they turned out all right. When you thought everything was fine, they suddenly said something. What would these be like? The big man, for instance, with the jovial red face and the walrus moustache who sat directly facing her. She knew his name — she had heard the landlady address him as Mr. Prout — and he had boomed 'Good morning' at her when she came in, uttering the words in three distinct notes, like a big clock chiming. He was talking to his wife now, a shrivelled little woman who looked as if she were wearing black even in her white summer dress. Or the two nice-looking young women sitting near the door? Students, or typists, they looked. Or the couple in front of the fireplace? Clara hissed to her husband. 'Joe. Look, Joe.'

Joe disposed of a mouthful of beef and vegetables. 'Herh?'

13

'That couple over there.' She spoke softly and urgently. 'I bet you they're ours.' The boys listened; they knew what she meant. 'Him, the husband; look at him.' She was excited at her discovery.

He looked. 'Nah. You're imagining. Anyway, you can't tell. Can't ask them either. They'd take a fit if you was wrong.'

'You can hint,' she said. There was a special technique for hinting; a host of private, innocent words and phrases to trail here and there in the midst of conversation, in the hope of a response.

He shrugged his shoulders. 'You can try. But be careful. I don't think they look like ours.'

Clara looked at her husband's broad and rubicund face, with the black hair well greased and brushed back from his forehead. There was nothing out of the ordinary in his mild Cockney voice. The bowl of a pipe protruded from the upper pocket of his jacket. 'Come to that,' she said, 'nor do you.'

'Mum,' Mark was nagging again, 'have you seen the aeroplane? The red one? It's been going up and down all the morning. You can go in it for five shillings a time. There's boards up about it all along the front.'

'So?' she asked shrilly.

'Let me go up, Mum. It's only five shillings.'

She uttered a cry of derision. 'He wants to fly now. And who do you want to take you? You want your mother to break her neck?'

'Please, Mum,' he pleaded. She had rarely heard such intensity in his voice. 'Mickey can take me.'

'Yer mad,' mumbled Mickey through his food, 'I don' wanna go up in one o' them things.'

'Dad?' Mark pleaded.

Clara warned, 'Joe!'

'That's enough.' Clara knew, when her husband spoke, that she was safe; he had little initiative but, goaded by her, he would make a show of authority.

'Don't worry your mother. Eat your dinner up.'

'Oh, Dad,' Mark moaned sullenly, 'it's only five shillings.' He bent to his food again.

Clara's breast was tight with pride as she watched Mark introduce himself.

'My name is Mark Strong,' he said carefully.

The older of the other two boys said, 'My name is Neil. This is my brother Eric. He is nine.' Eric bobbed primly towards Mark in the faint suggestion of a bow. Mickey stood loosely behind Mark, scowling and looking a lout.

It had all happened very simply. In the hall, with people pushing past, Mrs. Muncey had accosted them and asked if they would like to come down to the beach. Now the wives were walking together, the husbands strolling behind them, the four children circulating in an impatient pack in front of the party.

Clara was happy at the way it had worked out. The September day was glorious, the sun shining from an unflecked sky, the heat tempered by the wind from the sea. The children looked happy again; they had been strangely subdued after breakfast, a thing she could not understand on the second day of a holiday. She felt hungry, too, for the nervous sickness had passed, and she had not eaten any lunch. She had a half-pound bar of milk chocolate in her bag. She wondered if Mrs. Muncey would consider her common if she were to break it and offer it round while they were walking.

Clara listened alertly to the men's talk while she kept Mrs. Muncey's chatter at bay with an occasional word. 'Yes… Oh, so do I… I always use lard…' At times like this she was skilled at using words as a barrier behind which she could shelter and pursue her own thoughts. The men were talking about the British Legion and their old regiments. As the beach came in sight, she began to worry about the deck-chair money. There would be tickets to buy when they found chairs on the beach. What would Joe do? If they had been with trusted friends, there would have been no difficulty; a good-natured scramble to pay, nobody noticing the outcome. But now? If Joe was backward in paying, the others might talk. 'Just like them,' they might say; 'too mean to spend a shilling.' And if he rushed to pay? 'Just like them,' they might say; 'won't let you forget they've got the money.'

'My line?' Joe was saying, 'Tailoring. High-class ladies.' He fumbled for his tobacco pouch. 'Care for a smoke? It's Bondman.'

'Nice tobacco that,' Mr. Muncey acknowledged. 'I generally smoke a special my tobacconist makes up for me. Very nice mixture. Cool. I'll let you try some.'

Clara sighed: she wondered if she would ever begin to enjoy this holiday. She smiled sweetly as Mrs. Muncey finished a long harangue about the price of curtains. 'I bought my new ones last year,' she answered, hoping for the best, 'at the sales.'

They found four deck-chairs and made themselves comfortable. Joe paid. Mr. Muncey made only a mild protest, then hailed an ice-cream seller and bought four cornets. Clara felt easier. How well it had passed over!

She relaxed lethargically, letting the sun's glare dazzle her eyes until the picture of sea and sky in front of her was confused by whirling bolts of red and black. There seemed to be several layers of sound about her, each quite distinct, yet all mingling in her ears; the din of children — Lord, she thought, what a nerve-racking noise ten-year-old boys could make when they forgot their pretending-to-be-grown-up manners and began to shriek and scamper as they ought; the stupefying heat of the sea; the sound of traffic from the street behind her; a baby crying somewhere; a sudden uproar of laughter from a nearby group of deck-chairs; girls squealing at the water's edge; a portable gramophone, feeble but insistent; within this, the chatter of her companions and — remotely she heard herself speaking — her own voice.

She blinked herself back to awareness. Mrs. Muncey leaned towards her.

'It's a *blessing*, my dear, isn't it, to relax for once in the year and forget the housework?'

Clara said gratefully, 'Yes.' Embarrassed, she tried to think of something sensible to say. She could almost count the painful seconds of silence. 'Makes a change, doesn't it?' That wasn't good enough. 'I always think it's being able to sit down and have your meals served to you that makes all the difference.' She spoke carefully, trying to keep the Cockney whine out of her voice and to imitate Mrs. Muncey's speech; she sounded her consonants so carefully that the ends of her words clacked like typewriter keys.

'Where are the boys?' she asked anxiously.

The men were sprawled low in their chairs, luxuriating in the sunshine, their stomachs full of lunch, the blue pipe smoke wreathing over their heads. Joe said languidly, 'Worry, worry, worry. These women!' The two men laughed masterfully. 'They can look after themselves,' Joe said. 'They won't get drowned.'

'The tide's out,' Mrs. Muncey added. 'They're *probably* off behind the breakwater looking under the stones for crabs.'

'Ah' — Mr. Muncey's voice came out of the dazzle and chatter — 'that's what I could fancy for tea. A nice crab salad.'

Mrs. Muncey supported him with noises of delight. 'Do *you* like crab, dear?' she asked.

Clara hesitated for a moment. 'We don't eat it.'

'Ah,' said Mrs. Muncey gaily. 'Your *tummy*, I suppose. Lots of people dare not touch it. Then there's the *Jews*. They don't eat it, either. They're not allowed to.'

There was silence for a little while. Mrs. Muncey spoke again. 'It *is* getting hot, dear. Would you like my parasol to keep the sun off your head? I don't feel it, myself.'

Clara was tired, confused by the heat and by her own thoughts. She mumbled 'No, thank you' absently, and shut her eyes again, as if to discourage conversation.

But Mrs. Muncey was insistent. She was dismayed by the way in which the conversation had tailed off. She felt Clara's forehead. 'Poor dear,' she said. 'There's some shade by the breakwater. Let's move over there.'

They moved, the men taking up the chairs with a great show of gallantry.

When they were settled again Clara decided to reopen the conversation. Mrs. Muncey's kindness had penetrated her armour of preoccupation; she wanted to make up for the seeming indifference she had shown a moment before.

'Do you come here every year?' she asked.

'This is the third year.'

'It's our first time,' Clara said.

Mr. Muncey intervened through a cloud of tobacco smoke. 'You'll like it. It's just far enough from the centre of the town to be ideal for kids. No crowds.'

Mrs. Muncey took up the tale. 'And she's *such* a nice lady, too, Mrs. Maddox. Very genteel. She looks after us so well. We always have the same room. She sends us a card at Christmas. You can *always* rely on nice company, too, with her.' She smiled at Clara to underline the compliment. 'She's *very* careful who she takes.'

Joe said, 'We went to Bournemouth last year.'

'We went there once,' said Mrs. Muncey. 'Never again.'

'Overrun with Jews,' said Mr. Muncey. 'Swarming with 'em. Couldn't get away from them whichever way we turned. Could we, Edna?'

'No,' said his wife; 'it was terrible. Go and get a tea tray, Charles, dear. I'm sure Mrs. Strong will feel better after a cup of tea.'

Mr. Muncey stirred lazily. But Joe Strong was already sitting upright in his chair. His face was stiff and expressionless. Clara watched him in agony.

'We're Jews,' he said.

17

'What!' Mr. Muncey took his pipe out of his mouth.

Mrs. Muncey said 'Oh' faintly. Clara thought she looked genuinely upset. The part of her that was not writhing felt sorry for the woman.

'We're Jews,' Joe repeated, aggressively this time.

Mrs. Muncey expelled a long breath. 'Oh, *go* and get the tea tray, Charles. *Such* a silly thing. As if it mattered.' She assumed her sweetest smile. 'We meant the *foreign* ones, of course.'

Her husband was hanging over them anxiously, like a boy in his dismay. 'You know,' he said, 'you know what I mean. Why,' he turned to his wife, relieved, as the words came flowing back to him, 'nobody would ever dream, would they, that Mr. and Mrs. Strong were Jewish?'

Mrs. Muncey said, 'Ever so many of our friends are Jewish.' She chattered on, helplessly.

It was like broken bones grating inside Clara. The more they said the worse they made it. She wanted to leave them, abruptly, to leave the boarding-house and to flee to the sanctuary of her own home. She waited for Joe to speak.

'All right, old man,' Joe said. 'Say no more about it.' His bluff voice was sickening to her.

The men went off together for the tea tray.

Mrs. Muncey leaned over her. 'I still say it's a cup of tea you need, my dear, when you've been in the sun.' She displayed the sweet smile again.

Clara smiled back, and retired once more behind the glare, behind the strata of noise, into her private world, while in the distance she heard the voices, Mrs. Muncey's voice and her own, making conversation.

3

The growling roar swept suddenly over their heads and the red aeroplane appeared from behind the chimney-pots. It turned steeply over the pier and dived to within fifty feet of the sea. The four boys, standing at the water's edge, watched fascinated as it climbed past them and dwindled to a toy's size in the sky again.

Neil Muncey announced, 'That's an Avro 504K.'

He was annoyed when Mark answered, 'I know. There's one at the Science Museum. My dad took me there.'

'It's ever such an old type. It was designed in 1914.'

Mark asked, 'Do you know what kind of engine it's got?'

Neil replied hurriedly — he did not want to give Mark time to answer his own question. 'Of course. A Le Rhône Rotary.'

Mark said, 'A rotary engine goes round and round. They don't use them any more.'

Neil lost patience. 'That's a silly thing to say. Everyone knows that. When they're the same shape but they don't go round, they're called radial engines.' He had been delighted at first to find that Mark shared his passion for aeroplanes; but it was not proving easy to establish the prophet-disciple relationship that ought to exist between a boy of twelve and a boy of ten. He looked critically at Mark. 'His eyes look as if he's always sulking, or going to burst out crying,' that was what Mummy had said about Mark. 'Not like the other one. He looks a real ruffian.'

The four of them threaded their way in single file among the rocks, keeping close enough to the tide's ebb for the last rush of water from each wave to obliterate their footmarks in the soft, smooth sand. The two smaller boys took the lead, shouting to each other, and jumping from rock to rock. Neil and Mickey walked behind.

Neil could not think of anything to say to the other boy. He asked, 'Do you go to the same school as your brother?' — for he and Mark had already had a boasting match about their schools and there was a safe field of conversation here — but Mickey only replied with a scared, good-natured grin. His silly, long snout seemed to grow longer and rounder when he grinned. Neil asked desperately, 'Do you play cricket?'

Mickey answered, 'Nah. Foo'ball. Go up the Spurs every Sa'day, in the season. Mark don't. He don't like it.' When he spoke you thought at first he was lisping; then you listened more closely, and he wasn't. Neil thought that it was a funny way to speak.

Eric turned towards them and mocked Mickey's vowels. 'Gah-oow up the Spurs,' he chanted, 'Nah. Gaa-oow up the Spurs.'

Neil was horrified. He pulled faces of warning and hissed, '*Eric!*' He looked anxiously at the other two boys. Mark had hurried on a little way and had his back to them. Mickey was grinning stupidly. Neil felt sorry for him; he would probably go on grinning like that if you punched him in the stomach.

They stopped for a moment and solemnly inspected a huge and elaborate sand castle that two men were building. The men wore black suits. They had taken their jackets and ties off, but they still wore their waistcoats. They were barefoot and their trousers were rolled up to their knees. One of them wore a bowler hat and was sweating horribly. Neil felt sick looking at him. The castle was at least four feet high. It had turrets at the four corners and battlements all round. There was a courtyard in the middle and an archway, its roof held up by an oyster shell supported by two pieces of wood, leading into it. The castle was surrounded by a deep, broad moat, and the men were now busy building a wall round the moat.

They walked on a few yards. Mickey picked up a green, slimy rock and heaved it at the castle. Neil watched for a moment, startled, as one of the smooth-walled turrets crumbled and crashed in a heap of dark wet sand across the moat. The men came running at them, shouting. Neil ran, with the other boys, in a panic, panting and wondering if he should have stood his ground and told the men that he had nothing to do with such a deed.

They were safe now, on the other side of the breakwater. The men had gone back to their sand castle. The red aeroplane came snarling over their heads again. Eric extended his arms and ran among them, swooping and swaying and making a noise to signify that he was an aeroplane. Mark ran after him, clutching an imaginary joystick in a clenched fist and rat-tat-tatting like machine-guns. It was a silly way to behave, thought Neil. He was too hot to run, his skin red and prickling with sweat under the sun's heat. He felt, in his thin shirt, as if he were in a furnace. He said, 'Let's go in the water.'

Eric stopped snarling and said, 'Where can we leave our shoes?'

'Mr. Prout will look after them.'

Mr. Prout was sprawling in a low deck-chair at the foot of the sea wall. His face was turned up to the sun, his eyes closed.

The four boys made their way up the beach. Mrs. Prout, seated at her husband's side, opened one eye and inspected them apathetically. She did not speak.

Neil raised his cap. Mark and Eric followed his example. Mickey wore no cap, and stood timidly behind the others.

'Excuse me, please, Mr. Prout.' Neil spoke loudly and firmly, pronouncing his words as if he were reciting a poem at school. Mr. Prout grunted and turned his head away from them... 'Mr. Prout, sir.'

Mrs. Prout opened her eyes. 'Shshsh!' she said fiercely. 'Carncher seez sleeping?'

'Please, Mrs. Prout,' Neil said, 'we're ever so sorry to trouble you, but may we leave our shoes with you while we go in the water?'

Mr. Prout grunted again. His voice came up from the caverns of sleep. 'Yerss.' He did not open his eyes. 'Pleasure.' His head lolled the other way again.

With the cold sea water lapping at his ankles, Neil felt better. The sticky heat within his clothes disappeared. They waded out until they were knee-deep in the water, keeping close to the breakwater and collecting shells and pieces of seaweed for Eric to take home with him when the Munceys returned to London the next day. Back at the water's edge, they chased crabs, setting the little pink ones to race each other, tormenting the big, ugly green ones, daring each other to pick them up, and cracking their shells with rocks. Neil hated the sight of the white mess that came oozing out of a smashed crab; but when they caught a big, fierce, old one, he was the first to pick it up; he put it on the breakwater and as it scuttled away he threw stone after stone at it, shouting 'Bang. Bang. Bring up the cannon' as excitedly as the smaller boys; and when it escaped he pursued it through the shallows on the other side of the breakwater, threw it up in the air, and dropped a great, dripping rock on it as it fell.

They lay on the beach, using their handkerchiefs to help the afternoon heat dry their feet.

Neil smiled at Mickey, who grinned timidly back. 'Do you do gym?'

'Yes,' said Mickey, 'up the club. We got thirty-foot ropes. We climb up them and then we come down head-first. It's called the Spiral Butterfly.'

'We do rope-climbing at school. Only they won't let us do the Butterfly till we get into the Middle School. That's when you're fourteen. Do you have cadets?'

'No.' Mickey sounded uncomfortable again. 'At Mark's school, they got 'em.'

'What school do you go to, then?'

'Salamander Street.'

'Oh. An elementary school?' Neil heard the note of shocked surprise in his own voice and was sorry. He scrambled to his feet. 'Can you climb up the sea wall?'

He ran desperately at the wall. Mickey did not follow, but sat looking after him.

They had strayed a considerable distance from the section of the beach on which their parents had settled, and they made their way up an iron staircase on to the promenade to begin the walk back.

Mickey and Neil walked in awkward silence. Eric was saying, 'This time last year it was ever so stormy. The sky was all black, and it rained and rained. Didn't it, Neil? It got windy one day and the waves came right up over the promenade. We stood on the other side of the road, and when the waves burst we got wet with spray. Didn't we?'

The red aeroplane flew over. The two small boys raised an arm each and became anti-aircraft guns. They screamed, 'Bababababab,' and Mark shouted delightedly, 'We've got him, we've got him, he's coming down in flames,' as the machine banked over the pier and flew back to its landing ground. Neil was ashamed of their clamour.

'Have you seen that place along the front where they sell orange crush?' Neil said. 'They put the oranges in at the top and the juice comes out at the bottom. You see them do it. It's only sixpence a glass. It tastes lovely.'

'Let's ask Dad for some money,' Eric suggested, 'and buy some.'

They were standing now against the promenade rails above the beach on which their parents sat.

Mark said eagerly, 'I've got heaps of money. Seven shillings. Look!' He pulled out his purse. Neil was appalled. 'I'll get them all. I'll treat you.'

'Go on down, Eric,' Neil said, 'and ask Dad.' They watched Eric scuttle down on to the beach and stand in front of the semicircle of deck-chairs. Soon he came back towards them. Mr. Muncey walked part of the way with him, one hand on his shoulder, apparently talking to him with great earnestness; then he went back to his chair and Eric came on alone.

He rejoined them. Neil asked, 'Got the money?'

'No. It's tea-time. We've got to go home.' Eric was looking pale and scared. Neil thought he saw signals in his brother's eyes. He was puzzled.

'Let's wait up here for them.' Neil indicated the grown-ups, who were just beginning to stir in their chairs and gather up their possessions. 'They'll be five minutes yet. We can walk back with them.'

'No.' There was a frantic squeal in Eric's voice. '*We've got to go back now*. Dad said so.'

'Why?' The signals were unmistakeable. Neil followed his brother's darting eyes and strove to understand.

'We've *got* to.' Tears were starting in Eric's eyes, his voice was husky with fright. He beckoned Neil. 'Here. Come here. Let me whisper.'

Neil's throat turned dry with embarrassment. You just *couldn't* whisper in front of strangers. 'What's the matter, Eric?' he pleaded. 'Speak up, for Heaven's sake.'

Eric hesitated. He looked huntedly at Mark and Mickey, and spoke quickly. 'Dad says they're Jew-boys. We're not to play with them. We've got to go straight back to tea.' He began to blubber. 'Dad said I wasn't to say anything.' The ugly tears ran down his scarlet cheeks. 'It's your fault.'

Neil shivered, helpless. He thought Mark was going to be sick. 'Come on, Eric,' he said desperately. He grabbed his brother and hurried him away. This was not what he wanted to do; he could not find the words that he wanted to say or the courage to speak.

Mark too was walking away, alone, into the afternoon crowds.

Through the sunlight and the whirl of gay, trivial noises, Mickey's voice came to them, raised in a thick shout:

'Swine!'

Neil bowed his head as if he were walking against heavy rain and plunged on, not looking at his brother, whose arm he still clutched.

'Dirty swine!'

People were stopping and looking. Neil was terrified by the blur of empty white faces around them. He heard, uncomprehendingly, a woman's scream. The sun flashed on an object that flew past his head. The empty lemonade bottle which Mickey had snatched from a waste basket splintered on the road surface in front of them.

There was more screaming and angry shouting; and a voice still raised above it all:

'Swine! Swine! Swine!'

With his brother at his heels, he ran up the street towards the boarding-house, sick, breathless, his heart hurting and straining inside him as if it were about to burst.

4

Mark sat on the edge of the sea wall, kicking his heels against the rough stone. The others had all gone back for tea; he had fled, and he was lonely now, with the babble of pleasure going on all round him, the hordes of children still shrieking and scampering on the beach, the pavement behind him alive with the endless clatter of footsteps, and the white-fringed waves creeping interminably in from the skyline to the beach.

How could Mickey have done such a thing? He might be arrested for it and sent to prison. Perhaps they would both be sent to prison. The other two boys might say he and Mickey were both to blame. He had run away; they would take that as proof that he was guilty. Inside his hot body he felt the cold fear expanding. This thing: how could he escape from it? Why did it always come up between him and other people?

What was the curse on him that made Neil and Eric, playing with him one minute, run away from him the next?

He had examined himself, minutely, in the mirror a hundred times to find out what it was. He had listened to himself speaking, kept watch on his own actions, scrutinised other people, to discover what made him apart from the others. It remained more than he could understand. They had run away from him. Eric had burst into tears. Neil had seized Eric's hand, and they had run away. Unhappiness made a lump in his throat and a stale taste in his mouth.

A black-and-white terrier came trotting across to him and began to investigate him. He let the dog sniff at his clothes, stroking its wiry hair absent-mindedly. 'Hi, dog,' he said, 'What's your name, doggie?' He fumbled with the dog's collar, in search of a disc. Somebody whistled and the terrier scuttled off. Mark gave a long, bubbling sniff as he watched the animal vanish amid a forest of human legs, its bandy legs waddling rapidly and its stubby tail flickering to and fro. He smiled, and looked around for more dogs. He was often able to soothe himself like this, drifting away from his troubles on a tide of imagination.

Always, as far back as he could remember, he had wanted to be the same as other boys; he had no other ambition; always this word 'Jew' sprang up like barbed wire between himself and the world. Yet in his own life it had meant so little. He had never learned the strange language that other Jewish boys of his acquaintance spent their evenings studying. His parents were English-born; he was often proud of it when he listened to other boys' parents speaking broken English. Mum and Dad never bothered with all the queer religious things and holidays that he had seen and heard of in other Jewish homes. He had heard his father say, 'I make an honest living. I teach my boys the difference between right and wrong. What should I fill their heads up with religion for?' It made no difference to the others. As soon as they heard, it was as if you had diphtheria. The others. That was how he had come to think of them now. Yet all he wanted of life was to be one of 'the others'.

The earliest memory he retained of the flat in which they lived was of a Sunday morning, the street all quiet and looking somewhat cleaner than on weekdays. He could hear the bells of the parish church, the exciting *boom-boom-boom* of the Boy Scouts' band, the *ta-ra-ra* of their bugles. On the other side of the street the houses had no basements but boasted of front gardens, little bare, black plots of earth hemmed in by tall railings, each with its one stunted plane tree. But on the spring morning that he remembered, the planes in leaf changed the whole aspect of the street, breathing a pale green freshness into the grimy greys and blacks; and when the sun came out, it gilded every rustling leaf. He saw this picture through the front-room window, where he sat watching his weekday playmates, stiff and prim in their Sunday clothes, being taken to church by their parents. As they went by he tapped at the window, and they waved at him. But they walked away, in the sunshine; he stayed indoors, behind the closed window.

He remembered another morning, a Saturday, the first of the few occasions on which his father had taken him to a synagogue service. He was six years old at the time.

The synagogue was a hideous red brick building, set a few yards back from the pavement, in a gravel area, behind a low brick wall surmounted by railings. Mark followed his father through the gate. The short gravel path was crowded with congregants who had escaped from the service. To the small boy, lost among their legs, their noisy talk sounded like the chattering of a street market, shrill and sonorous voices intermingled; behind them, from within the building, came the rumble of many voices, rising and falling in prayer and response, like the sound of the sea. All about him, as he looked up curiously, there seemed to be huge, overfed bodies, trim beards, trilby hats and black skull caps, the smell of hair oil and good cloth. He did not want to go inside. He wanted to stay in the sunlight, to fill his pockets with pebbles, to slip out into the street and explore the vast world. Instead he followed his father into the gloomy hall, past a fierce, fat beadle with a beard smelling of tobacco, and into a pew. The hall seemed enormous to him, the roof remote beyond the dazzling candelabra, the women's gallery scarcely visible in the shadows that gathered behind the blur of many lights. The shawled priests huddled together on a central platform, behind an ornate balustrade, yellow, shrunken old men, bowing endlessly towards the altar, muttering and whispering their prayers, breaking into wailing, sing-song chants. Mark became frightened and confused. The lights, the noise and the heat upset him. He ceased to observe and crept after his imagination into a world of fantasy. The old men in their robes and shawls, bringing the Scroll down from the altar, and bearing it back in discordant triumph, were coming to take him through the tall, carved altar doors into a darkness where beasts and serpents prowled. The beadles bobbing and mumbling together in the aisles were plotting to snatch him from his father. He was lost in a nightmare of alien words, of strange chanting, of hostile, porcine faces. His home was a million miles away, somewhere in the sunlight. He pushed past his father, scuttled down the aisle, bolted past the fat beadle and through the swing doors into the blessed sunlight. He stood on the pavement, sick with relief. He could still hear a faint chanting from inside the building; but he was out of the nightmare, back in the same world in which his playmates lived.

The mist of dream dispersed as a boy walked past carrying a model yacht, a wonderful vessel, three feet long, with a great deep keel, a polished deck with brass rails, and beautiful, tall white sails. He must be taking it to the pond that lay behind the promenade, a few hundred yards further on. Mark thought for a moment of following him, so that he might watch the yacht sail across the pond, heeling with the wind and cleaving the green water; but the languor of dream had made his limbs heavy, and he did not move.

'The others.' Most of the time, at the elementary school, his life among the other children had been happy; except for the days when, inexplicably, they would turn on him and lock him in the lavatory in the playground, or tie him to the railings, or push him over into a rainy gutter, shouting that word.

How could Mickey have thrown the bottle? Didn't he know it only made things worse? It made you different and it made the others 'the others'. Sometimes he blamed his parents, fiercely, because he had been born to them. Why could he not have been born to Mr. and Mrs. Muncey? He would have had a tall, cool, grey-clad mother and a big, hearty father. He would have been able to speak as nicely as Neil and raise his cap as gracefully. He would have been the same as all the others.

Loud voices came to him from the babble of background noise on the promenade.

'Twice round the bloody gasworks. That was 'er.'

'You always did like an armful, didn't you?'

English voices; they disappeared in the babble again. He had hoped, when he had started at the Grammar School last term, that everything would change. He would learn to row, to shoot, to play fives, to talk a new language; in a year or two he would be old enough for the cadet battalion; he had entered into a world where masters whisked about in grave, black gowns and spoke to ten-year-old boys as if to adults; where the scholarship boys were lined up twice a week by the singing teacher to have the Cockney intonations drilled out of their speech. Perhaps he would be accepted into this world completely, without reservations. So far he had been happy enough. His only disappointment had been that there were many more Jews at the Grammar School than there had been at the elementary school, the sons of local tradesmen, sleek, greedy, over-intelligent boys whose parents gave them wallets filled with notes to display at the tuckshop, in the hope that they might buy off the hatred which Mark could only fear. They had their own morning service, held in a classroom, and Mark had to attend it. The rest of the school went into Chapel every morning. Mark dreamed of going into Chapel with the others; it represented all that his heart desired; the ranks of boys kneeling, all one, all together, in the shadowy coolness, the hymns that sounded to him, lurking in the corridor outside, like angels' voices, with the organ music rich and deep beneath; the pale green lustre around the stained-glass windows, the grey, fluted pillars, the gilt-lettered Roll of Honour of war dead on the walls.

The red aeroplane circled overhead. It was probably the last flight of the day, for the glare had gone from the sky, streaks of purple and green were thickening above the horizon, the breeze was livelier and more chilly, the waves rearing themselves more fiercely against the breakwater. The crowds had thinned, and a feeble-looking old man in a fawn smock was stacking deck-chairs beneath the sea wall.

Mark climbed to his feet. His limbs were stiff with inaction, his buttocks numbed by the cold stone on which he had been sitting. His bandaged knee was painful now. He swung on the rail and watched a red-sailed barge creeping in from the sea.

The exercise brought the warmth back to his body. The barge moved slowly across his line of vision; far beyond, a faint black stain of smoke smudged the sky as a steamship headed out to sea. It was good to be at the seaside, standing in the fresh, salt evening breeze.

He realised that he was hungry. The fear returned, like cold fingers searching inside him, at the prospect of going back to the boarding-house. Tea must have been finished an hour ago. He felt the purse in his pocket. He could buy a meal. No, he had other plans for his money. He started back for the house. Passing a row of slot machines, he could not resist the temptation to buy a twopenny bar of milk chocolate. He ate the chocolate quickly. It tasted delicious. He sucked at the last melting fragments in the corner of his mouth. He bought a second bar and walked on, munching.

5

The bedroom reeked of scented soap.

Joe Strong took his shoes off and sat heavily on the bed. 'My feet are killing me. It's these thin socks. They rub if the shoe's on the large side.' He massaged his right foot. 'What did we do? We came here for a holiday. Is that a crime? Did we rob anyone? Did we set the house on fire? Did we interfere with anybody's business?' He set his foot down and let it take the weight of his body. 'She took our deposit, didn't she? She made us welcome. What does she want us to do? Wear badges?' He walked across to the dressing-table and examined his reflection in the mirror. 'I'm catching the sun already. Just beginning to peel.' He turned to his wife again. 'We didn't start anything. It was their idea to go down to the beach. We didn't push ourselves on to them. Now they all look at us as if we'd crucified Christ personally.'

Clara said, 'What shall we do now? I can't stay here another day. The food chokes me when I sit in that dining-room.'

'They speak to us still.'

'But can't you feel what they're thinking?' she protested bitterly. 'And *she* wants to get rid of us. That one. The landlady.'

There had been a terrible scene in the hall the evening before last when Eric had told his tale to his parents. Mrs. Muncey who, a moment earlier, had been talking pleasantly with Clara, turned on her and said gratingly, 'You could have *murdered* my boy. Throwing a bottle at him. Bringing your Whitechapel ways among *decent* people. You ought to think yourself lucky I don't like scandal.' She was trembling, as if the hysteria were forcing its way up from within her; she spoke in short outbursts, as if each sentence forced her to utter the next. 'Otherwise I'd put the police on to that boy of yours. *Borstal*. That's what he'd get. That ugly big snout of his.' The tremor found its way into her voice. 'We can't get away from you people anywhere. You ought to be *barred* from respectable places.' She turned on the landlady. 'I'm surprised at you, Mrs. Maddox. We always thought we could rely on *you* to keep their kind out of your house.' Mrs. Maddox had murmured a torrent of conciliatory words at them both; but her eyes had made excuses to Mrs. Muncey. Clara had been too overwhelmed to speak.

Mrs. Maddox had not said anything to them about it since, but yesterday, when the Munceys had left, she and all her boarders had crowded in the front garden to give them a clamorous send-off. Joe and Clara, watching from behind the curtains through their bedroom window, saw in it a demonstration against them.

Since then, Mrs. Maddox had been very abrupt and formal in her manner. In everything she said to them they fancied that they discovered some insolence, some hint; as when she asked them if they could tell her exactly what time on Saturday they planned to leave, so that she could get the rooms ready for their successors; or when she asked Joe off-handedly, if she had mentioned when they arrived that she never accepted cheques. The other boarders greeted them in the mornings as ceremoniously as before, but otherwise left them to themselves.

'Well,' Joe said, 'do you want to go home? It's all the same to me. There's not another place to be found here. My feet still hurt from looking. It's the good weather. They'll take bookings for next week, but you can't get the three odd days. Not at prices we can afford, anyway.'

Clara moaned, 'I don't know. It's the boys. I'll be glad when I'm back in my own house. Some holiday this has turned out. But the boys — they've been looking forward to it for so long.'

The boys were sitting by the window, listening.

'Do you want to go home, Mickey?' she asked. She knew that Joe was ashamed to speak to the boy. On the night of the incident with the Munceys he had begun to lecture Mickey, had lost his temper, and, beyond control, had struck his son across the face. Now he regretted the blow.

'Wha' do I want with the seaside?' Mickey said, 'paddling an' making sandpies, and pickin' up sea-shells. I ain't a kid. I can have a game o' football at home, anyway. 'At's more'n I can do here.'

Mark knew that his brother was lying, and that Mickey felt as sick at heart as he did when he, too, said, 'Take us home, Mum.' It was good at the seaside; all the other things were easy to forget when there were ships to watch heading out towards distant lands, and jellyfish to discover at the water's edge.

'I'll pack tonight,' said Joe, 'and pay *her* in the morning. We'll be home tomorrow night and have a good supper, for a change, in peace.'

Clara asked, 'Will you tip the servants?'

Joe shrugged his shoulders. 'Might as well. They done nothing to us. Anyway, imagine what they'll say if we don't.'

'They'll say it, anyway.'

Mark heard no more; he slipped out of the room and closed the door quietly behind him.

This was his last chance. He felt a sudden panic on the stairs in case he had left his purse in the bedroom; but it was safely in his pocket.

He had not thought, watching the Avro drifting in over the rooftops and disappearing quickly behind the houses, that it would be a long journey to the landing ground. But he seemed to have been walking for hours, through a maze of streets, before the rows of villas petered out into a litter of bricks and scaffolding amid the brambles and the field came into sight.

He ran the last hundred yards. It was late in the afternoon. The sun was obscured by massive grey clouds beneath which scurried smoky tendrils of darker vapour, driven by the same wind which made the trees on the far side of the field whisper and shiver. Mark expected to feel the pellets of rain driving into his face at any moment. Then there would be no more flying; and for him, a long walk home in the downpour.

There was the red Avro, with its comma-shaped rudder and its heavily-staggered wings, crouching over the long wooden skid between its wheels, at the far end of the field. A windsock, bloated now, swooped and tugged at the end of a short mast. The gate into the field was open, and just beyond it a man sat at a small wooden table, from the front of which flapped a red poster. Two other men, both bare-headed and in raincoats, sat on the edge of the table, their hands in their pockets, their heads pulled down inside upturned coat collars.

Mark tried to speak. His throat was parched and he could only make harsh little noises.

'What's that, laddie?' One of the men leaned towards him.

He croaked, 'Is this where they have five-shilling flights?'

'It is indeed.' The man laughed, and the other two men laughed with him. 'When they have the customers.'

Mark's voice returned. 'Please, sir, I'd like to go up.' He fumbled with his purse and counted five shillings on to the table. He dropped a sixpence; his fingers were numb. He crawled under the table, weak with shame.

He was on his feet again; he had not found the sixpence, but he was too frightened of the men to go on looking for it. He took another from his purse.

'Found your sixpence?'

'Yes, sir.'

'Hold on to this, then.' The man gave him a long, blue ticket. 'You'll have to wait till someone else turns up. We don't take less than two five-bob passengers at a time. It's not worth our while.'

He whispered, 'Yes, sir', and clambered up on to the fence to wait.

He waited. All his other troubles were forgotten now; there was only the tingling suspense of waiting and the fear, as the clouds grew darker and the first drops of rain blew into his face, that there would be no more flying for the day. The men were huddled together, evidently discussing what to do. The grass stirred wildly. He was almost beside himself with impatience; it made his gums itch intolerably.

Then one of the men sitting on the edge of the table stood up.

'Come on, laddie. I'll give you your joy-ride before the waterworks start.'

Mark tumbled down from the fence. His legs buckled under him; he picked himself up and trotted after the man, who, with one of his two companions, was walking down the field towards the aeroplane.

The rain had stopped, although there was still a fresh dampness in the wind. The clouds parted and a broad shaft of sunlight poured down upon the field. The wall of dark cloud still reared all along the skyline, towering over the trees to his right and the houses to his left, but all around him the light grew brighter as if he were walking across the bottom of a great bowl that was filling up with golden light. The tree-tops, a mass of black a little while ago, were green and lustrous. The blue patch in the sky widened until there was no cloud left overhead; then, at the foot of the gently sloping field, the mists dispersed and the sea became visible, a sheet of rippled silver, with tracks of sunlight glittering across it.

Mark was given to fantasies. He had imagined that, for his first flight, he would invent and act a suitable story, becoming an air ace of the last war, or an explorer about to set out; but now his imaginative faculties were paralysed; he was nothing but a bundle of physical sensations.

He let them swing him up into the back cockpit and settle him in his seat. He looked over the coaming at the ground; it seemed a long way down. One of the two men clambered up on to the lower wing and eased himself into the front cockpit. Mark had been looking for a pilot; someone in a leather coat, wearing helmet and goggles. He was a little disappointed that the pilot should turn out to be this tall, thin man in a raincoat, with a tanned, creased face and thin, curly hair; a man who looked as old as his father.

Thought ceased as the second man swung the propeller. The rotary engine coughed, popped, and burst into a harsh, rattling roar. The gleaming wooden propeller blade jerked over once or twice, then quickened its revolutions until there was only a shimmering blur before his eyes. The slipstream battered at his face, tugged at his hair, flattened the grass behind the machine and sent a fury of dust and dancing leaves whirling back towards the fence. He felt the slender wood-and-canvas fuselage trembling around him; the spars on which his feet rested were vibrating at the impatient tug of power. The mechanic, below, jerked the chocks away and ducked aside. The Avro moved forward; the rudder flapped and the tail slewed round. The machine, facing now into the wind, bumped and swayed across the field, gathering speed. The fence and the houses streamed backward past them. The table and the third man, both become strangely small, whirled suddenly beyond the tail and out of sight. The grass straining beneath them became a blur. The whole machine seemed to be filled with a restrained buoyancy. Looking forward past the pilot's head, over the circular engine cowling, through the propeller's blur, Mark watched the line of trees come racing towards them. There was a beautiful moment when the vibration stopped; everything felt smooth and free; the trees, hurtling at them, bigger and bigger, suddenly sank away out of sight. The wings were swaying gently; the tree-tops, like a little fringe of dark green wool, appeared behind them and raced past the tailplane. Mark could see the whole shape of the field now; it dwindled rapidly, became the centre of a pattern of fields and hedges and was lost in the patchwork as the pattern grew. To his right and left the wings rocked slightly, the ribs showing beneath the tight, gleaming canvas as subtly as the muscles beneath human skin. There was no sensation of height; no gap discernible between the machine and the map of dark woods and golden cornfields across which it crawled. Only when the machine lost a few feet of altitude and sagged into a sudden patch of emptiness did his stomach contract. The high-pitched din of wind and engine was terrifying. He shouted at the top of his voice, but he could not hear himself. The wind beat against his face, as hard and resilient as rubber. He could hardly breathe. He was numb and deafened.

The map tilted up steeply and slid round the Avro. Again Mark felt the swooping feeling in his stomach. A dazzling expanse of sea was visible now, to his left at the moment but moving gently round and under the tail; a dirty, black-and-grey pattern of houses as the town passed beneath; a road like a grey tape and vehicles like lopsided black beetles; the whole sliding sideways out of sight.

The engine's roar faded. One field leaped up towards them out of the pattern; grew larger until its boundaries passed beyond the limits of their vision; the wind soughed mournfully through the wires; the smooth green blurred again and became grass rushing beneath the wheels. A bump, a gentle, swooping bounce, another bump, and the machine was lumbering to a stop. Bewildered, and lost for a moment, Mark saw with surprise the fence, the row of red brick houses, the man at the table a hundred yards away, and the sea gleaming at the foot of the field.

Numbed and frozen by the wind, he huddled in the cockpit seat, unwilling to stir. He had opened to the sun. Somehow he knew that his life, his real life, had begun.

1935

1935

1

The north-east quarter of London is a dreary warren of little streets. For the motorist, speeding towards the pleasanter suburbs or pursuing the ever-receding countryside, there is nothing to seize the attention. He later remembers the area, not in terms of scenes encountered, but as a lapse of time, during which he glanced, indifferently or impatiently, at the dashboard clock while for five, ten, fifteen minutes a grey sameness of street corners went sliding backwards past the windows. Certainly there is no reason why he should have noticed Khartoum Road, which he would have passed, hastening on his journey northwards, less than a minute after the traffic jam at Dalston junction had disgorged his car.

Khartoum Road is a noisy, child-infested thoroughfare, lined on one side by houses that are as uniform and devoid of feature as black brick boxes and on the other, through some caprice of a Victorian builder, by tall, decaying houses with gloomy basements and with high front steps flanked by balustrades of peeling plaster. Stone animals squat on short pillars flanking each flight of steps, their outlines battered and corroded by time and the sport of generations of children. The area railings are hideously ornate, and from the roofs of many of the houses there rise, like faded green cocks' combs, fretworks of cast iron. Each house is filled with the squawling and brawling of several families.

It was here that the Strongs lived. On a Sunday morning in the autumn of the year 1935 Joe Strong was sitting at the window of his workroom, looking down at the street. The October mist was not yet thick enough to obscure the houses opposite, but fifty yards along the street on either side it reared like a white wall. He was alone in the flat, awaiting a promised visit from his brother Moss. Clara had gone to the Petticoat Lane market with Mark. Mickey had left early, in spite of the lowering fog, to kick a football about with his cronies on Hackney Marshes.

He moved away from the window and picked up the pair of big tailor's scissors from the bench, clashing them absent-mindedly. He put the scissors down abruptly as he heard the rumbling sound of someone stepping on the lid of the coalhole at the foot of the front steps. Heavy footfalls echoed in the porch. There was a long ring at the doorbell. Joe made no move to answer the bell. He was hoping that the people downstairs would open the door, especially as Moss had only given one ring instead of the two required for the upstairs flat. Joe was only forty-two, but, sitting in his workshop day after day, he had little occasion for exercise; he was running to fat and his legs were stiff and sluggish. There was another ring at the bell. After the visitor at the door had released the knob the bell went on jangling loosely, its sound echoing in the empty hallway. The people in the lower flat were probably still in bed. Joe went downstairs.

He opened the street door and greeted his brother Moss, who, enormous in his heavy tweed overcoat, was beating his arms across his chest and stamping his feet impatiently.

'Ha! Stranger!' Joe said, 'Come in.'

Moss stepped into the hall, still stamping his feet. He grunted, 'Bloody cold. Gets in y' throat. Takes a drink to get rid of it.' He followed Joe up the stairs.

'Come in here.' The dining-room into which Joe ushered his brother was on the lower of two landings which the flat occupied. When he and Clara had been married, twenty years ago, they had taken the top flat. Some years later, when their second son was born, they rented the lower landing. There were three rooms on each floor; on the top floor a bathroom and two bedrooms (one for Joe and Clara, one for the boys), and on the lower floor, the dining-room, the kitchen and Joe's workshop.

Joe lit the gas fire, opened the doors of the walnut side-board and surveyed his stock of wines. 'What'll it be?' he asked. He knew what Moss would drink, but he could not resist the opportunity to show his rich brother that he, too, could receive a guest in the right way. 'Brandy? Whisky? Kümmel? Benedictine? Sherry?'

'Sherry?' Moss jeered. 'I wouldn't give it to the cat. As if you didn't know!' His voice sounded like simmering fat; thick, prosperous, with a bubble at the back of his throat. There was an overtone of insult to his voice that never left it. Even when he was cordial he made Joe feel resentful. He took the glass of whisky from Joe, said, 'Cheers,' and threw the drink at the back of his throat. 'Nice drop o' schnapps. You ain't been doin' so bad lately, eh?' He looked around him, with benevolent contempt, at the shining brown veneers, the prim brown settee, the stiff-backed chairs, the tall vase full of paper flowers on the table and the clock disguised as a Greek temple on the mantelpiece.

'Mustn't grumble,' Joe lied. 'How's Jin? Her back better? Clara says she was complaining the other day.'

'She still gets the spasms. I been gettin' a specialist for 'er. Geezer from 'Arley Street. Ten guineas a time. All right, eh? Wants 'er to go away, 'e does. Vichy.'

'Vichy. Where's that?'

'Gawd knows. On the Riviera somewhere. Must be good, though. Most expensive place there is, they reckon. All right, eh?'

Joe smacked his lips admiringly. 'Class, that is, and no mistake.'

'Herh! Herh!' exulted Moss. 'See my ol' Jin comin' back best of pals with Lady Love-a-Duck, eh? Pour me out another drink an' give yourself one. Generous, ain't I?'

Joe refilled the glasses with whisky. Moss raised his glass and cleared his throat deafeningly. 'Well,' he rumbled, ''ere's to our ol' Bella, bless 'er. Seven more days an' she'll be gettin' 'er little bit o' squeeze. About time, ain't it?'

Their sister Bella was getting married on the following Sunday. She was a big woman, with cheeks like great red apples. For years she had been trying, with the assistance of the whole family, to find herself a husband. Now, at the age of forty, she had got hold of one, an asthmatic, yellow-skinned little tailor's presser; and the whole family were combining their resources to make a great occasion of the wedding.

'She'll kill the poor little bleeder,' said Moss enthusiastically. 'She'll crush 'im to death. She'll pulverise 'im. My life, she will!'

Joe laughed uneasily. He did not approve of this kind of talk. 'I bet the wedding's keeping you busy,' he said.

'Busy?' Moss exclaimed. 'Don' ask me! I'm giving that girl a 'undred pounds' worth o' my time. I 'ope she appreciates it. Who sends out the invites? Me. Who keeps an eye on the presents? That old swine Friedlander sent two guineas. I tore the cheque up in 'is face, I did. "Never mind 'er," I said to 'im, "It's an insult to *me*. Me! The name is Mossy Strong, in case yer don't know. Don't tell me business is bad," I says to 'im. "I know where them razor-blades come from you been 'olesaling for the last month." Like a lamb, 'e was. Wrote me out a cheque for ten guineas on the spot. I shook 'is 'and. "Abe," I says, "so long as you can keep a soft spot in yer 'eart for a motherless girl the One Up There won't forget yer." "Never mind the One Up There," 'e says. "It's you I can't afford to cross, Mossy Strong."'

He reached for the whisky bottle and filled his own glass. 'Cheers! I 'ad a run-in with the caterers, too. Swindlin' sods, they are! Lucky you got me there to deal with 'em. They said they couldn't do it on the price we agreed. Wanted another twenty-five quid, they did. They knew it was too late for us to go to another caterer. "What's this?" I says. "Blackmail? I don't like that!" Anyway, we struck a bargain. An' that's what I come about.'

'Why?' Joe was anxious at the mention of money. He had already given ten pounds towards the cost of the wedding. There would be another five guineas for a present. More money had gone on wedding clothes for his whole household. Most of the last year's savings had been swallowed up already. Joe did not begrudge the money, but he was beginning to feel the pinch.

'I agreed to pay another twenty quid. Won't come to much between you an' me an' Sid. But I made them promise to do something about the floral display. You ought 'a seen the bloody floral display they was thinkin' of. Disgrace, it was. I wouldn't send those flowers to bleedin' 'Itler's funeral.'

'For Hitler's funeral,' Joe said, 'I wouldn't begrudge spending a bit. So what happened?'

'For the extra money, they'll smother the bleedin' 'all in flowers.'

'Here,' said Joe; 'wait a minute. This is our Bella that's getting married, not Queen Marie of Roumania.'

'Don't you want our Bella to get married like a queen?' Moss eyed his brother menacingly. 'Look, it ain't much. I'd put the lot up myself, but it's a matter of family affection, ain't it? I didn't think you'd want to miss the chance. I'll come in for a tenner if you an' Sid put up a fiver each. All right?'

'That's fair enough.' Joe tried to conceal the edge of bitterness in his voice. Moss had a flourishing fishmonger's shop, a growing connection as a street bookmaker and lucrative interests in a wide range of enterprises of varying underhandedness. Sid, their younger brother, was a professional gambler who could have spared the money out of one night's winnings at the dog track. But Joe did not demur aloud, for he knew that both his brothers despised him for the timid honesty and the lack of what they called 'ambition' that had kept him a workman at the bench for thirty years, and he did not want to make yet another admission of his poverty. Nor did he want to seem lacking in generosity. 'Want the money now?'

'Nah. Any time. Good boy, Joe.' Moss rose mountainously from his chair. 'Be runnin' now. Promised Jin I'd be back early for dinner.' He began to button his overcoat. 'Both the boys are comin', ain't they?' he asked suddenly. 'In dress suits, I 'ope?'

'Of course!' Joe assented indignantly. 'What did you think? A pretty penny it's costing us, too, hiring three suits at once.'

'Mickey bringin' 'is girl?'

'Mill? Yes. I'm making up a dress for her. It's in the workroom now, waiting for a fitting.'

'I'm glad that boy's going steady,' said Moss. 'Sid says 'e don't see 'im at the track no more. Pity 'e wastes 'is time in a cabinet-maker's workshop, though. I could do a lot for that boy if 'e come in with me.'

'He likes it,' Joe said. 'He's wonderful with his hands. Look at the things he's made in here.' He indicated the lamp standard in the corner, the fire-screen and the tea trolley. 'Anyway, I don't have to worry about him. That's more than I can say about Mark. I don't know what's to become of the boy. He's like a stranger in the house.'

Mark was indeed the greatest problem in their lives. For seven years he had been going to the Grammar School, and each year he had grown more apart from his family. Now his attitude to them varied between a nervous, absent-minded affection, a sullen remoteness and outbursts of irritable complaint. He would come in from school, fling his case into a corner and vanish into his bedroom. If they called to him to come and eat he would break out in hysterical rage. One day last week he had shouted, 'How can you have an appetite in this house with that horrible smell on the stairs — oilcloth and cabbages and the babies' napkins from downstairs?' Clara, her own repressed anxiety turning to anger, had cried, 'Perhaps you'd like us to move, eh? Perhaps you'd like a house in the country with goldfish pools? Or Buckingham Palace maybe? Why do you think we've lived here for twenty years? We might have been able to move if we'd sent you out to work at fourteen like your brother, instead of keeping you at school.' Mark, white-faced, had muttered, 'Oh, you're impossible,' and although he greedily attacked the meal his mother set before him, she regretted her words already, for she knew that they would fester in him for weeks.

Joe knew that Clara, too, must have been upset by the incident. She had told him about it in bed, unemotionally, but her calmness had not deceived him. For most of the last twenty years it had been her consuming ambition to move to a house of their own. She had haggled with shopkeepers, gone without new clothes, refused to spend money on holidays, in order to save. She had studied advertisements, scrutinised house agents' lists, tramped the suburbs, in search of a cheap house, but in vain; and meanwhile the earnings of Joe's prosperous seasons were frittered away in seasons when there was no work; there were illnesses; Mark's schooling cost much more than his scholarship grant; and they were still living in Khartoum Road, with as little money in the Savings Bank as ever.

'I know,' Moss was saying. 'Jin was telling me. 'E's got some funny ideas, that boy. Sneering at Bella's wedding, 'e was. Said it was degrading, marryin' Bella off to a little worm like that.'

Joe shrugged his shoulders. 'His nonsense!'

'Nonsense?' Moss fumed. 'I'd give 'im nonsense if 'e was my boy. Ain' 'e got no family affection?' This was the supreme sin to Moss. 'Bella's 'appy, ain't she? Is that a crime? She's got a nice, respectable feller. 'E ain't after money. It's 'is side that's buyin' the business.' The family, prepared for a bout of hard bargaining, had learned with relief that the bridegroom's relatives were prepared to set the couple up in a small business. 'If that ain't a love match, what is it?' He had crossed the room and was standing with his hand on the door-knob. 'Keepin' that boy at school was your mistake. My Aubrey won't go to no Grammar School. Fourteen at Christmas, an' out 'e comes, into the shop. That's where 'e'll get 'is education. Latin? Lit'rature? They don't put money in a boy's pocket. Smart boy, my Aubrey. Jin says 'e was born a business-man.' He opened the door. 'When's Mark leaving school?'

'Next summer. He's got two more terms.'

'Put 'im in with me. There's money in bookmaking. Might as well keep it in the family.'

'He's got his own ideas.'

'Send 'im round to me. I'll 'ave a talk with 'im. I'll tell 'im a thing or two. Time 'e got to know the facts of life. Any night in the week. You send 'im round.'

'I will,' said Joe gratefully.

'I'm orf now. Regards to Clara. Don't see me out.'

But Joe followed his brother deferentially down to the street door.

2

Mark and his mother had gone to visit his grandfather and Bella, the bride-to-be. While the women chattered about clothes, Mark talked with his grandfather, of whom he was sentimentally fond.

Jacob Strong lived in a little alley with cracked, sunken pavements, just off Whitechapel Road. He was short and thickset, like a cube, with a little square head set on it, waddling along on a pair of stumpy legs. His face was red and veined, with crooked blackened teeth and little eyes that peered suspiciously through the lens of a pair of gold-rimmed spectacles. His hair, which he wore cropped with a schoolboy fringe coming down over his forehead, was silver, as were his drooping moustache, the stubble on his cheeks and the tufts that protruded from ears and nostrils. Usually, he wore no jacket and his dirty, collarless shirt was open almost to the waist, revealing a thick woollen vest over the neckline of which sprouted another tangle of grey hair. The glittering, wiry hairs were thick, too, on his arms and the backs of his hands.

He was sixty-four years old, and until a few years ago he had worked as a fruit-porter in Spitalfields Market, one of the many Jewish porters there who are only distinguished from their Gentile workmates by the fact that they are burlier, their Cockney accent more pronounced, their language more obscene and their capacity for beer greater. He now lived on the charity of his children, and on the kindness of his neighbours, who kept him busy with all sorts of odd jobs and mysterious missions.

His wife had died several years ago, after giving him four children: Joe, who was now forty-two years old; Bella, two years younger; Moss, born a year after Bella; and then, the youngest by eleven years, Sid.

His acquaintances referred to him as a 'Dutch' Jew, although it was nearly three hundred years since his ancestors had come over from Holland, and although his speech, so far from being guttural, was of a wheezing, archaic Cockney which Mark delighted to hear.

After an entertaining hour in the old man's company, Mark and his mother went on to Petticoat Lane, to make some purchases in the market.

There was a tender and helpless side to Clara, a peculiar innocence which her son Mark sometimes perceived. It touched him, and moved him to remorse at the pain and bewilderment which his outbursts of fury inflicted on her. It was in one of these spasms of affection that he had offered to go shopping with her.

He pushed through the crowds, trying to keep up with his mother. He had been trying, in his secret thoughts, to face the same problem that, unknown to him, his father was discussing with Moss at this moment: that of his future. What was he to do when he left school? Each time he put the question to himself his thoughts crumbled into doubt and confusion. His secret and hopeless longing was to fly. But how? The training for a career in civil aviation was too expensive to be considered.

To enter the Air Force meant (for a lower-class boy who could not get a direct commission) years of apprenticeship on a few shillings a week, with only a ground job at the end of it. In neither case would he be able to help his family; and, although his mother hoped that he had forgotten her words, he still repeated them bitterly to himself each time he considered the subject. 'We might have been able to move if we'd sent you out to work at fourteen.' He could not drive the words from his mind; they burned there, leaving raw wounds of guilt.

The press of people added to his confusion, and he gave up the attempt to think clearly. He felt as if he were struggling in a nightmare, with the naphtha lamps flaring through the white fog, the rawness in his nose and throat, the hoarse clamour that besieged him from all sides, and the endless surge of bodies against him. Each time he found himself for a moment on a clear patch of pavement, another wall of dark bodies would burst upon him out of the whiteness and the tide of humanity come swirling around him. At times the people were jammed so tight that they could not move; they stood between the stalls and the warehouse walls that rose like black cliffs, and it was as if their bodies were one great mass, blending into the fog, and their heads were growing like cabbages out of this mass, immovable and helpless. At these moments the people turned their faces up towards the invisible sky, as if they were drowning, and those who wanted to talk to others shouted upwards, unable to turn their heads, but hoping that their companions would hear their voices raised above the din. Then the people would begin to move again, grinding past each other in two streams, and still they were so close together that they were not conscious of separate human bodies, but saw the other faces moving past like a succession of disembodied masks.

His mother loved this, he thought, as he watched her, small and pigeon-shaped in her shiny black coat, weaving her way through the crowds. Occasionally she would look over her shoulder to make sure that he had not lost track of her and she would offer him a bright, timid smile that at once annoyed him and awoke a wrench of tenderness inside him.

To her all this was a gay carnival. He saw her look up with delight at a mass of balloons floating over her head as she waited for him on the corner of Wentworth Street; she loved colours like a child. A few moments later he caught up with her again and found her watching a hawker who was making little clockwork geese scuttle to and fro in front of him. She pointed at the geese; her cheeks were shining with laughter. On the fringe of a large crowd surrounding a stall from which cheap dresses were being sold she took his arm and made him listen. The salesman was haranguing the crowd with the eloquence of a mob orator. 'Here you are, ladies,' he bellowed. 'Here's a nice maternity dress. Plenty of room round the bread basket, and buttons down the front. When baby's hungry, you just undo a button or two and both your bubs come tumbling out.' Mark heard his mother shriek with outraged laughter next to him. At another stall she kept him waiting for five minutes while she examined in detail an array of cheap brooches. She stopped him by a fruiterer's stall. 'Doesn't it look nice?' she shouted to him above the noise. Oranges were stacked in great banks, with pyramids of shining green apples and waterfalls of black grapes, with huge, hanging bunches of bananas and boxes of dates and tangerines in nests of silver paper; the naphtha lamps roaring and flaring and casting a flickering light upon them all.

A file of Lascar seamen, in denim dungarees and woollen caps, pushed past him. Their speech sounded to him like the chatter of parrots. He heard fragments of conversation in Dutch, in French, in German, and once, at his ear, somebody's voice saying, 'Ah, I went upstairs and told him his horse had lost, and he just smiled, and when I'd gone, he put his head in the gas oven. He was a good gambler, though.' He nearly lost his mother trying to hear more, but the voice had vanished in the crowd.

The voices of vendors assailed him.

'Buy, buy, buy!'

'One-and-six a bunch!'

'Step right in, ladies. The best value in the market!'

A quack was selling medicines, lecturing with the aid of a porcelain statuette on which were painted horrible reproductions of the human organs. An old man was standing at the corner of Bell Lane mournfully selling *The Daily Liar*. A barrel organ made itself heard above the din from the direction of Commercial Street and behind him, in the fog, Mark heard the thumping and braying of an ex-Serviceman's band. The voices of the stallholders sounded thick and raucous to him, their faces mocking and ugly. His own people! He hated them, clamouring to him with outstretched hands like Oriental beggars, screaming and supplicating for custom, spitting and snarling at each other over a disputed victim as cats might over a scrap of food.

Tonight they would be in the West End, sleek, well-dressed, arrogant, stuffed with money and behaving like the lords of creation. This morning they were lining the crowded roadway like a living frieze of frenzy, tearing the money from the pockets of the gaping shoppers. It seemed to Mark that it was towards him that they were reaching out, to pluck him out of the clean, tidy world in which he was trying to make a place for himself, to hold him fast and drag him down into a screaming underworld.

He followed his mother into a shop. It was quiet inside; the voices of the assistants and the thud of bolts of silk on the counter sounded louder than the uproar in the street. There was a warm smell of cloth.

The proprietor came forward, and Mark turned away as his mother and the man began to talk. He heard her discussing fabrics and prices and examining material.

'How much is this spun silk?'

'Five and eleven a yard, lady.' The shopkeeper was a swart little man. 'And I'm not making a penny on it. By my life.'

'I'll give you three shillings a yard.'

'Three shillings!' The little man banged the bolt of silk down on the counter. 'The bread from my children's mouths she wants to take!' he announced. He assumed a pleading attitude towards Mark's mother. 'Where else in the Lane can you get a bit of material like this for five and eleven? Where, lady? Where? Go on, tell me!' He turned to his cashier and flung out his arms. 'Tilly, give me five pounds out of the till. There you are, lady, five pounds, you can have it if you will tell me where else in the Lane you can get a piece of material like this.' He mopped his brow. 'Feel it. Go on, feel it. See how it suits you. See!' He knelt suddenly at Mrs. Strong's feet like an impetuous lover, and draped the fabric from her waist to her ankle. 'Look at it in the mirror. I won't charge you nothing for a look. A pleasure it is. A queen you look!'

Mark saw his mother look approvingly at her reflection in the mirror. 'It's not for me,' she said placidly.

'All right,' said the shopkeeper. 'So it's for your daughter. She takes after you, doesn't she? If it suits you, it suits her.'

'I haven't got a daughter.'

The man stood up. 'Three shillings she says,' he moaned. 'My dear wife should be in the shop to hear her trying to ruin me. Make it a dollar, lady,' he ended briskly.

Mrs. Strong countered, 'Four shillings.'

Mark edged away towards the door. Time after time he begged her not to do this; but she would answer defiantly, 'You keep quiet, Mister Aristocrat. Till you start earning money don't you tell me to throw it away.' He knew that it was not only the need to economise which led her to haggle; it was a pleasure to her, a sport. Now, as he watched her, her cheeks were flushed, she was as alert and as quietly excited as a huntress.

The little shopkeeper returned to the attack. 'Look at her,' he shouted, pointing dramatically at Mrs. Strong and clutching his hair as everyone in the shop turned to look. 'Four shillings, she says. She thinks I'm a philanthropist.'

Mrs. Strong said, 'And maybe you think I'm Lady Rothschild. Four-and-six. Not a penny more.'

'Impossible.'

'Come on.' She took Mark's arm and turned to leave.

The shopkeeper, cradling the bolt of silk like a baby in his arms, darted between her and the door.

'I'll tell you what,' he announced. 'I'm a sport. For you only I'll do it. My wife will curse me for it. My assistants will think I'm a fool. My customers will point at me and say, "Look. There goes Polatchik. Soft in the brain he's gone. A tragedy!" What does it matter? Split the difference, eh? Four and nine a yard.'

'Wrap me up three yards,' said Mrs. Strong.

3

On the following Wednesday evening Mark had his interview with Moss. When his father had asked him to go he had flushed and looked up from his supper with an angry reply on his lips; but his mother, knowing that at the moment he was especially fearful of hurting her, had quickly said, in the shy, small voice that always touched his heart, 'Why not, Mark dear?' Mark had answered despairingly, 'All right, Mother. I'll go.'

He disliked his uncle, but he hated his aunt, and it was she whom he dreaded to meet as he lingered outside Moss's house. He was terrified that he might be left alone with her. She opened the door to him. 'Hallo, Mark. Come in. Moss'll be down in a minute. How are you keeping?' She was a slim, hard woman with dry, bleached hair. He heard himself answering meekly, 'I'm all right, thank you, Aunt Jenny', as he followed her into the house.

At seventeen, Mark was broad and well built, with only a pallor in his skin and an alert grace in his movement to remind him of his childhood puniness. His eyes were watchful and scared as he faced his uncle's wife, for whenever they met she eyed him with a calculating lust that belied her conventional greetings.

Yet, however much this look of hers played havoc with Mark's adolescent imagination, and however often it was misunderstood by men, it was misleading, for she and her husband were a happy and faithful couple. She was a Gentile, and had been married to Moss for fifteen years. She was bound to him by an affinity which was stronger than any racial differences, for both of them boasted of possessing 'a head for business', and they ran together on the track of profit like bloodhounds in a twin leash. What kept them together, Mark imagined, was their need and appreciation of each other's business abilities and their common absorption in the progress of Moss's many enterprises. They had the same passion for cards, they both displayed the same gluttony, they both enjoyed the same kind of rowdy company, and they publicly rejoiced in each other's heroic sexual appetites. Out of all this there must have grown up a squalid comradeship that was as binding as love.

'Sit down,' Jenny said. 'I'll get you a drink.' Mark demurred. 'Go on,' she urged; 'you'll like it! Time somebody treated you like a grown-up, isn't it?' He took the glass of whisky from her and drank it hurriedly, in an attempt to imitate Moss. 'My!' Jenny said. 'You can take it, too!' There was a quality in her voice which reminded him of the inhuman crackle of tinfoil. 'How's your Mum and Dad?' She was coiled on the settee opposite his armchair, watching him intently from a nest of brightly-flowered silk cushions, her yellow hair lustreless against the gleaming patterns of black, red and silver. He stared at the carpet to avoid the sight of her silk-clad legs and mumbled, 'All right, thank you.' She lit a cigarette. 'Want one of these?' Mark refused. 'I've got a nice pair of kippers from the shop,' she said. 'You can take 'em home for your mum.' He thanked her again, still avoiding her look. He knew that she was mocking him. She could play on his adolescence as on a violin; she was interested in no more than that. 'Well,' she asked, 'got a girl friend yet?'

'No time for that sort of thing,' muttered Mark. His face was flushed; when he tried to talk the muscles were stiff and resistant.

'Not much!' Jenny jeered. 'Fancy making a boy of your age walk about the street with a silly little school cap like a pimple on his head. I bet you feel a fool when a pretty girl looks at you!' She heard footsteps on the stairs. Mark heard them, too, gratefully. 'Ah,' Jenny said. 'Here he is.'

Moss came in. The room was in shadow, a tall standard lamp casting its rays in a circle, white and bright and soft as moonlight, about the settee on which Jenny sat. 'Hah!' Moss grunted, 'Let's 'ave some light on the subject.' He pressed switches and shaded lamps glowed in the corners of the room, revealing the walls hung with black tapestries on which red and silver peacocks spread their dazzling fans. Jenny had decorated this room.

'Glad you come, boy,' Moss said. 'Drink?' Mark said, 'I've had one,' and waited, warily, while his uncle filled and emptied a glass.

Moss walked across the room and leaned against the mantelpiece, in the glow of the electric fire. 'Gettin' on all right at school?'

This ponderous diplomacy annoyed Mark. He answered, 'I'm leaving in two more terms. That's what you wanted to see me about, wasn't it?'

'Ah,' Moss assented. ''Ow'd yer like to come into business with me?'

Mark stared dumbly at the electric fire.

'You know me,' Moss went on. 'Always think of the family. Put 'em all in clover, that's what I'm gonna do.' He spread himself in front of the fire. 'Next year, I'm branchin' out. I'm wastin' no more time on the fish-shop. Jin's gonna run that. Ain't yer, gel? Big-time bookmakin', that's me in future. Finished with street betting. Time you finished payin' orf the coppers, there's only chicken-feed left. Offices in the West End, that's the way to do it. Call yourself Turf Agency, Sporting Accountant, that kind o' thing. Big stuff only. Millions in it.'

'It's respectable,' said Jenny; 'you pay income tax. Some o' these big West End bookies, they give money to charity, they sit on hospital committees, the best people aren't too proud to shake their hands.'

Moss expelled a rumble of laughter. 'She's got ideas, my wife. High society she likes. She's right, though. There's a career in it. Your Uncle Sid's in already. I'm putting my Aubrey in next year when 'e leaves school. I got a job for you, too. Like the idea?'

Mark looked for courage in the bright heart of the fire. His first attempt to answer only produced a harsh noise in his throat. At last he croaked, 'Not much.'

'Five quid a week for the first year. You'll be doing nothin' but travel round with me learnin' the business. A lord's life. When you're nineteen I'll start yer on ten quid a week, maybe more. Well?'

Mark struggled to speak. His heart was fluttering with fright. 'It's not the kind of job I'm interested in,' he said weakly.

'You'll learn the ropes, make 'undreds for yourself on the side, you will, bit o' smart bettin', inside information. Ask your Uncle Sid! Your Mum and Dad could do with the money. Eh? Couldn't they?'

Mark did not answer. He sat with his hands clasped in his lap and his head bowed as if he were on trial.

'What's up?' Moss's voice was less genial. 'Struck dumb? What's wrong about it?'

Mark did not speak. He was trembling slightly.

'I know,' Jenny said sharply, stretching her body among the cushions. 'It's beneath his lordship's dignity.' She imitated Mark's careful grammar school accent. 'He likes *nice* people. He wants to get away from *horrid* people like us. Don't you, dearie?'

Mark looked at her in impotent fury. How easily she could read every one of his thoughts! He was pale, and his voice was shaking, as he replied, 'That's not a crime, is it?'

'It's a bloody tragedy,' Moss growled. 'What you gonna do? Tell me.'

'I want to live gloriously.'

If Mark had dared, this is what he would have answered, for he was at the age when he still foolishly believed this to be his birthright. At seventeen a boy is still sustained by dreams. He has not yet been flung into the middle of a dunghill existence in which it is necessary to be mediocre to survive, heartless to avoid distress, dishonest to flourish. He must 'grow up' — that is to say, his spirit must be broken — before he can accept all this and settle down to his allotted ant's life.

Instead he answered: to him it meant the same thing, 'I want to fly'.

There were other things he could have added, if he had thought it possible to make his uncle understand him. He wanted to escape from his own people, who seemed to him to have accepted the world's evils as their conditions of existence. He wanted to belong where he lived. He wanted to attune the rest of his life to the atmosphere of sanity, stability, tradition that surrounded him at school. He longed for the calm that came of settled centuries and sound nerves.

'Fly? You're barmy,' Moss said. 'Where's the money in it?'

Mark shrugged his shoulders.

'It's a rich man's game,' Jenny said. 'Flying for pleasure costs a fortune. Come in with Moss, get some money in your pocket, and you can do all the flying you want.'

Mark still did not answer.

Jenny asked, 'Are you going to do anything about it when you leave school?'

'I don't see how I can. I can't get a flying commission in the Air Force, and it costs as much to train for commercial flying as it does to go to Oxford or Cambridge. I shall have to get some other job for a while.'

'What sort of job?' It was still Jenny, questioning calmly.

'The school finds jobs for you,' he answered sullenly. 'In the City, generally.'

Moss broke in, 'Thirty bob a week, eh?'

'Well?' Mark snarled.

'Look!' Moss came over and gripped Mark's shoulder. 'You're in for a bloody big shock, boy, if you try an' crawl in with *them*. You're one of us.' Mark glared denial but lacked the courage to speak. 'You're safer among your own,' Moss said.

'My own,' Mark shouted in a sudden rage that was fed by his growing indecision in face of the prospect of comparative wealth, and by the wrench of recognition he had felt at Moss's latest words. He stood up. 'I don't know,' he said unsteadily.

'You'll see the world,' said Moss. 'Brighton, Newmarket. Your own car.'

Jenny came and stood behind Mark. 'Leave him alone,' she said. She put her arms loosely about his neck. 'Plenty of time to make up his mind. Think it over, Mark.' Her arms were warm, and awoke the luxuriousness in his blood. 'You know,' she said softly, 'you're missing things.' She squeezed his shoulders and smiled as he shivered. 'We'll see you at the wedding. You can tell us then.' She removed her arms. He was relieved; yet, to his horror, he missed them. 'You'll spare a dance for your Aunt Jin, won't you?'

Mark was in a state of stunned confusion when he left. He let Moss force another drink on him. He felt strong and angry for a moment as the heat of the alcohol spread through him, but as it died away the fog of doubt, unhappiness and physical fear closed in on him again. He hardly knew where he was going as he made for the door.

'See you at the wedding,' grunted Moss.

'Don't forget the kippers,' Jenny called after him; and he recognised the mockery in her voice.

4

Bella's bridal feast was held in a hall in an East End back street. On Sunday afternoon, after the wedding service at the synagogue, hired Daimlers brought the guests here in relays. As they entered they crowded to the buffet where, although there was soon to be a wedding breakfast and later a gargantuan dinner, they stuffed themselves with thirst-provoking snacks and whetted their appetites again with glasses of brandy.

Jacob Strong stood by the door receiving the guests. He wore a morning coat and a furry silk hat, and peered about him at newcomers like an old bruiser in the ring. He shook each proffered hand vigorously, as if testing it for strength and flinging it contemptuously aside. When his cronies appeared he led them to the bar and drank with them, swallowing glass after glass of whisky as if it were water.

His youngest son Sid, in white tie and tails, was supervising at the buffet, goading guests to help themselves and distributing carnation buttonholes. He was less than five feet in height. His face was thin and grey, with a huge angular nose like the finger of a sundial fastened point downwards in the middle of it. His movements were quick and birdlike, his voice high-pitched but assured.

Joe Strong and his family arrived, Joe and his sons in hired dinner jackets, Clara and Mickey's girl, Mill, in evening dress. Mark, whose inborn precocity had overcome for the moment his critical sense, felt proud to be dressed like a grown-up and to be drinking whisky without restraint. He thought of himself among his schoolmates as a man amongst boys.

'Mark, dear, I've got a nice partner for you.' He was standing at the bar, and turned to find his Aunt Jenny face to face with him, her body so close that he caught fire from its warmth, her perfume heavy in his nostrils.

'Well, well!' she laughed. 'I only have to mention a girl and you blush. You're not much of a Romeo, are you? Or do you only operate in the dark?'

He knew that she had seen and understood the reason for his flushed cheeks. He managed to speak at last. His voice cracked absurdly, exposing his embarrassment to her, 'Have a drink, Aunt Jenny,' he croaked.

She laughed again. 'Changing the subject, eh? All right. I'll look forward to hearing your confessions some other time, when it's not so crowded.' She busied herself with the seating chart which she held. 'Anyway, you're not sitting with your Mum and Dad. I've put you with the young people on the left-hand table. You'll enjoy yourself better there. You can look after Dave's cousin, Ruth. You met Ruth?'

'No.'

'She's a nice girl. Your own age. Educated, too.' She winked. 'Let me know what luck you have.' She squeezed his arm as she left him, and he looked after her with hatred; but he could not help looking appreciatively at her hair, piled up and glossy after a morning of expensive attentions, and at the smooth-fitting black-and-white afternoon dress which moulded her hard and shapely body.

He sweated, and felt dizzy with drink for the first time. The hall was full now. The chatter beat like surf on his giddiness, a muttering bass with women's shrillnesses rising and falling against it in fluttering cadenzas. Many of the guests were already straying impatiently into the dining-room, where waiters hurried to put the final touches to the three long tables which ran the length of the room to join the short, transversal table at which the bride and groom would sit with their closest kin.

He was glad when the meal was announced, and let himself be carried by the rush into the dining-room. He felt as if his two feet stood on separate floors which were rising and falling like the pedals of a bicycle. He saw, through the crush, his mother looking at him with concern and, over someone's shoulder, Mickey grinning derisively at him.

He found his chair and slumped into it without waiting for his partner to take her place. He was aware of her sitting down next to him, and he heard himself making some silly remark to her, not able to grasp his own words, not daring to look at her; she was only a dark bulk to one side of his field of vision; he had the impression, among the yellow grease-spots that swam before his eyes, of thick black hair falling over a pale skin. Other people were finding their seats; their dutiful pleasantries came at him from all angles, bewildering him. He remembered the advice his father had often given him. 'You'll never get drunk if you keep on eating,' and without paying any attention to his neighbours he broke a roll and stuffed the pieces hastily into his mouth. He chewed and swallowed, and felt better.

He heard the girl next to him expostulating. 'The Rabbi hasn't broken bread yet.'

He reached frantically for another roll. 'It's very bad manners to talk about bad manners.' The words seemed too big for his mouth and floated away from him like bubbles.

Her voice came to him again. It was cool, not affected, yet without the Jewish vibration. 'Here,' she was saying, 'I know what's the matter with you. Have a drop of water.' She was laughing.

He turned to her solemnly and dared to look at her for the first time. 'Are you suggesting—?' Her hair was dark and gleaming and, although it was gathered somehow, fell in a thick mass almost to her shoulders. It framed a neutral, pleasant face with clear, pale skin. She smiled at him reassuringly. He noticed that her face came down to a pointed chin and that the only hint of the exotic was in her broad cheekbones. He felt ashamed of himself and said, 'I'm sorry. I've spent half the day pouring out drinks for other people. I've lost count of the number I've had myself. I'm Mark Strong. I suppose you're Ruth.'

'Yes,' she said. 'We've already been introduced. You wouldn't remember. That was two or three dozen drinks ago.'

He lowered his gaze carefully to look below her shoulders. She was — he could not decide; no, he certainly wouldn't call her fat. Full? No. Solid? No. Plump? Well, perhaps. She seemed slim, yet there was a kind of abundance about her that strained at her dress and made her look older than seventeen.

They fell quiet for a moment as the Rabbi intoned a blessing upon the meal and broke bread ceremonially.

'Wine?' Mark asked.

'No,' she said. 'Lemonade. That's what you'd better stick to, as well.'

As he leaned towards her to fill her glass Aunt Jenny's banter rose unbidden in his mind. He remembered his humiliation and the happiness died suddenly within him. The girl was talking again, eagerly; the ring of happiness was still in her voice; but he could not respond. He turned abruptly from her and began to eat his hors d'oeuvres, staring down at the plate. There was a note of bewilderment in the girl's voice now; he could feel the enquiry in it; then she desisted and bent to her own plate. He looked furtively at her and saw that her cheeks were red. He felt another pang of shame, but did not know how he might reach out to her again.

It was she who made the attempt, after the fish had been served. His mouth was full of boiled fish and sweet yellow sauce; he was enjoying it, and trying to stir himself to feel resentment at her silent, persistent presence, when she said, 'Don't they all look a funny lot, stuffing themselves?'

He followed her gaze down the tables, at the rows of guests eating noisily and furiously as if there were a gigantic contest in progress.

'Like a row of pigs at a trough,' he said.

'Oh, no,' she protested. There was anger in her voice. He realised that he had mistaken the light, trivial remark, meant only to draw him from his absorption, for an expression of the same contempt that he felt. 'What a horrible thing to say!' After a pause, she added, 'When my father's family lived in Poland they never knew what it was to have more than a bowl of thin soup and a bit of black bread every day. Once a week they had a proper meal, with meat. When my father was a child he fainted more than once in the streets with hunger. Three of his six brothers and sisters died. He went to work when he was seven years old. I don't blame them for loving their food.'

Mark had never encountered anyone among his own people as articulate and forthright in answering him as this girl. When Jenny had spoken to him he had expected a partner who would overwhelm him with shrill, silly table talk. He was disconcerted, and was relieved when they rose from the table.

'I'm going home to change,' she said pleasantly; but he muttered, 'Excuse me,' as if they were strangers, and thrust past her. Her cheeks darkened again; then she entered into conversation with someone else and, lagging at first so that she might not catch up with Mark and making a wide circuit in the ante-room to avoid passing close by him, she escaped to the cloakroom and looked about for her mother.

At six o'clock the second bout of festivities began. After the wedding breakfast many of the guests had left to change into evening clothes; others remained sitting about in groups in the hall.

The guests came streaming in again, all of them now in evening dress, some of the men wearing dinner jackets, some in tails. It was impossible to tell the rich from the poor among them; the sprinkling of wealthy relatives who had condescended to come were indistinguishable from the press of little tailors and furriers and cabinet-makers; for all, whatever their means, were gorgeously attired.

The crowds flocked round the bar again, reaching for snacks of black bread and pickled herring with seemingly inexhaustible appetites. A quartet of Strongs, bullet-headed, red-necked youths in full evening dress, had taken command of the bar, and were watching like a bodyguard over the whisky.

The hubbub increased as the band arrived. They disappeared into the dining-room to prepare their instruments and their music; then they reappeared and, keeping close together, fought their way with a teamwork born of long practice through the scrum until they were at the bar.

They were greeted with cordiality by the bartenders, for Joey de Jong and his Dixieland Devils were the pride of the 'Dutch' colony in the East End. After satisfying their thirsts, Joey and his men trooped off to the kitchen, where the chef allowed them to prowl among the trays, stuffing themselves with whatever offered in preparation for the gruelling evening's work that lay ahead.

At eight o'clock Joey de Jong and his drummer emerged from the kitchen, wiping their greasy mouths. The drummer commanded silence with a roll of drums and Joey with a blast on the trumpet. The guests' voices were stilled; only in the background was there discernible the same murmur of anticipation that can be heard on a race-track as the horses rear and fidget at the start. The Master of Ceremonies, a huge and magnificent personage in a scarlet uniform and white knee-breeches, looking like the majordomo of an Italian palace, appeared in the doorway of the dining-room and bellowed, 'Ladies and gentlemen! Dinner is served! Kindly take your seats!' He stepped aside — the movement was a masterly combination of speed and dignity — as the guests flooded past him.

The band were all seated. After much clattering and scraping of chairs, the guests were in their places. The tables, laid anew for the meal, were ablaze with flowers. Masses of lovely blooms filled bowls along the middle of each table. Great arches of blossom rose between the tables. The principal table, at which the bride and bridegroom were to sit, was a bower of colour and beauty. The damp freshness of the flowers, their delicate scents, brought a sweet coolness to the room, prevailing over the heat and the smell of cooking.

The Master of Ceremonies took up his station behind the empty chairs of the bridal couple. He raised his hand, and once more a drum's roll brought silence. His chest swelled. Joey de Jong watching him, raised both his hands. The band leaned forward on their chairs with their instruments ready. The Master of Ceremonies puffed out his cheeks; his lips parted and once again his parade-ground roar echoed across the tables: 'Ladies — and — gentlemen. Kindly — be — upstanding — to receive — the bride and bridegroom!'

Joey brought his hands down and doubled himself up in a kind of monstrous obeisance. With a deafening flourish, the band struck up the *Wedding March*. Chairs rumbled as the guests rose to their feet, and everyone in the hall turned towards the far door, through which appeared the bride and bridegroom. Bella, upon whom many handmaidens had toiled for the last hour, was as fresh as if the day were just beginning, massive within her shimmering veil, hugging her enormous bouquet to her with one hand and linking her other arm in the groom's with such possessiveness that she gave the impression of walking with the little man tucked like a parcel under her arm. Her long train of silver satin was borne in triumph by four bridesmaids. Jacob Strong and the groom's parents followed, and behind them walked Moss and Jenny, carrying themselves as if they realised that everybody attributed to them the real glory of this moment.

As they moved in stately progress round the room there broke out such a din that the band, playing with all its might, could only be heard as a throbbing in the background. Guests battered at the tables with spoons, stamped, clapped, shouted, cheered and sang. The more noise the guests made, the more Joey de Jong urged his players on to mightier efforts; the more frenziedly the band blew and drummed and scraped, the more the tumult grew, to render the band inaudible once more.

At length the bridal party were in their seats and the guests, in turn, subsided gratefully into their chairs and mopped their streaming faces. Joey and his boys, breathless, their hair awry, allowed themselves a brief rest while the Rabbi rose to utter his customary prayers; then they struck up again, this time with the *Merry Widow Waltz* as a procession of waiters, each bearing aloft a large, silver tray, streamed in from the kitchen with the grace and precision of a troupe of skaters swooping on to the rink, broke formation and moved ceremoniously along the tables.

Now there rose to mingle with the music the munch and guggle of two hundred busy mouths consuming food and drink, the clatter of cutlery and the clinking of bottles and wine-glasses, the many-pitched hum of conversation broken by the grave, enquiring voices of the waiters and by the sudden explosions of laughter that burst, in a haphazard bombardment of noise, in different parts of the room. Hands, clutching their shining implements, rose and fell to scoop up and deliver their loads of food, like racing shuttles. Two hundred jaws opened and shut as if they were all worked by one vast machine. Beckoning hands shot up from time to time, summoning the waiters back for extra portions. Cockney faces shone as full and red as big Dutch cheeses, the cheeks distended with good things. White-skinned, blue-bearded foreign faces were pushed low over the mounds of steaming food as if to examine every inch of it minutely before consuming it. Course after course disappeared, the sweating and tireless musicians launching into a new tune each time the procession of waiters reappeared. Hors d'oeuvres, massed in bewildering array on trolleys, wheeled from place to place. Clear soup, or thick, both augmented with meat balls, a chicken course, an even bigger meat course with tongue, crisp meat patties, peas and grated fried potatoes, the dessert, ices, many-hued and elaborate, and at last, when the daintiest were already gasping and grunting and wondering how to dispel the horrible, clogging pressure across their chests, came the cups of clear, pungent black coffee. The waiters were moving again from place to place with whisky for the gentlemen, to help them dispel from their mouths the rich flavours of pungent, greasy gravies, so tasty five minutes before, now so unpleasantly lingering. Cigarettes followed, and cigars. The ladies fluttered gratefully the fans — an ultimate inspiration on Moss's part — which each had found by her plate. Another signal from the Master of Ceremonies, another rattle of the drum, and the guests lapsed into somnolent silence while the Rabbi gabbled through his after-dinner prayers. Speeches followed. First Moss, his voice thicker and fattier than ever, his oratorical abilities, sharpened by years of crying his wares in the fish-shop, sailing away on a sea of whisky — his crowning witticism coming when he patted the timid little bridegroom on the head (swaying dangerously as he leaned towards him) and said: 'Englan' expects 'at every man tonight will do 'is duty! And, by God, our Bella won't give yer any sleep till you do!' More toasts, during which the guests rose and subsided like sleep-walkers, pouring down drink after drink. By the time the groom was hauled to his feet to peer at a piece of crumpled paper and stammer his reply the guests were thoroughly stupefied and stood swaying in their places, clapping perfunctorily at the wrong places so that the groom could not make himself heard and sat down in a panic amid a final thunderous burst of cheers.

The hall was filling now for the ball. Droves of new guests were arriving, and Sid, together with a couple of the hefty young men from behind the bar, was on guard at the door against gate-crashers.

Mark saw Ruth standing on the other side of the room. She looked graceful, and taller than before, in a pink satin evening dress with a long, flared skirt, cape sleeves and a dark sash hanging loosely from the waist. It would have pleased his vanity now to be seen standing at her side. But when she looked his way and he thought he might have to meet her eyes, he took fright and turned abruptly away into the crowd.

People were moving from the centre of the dance floor, leaving a clear space. The lights dimmed, and the band began to play the first waltz. The bride and bridegroom took the floor, amid a rattle of applause. Mark caught a glimpse, through the crush, of them waddling gracelessly past in a moving pool of brilliance as a spotlight followed them; then other couples moved on to the floor, coloured limelights began to steal among the shadows, and the dancing became general.

He could not see Ruth anywhere. An arm fell across his back. Jenny was at his side again. With her arm around his shoulder, she gave him a hug. She led him to the bar, and as they stood together he felt her flank close against him, her side blazing through the electric silk of her gown. He could not speak when she asked him if he wanted another whisky; his throat was parched and the back of his mouth felt closed. He quivered violently against her; she released him, gave him his drink and negligently swallowed her own. He gulped at the drink and the alcohol spread through his body, a spine of fire descending from throat to loins. He felt a new surge of confidence; his voice was thicker and stronger as he asked her to dance, and when she came into his arms he held her close. They moved round the floor. He seemed to be wrapped in a flame; he melted in her heat. Within his arms he felt her as an elastic hardness. He could not see her face. The floor rose and fell beneath his feet. When he bumped into people he did not notice them and uttered no apologies. Above the scent that she wore he caught the odour of her body. He felt male, and crazy; until, turning giddily, he came face to face with Ruth, who was dancing with another partner.

The flush drained from his face. She smiled, as if she had been expecting to see him at that moment, and vanished. Suddenly he felt weak and clumsy. Jenny was too close to him. The sweat was starting up through the powder on her cheeks, the contrived lustre fading from her hair in the heat of the ballroom. The cleft of her breasts, beneath his eyes as she clung to him, was white and chalky. He wondered how to get rid of her; he hated his own callowness, his lack of diplomacy. When the dance ended he could think of nothing better than to mumble his thanks and to plunge away from her into the crowd. Even when he had reached the other end of the hall he felt as if her eyes were still on him, mocking and cruelly understanding.

He found Ruth. He said 'Hallo,' and kept control of himself while she introduced him to her mother. He led her away to dance. The band was playing a quickstep; he was unskilled, and too absorbed in trying to maintain the step to be able to surrender himself to her presence. He held her aloofly, his arm muscles hard with embarrassment. The Dixieland Devils had worked themselves up to such a frenzy that he could not distinguish the tune they were blaring, but only the thumping rhythm. The hall was crammed now. Sid must have given up his guard on the door, for strangers were streaming in unchecked. He was bumped and jostled at every step. A final scream from Joey de Jong's upraised trumpet and the dance ended. Mark grinned foolishly at Ruth and, without speaking, opened his arms to her again as a waltz began.

She said, 'Still drinking?' She moved coolly and smoothly in his arms. The rhythm of her dancing was not spoiled when she spoke.

Mark boasted, 'Everything under control. I can go on till Doomsday now that I've got some grub inside me.'

'You'd better not.'

His self-consciousness left him as they talked. He relaxed, and drifted with her. She was not like other girls with whom he had danced. She did not hold herself braced away from him, nor did she thrust herself greedily against him; but she seemed somehow to receive him, to envelop him softly and warmly, so that the rigidity and strain vanished from his body and he moved easily with her, dancing in a trance. There was no scent about her, but a sort of feminine milkiness. He could have put his head on her shoulders and slept, still dancing.

'Are you enjoying yourself?'

In reply he only shrugged his shoulders. He did not like to admit it, but he was. To be drinking, to be dancing, to be excited and close to women, to be wearing a dinner jacket; he wished his school friends and his teachers could have seen him. But, he recollected quickly, aware again of his surroundings and guiltily conscious of the way in which his attitude had been changing, not among these people! He sneered, 'It's like the Darktown Strutters' Ball.'

Now that he was more sure of himself he wanted to provoke her again; he was ashamed of the way in which, by his rudeness, he had capitulated before, and wanted to renew the quarrel on equal terms. But, instead of bridling, she laughed indulgently and said, 'Silly!'

The festivities grew more furious every minute. The Dixieland Devils, in response to repeated and clamorous requests from the bridegroom's family, were playing a *Kazatske*, a wild, interminable group dance that earlier generations of immigrants had brought with them from the ghettoes and villages of Eastern Europe.

Unwearied by his previous endeavours, Joey de Jong, his hair falling over his eyes, his dress shirt crumpled, blew at his trumpet with puffed cheeks and bulging eyes and, setting it aside, began to caper and convulse himself as he urged his players and the dancers on. On to the dance floor flooded all the older folk, bald, shrivelled little men, stooping grey-beards, well-preserved business-men, hobbling grandmothers and vast-bosomed matrons, all shrieking with delight, marking the rhythm of the tune with quick shouts as if they were calling the step, *hup-hup-hup*, on a parade ground, stamping, clapping, whirling each other about, sinking down on bent knees and leaping gymnastically from one foot to the other; while those who did not dance stood in a ring around them, swaying, clapping deafeningly to mark the time, shouting the rhythm and cheering the dancers on. The rhythm of the dance increased in speed. In every part of the hall onlookers were stamping and clapping faster and faster. Even the old women who sat, exhausted, against the walls, swayed in time to the raucous music, and the waiters, circulating endlessly under the malignant eye of Sid Strong with liqueurs, ices, chocolates, fruit and coffee, swooped through the throng with their trays as if they were on roller-skates. The bride and bridegroom had already been stuffed into a car and noisily dismissed to their honeymoon; few noticed their departure, for they were far from being the most important people at this gathering.

Mark, who was exchanging small-talk with Ruth on the fringe of the crowd, had the sensation of being several people at once. One was oppressed by the unbearable din and by the frenzy that gathered in the stale and overheated air; one was mellow with good food, alcohol, and the company of the girl at his side, as she artlessly drew for him a picture of herself... she was a typist... she would like to go abroad... she dreamed of faraway places... she believed in God, but she didn't care for religion... next year her parents were going to let her spend her holidays away from them for the first time in her life... she was (a reluctant admission) the same age as Mark... did he like J. B. Priestley? A third of his selves had withdrawn, far from her chatter, to dream in quiet places.

A sound vibrated in his consciousness, thin, persistent and peremptory as the quiver of a tuning-fork. His head jerked up in response as the sound penetrated the layers of dream. Ruth had stopped talking. Her face was white, her mouth open. He heard the sound again; a woman was screaming.

A man had just come into the hall. He sagged in the doorway, clutching at a chair for support. His face was bloody, and blood was staining his white dress shirt.

More women screamed. The hall was full of white faces turned towards the door. From among them there was a subdued babble of alarm which seemed to be contained by a greater silence. The babble expanded shrilly to fill the hall again. The dancing had stopped; the music thumped on, unregarded for a few moments, then ended in a blast of discordant surprise. The injured man lurched towards the bar; and the assembly, drawn by his movement, crowded in towards him from the dance floor.

A voice boomed throughout the clamour. The guests paused in their onrush and swirled for a moment in hesitant groups. Moss Strong had appeared between them and the bar, enormous and forbidding, with legs astride and both hands raised commandingly. 'Quiet!' he bellowed. His brute power was a wall between the guests and the bleeding man. 'Quiet!' This feast was his; he was the real host and the glory was his to reap. He was not going to let any mishap spoil it. 'All right, everybody,' he roared. 'It's an accident. Man walked into a door. Too much to drink. 'E's all right.' The crowd swayed. Blank faces emitted an interrogative twittering.

'What yer waitin' for, Joey?' Moss shouted, 'Let's 'ave some music!' The band began to play. 'Come on!' Moss uttered the words like a parade-ground command. 'Everybody dance!' Several of his hefty young kinsmen had taken their places at his side, and they moved forward, shepherding the crowd back on to the dance floor.

'Everybody dance!' The beat of the drums echoed Moss's command. Obediently and unhappily, the guests began to drift about the dance floor again. There were few dancing at first, and many faces were still turned towards the bar. The number of dancers grew; the shrilling and screeching of the violins intoxicated the assembly again; the injured man had vanished; the incident belonged to the past and in people's mouths it was only gossip; Sid Strong launched his waiters like a fresh wave of attacking troops, their trays loaded with strong drink; alcohol flowed, the air became overheated once more; the feeling of flatness and alarm was dissipated and the tribal frenzy was again supreme.

But, unnoticed in the din, Moss's young men had moved quietly out through the door and Mark, trembling and alert, aware of the core of sick fear inside him but obedient to the summoning touch he had felt on his shoulder, was among them.

The man, who had gone outside for some fresh air, had been attacked.

They emerged into the street and looked about them in the gloom.

'Over 'ere, yer bastards!' The shout came from the right. About fifty yards along the street they saw a group of youths crowded on the opposite pavement in the pallor of a street lamp.

The young Jews, a dozen or more, advanced slowly along the street, closing together to form a pack. Mark moved unwillingly to the front of the group; he was dazed with terror, but his vanity propelled him. There they were, 'the others', half a dozen pale faces in the grey darkness, shouting derision. The pack continued to advance, driving Mark forward. The enemy were standing their ground; weedy youngsters in frayed, stained, navy-blue suits, their shirts dirty and collarless, their cloth caps worn rakishly; unemployed, they looked. Their shouting hurt Mark. It was not the words that they uttered that made him flinch — he was used to such things — but the note that he detected in their voices; a pitiful ferocity, born of misery and envy, a weak, half-weeping schoolboy defiance. He knew that they were frightened. He wanted to run across and plead with them, to tell them that many of the men who strutted about in monkey-suits inside the hall were unemployed like them, and had pawned, sold, borrowed, had condemned themselves to live on short commons for weeks to pay for these few hours of ostentation. He wanted to seize their hands and beg for their friendship. Yet he continued to move towards them, his fists clenched in his pockets, his head lowered, his temples throbbing in angry preparation for battle, his blood warming against his will in animal solidarity with the rest of the pack.

Still shouting, the ragged youths began to retreat slowly, daunted by the ton or so of beef and bone that was bearing down on them. They backed away, unsteady on the worn paving-stones, flimsy shadows passing between the lamplight and the gleaming windows of dirty little slum houses.

Their withdrawal increased the feeling of suspense which tormented Mark, a feeling which in turn bred an itch of anger within him. He was the first in the pack to raise his voice. 'Yellow!' he shouted, and quickened his pace. He heard the quickening clatter of footsteps as his comrades hurried to keep up with him. The pack closed in approvingly around him. Vanity rushed to his head and made him giddy.

One cloth-capped boy lagged behind the others. He looked younger than his companions; perhaps he alone was too young to withstand

Mark's taunt; perhaps, like Mark, he was driven by vanity or by the fear of not playing a man's part. Mark shouted again, 'Yellow!' The boy turned at bay and swore at Mark in a thin, scared voice. Mark came up to him, too excited by anger, too aware of the eyes watching him from behind, to take pity on the featherweight, chicken-boned little body or to be deterred by the fear that distorted the peaked and innocent face. Mark shouted in his face, 'You little rat!' The boy's eyes filled with tears. He hit Mark.

Mark expelled a long, harsh breath, as if he were experiencing a blessed relief, and drove in with his head down and both fists swinging. Many boxing lessons in the school gymnasium had taught Mark that the only way to overcome his natural lack of confidence and staying power was to attack with all the ferocity he could muster. He had the advantage of training, weight and a natural delicacy of movement. He crowded the boy back to the kerb, not troubling to keep his own guard up, provoked to greater fury by the few light blows that the boy succeeded in landing on his face, and driving a rapid succession of short, powerful jabs into the boy's soft midriff. His adversary, gasping with pain, his face deathly white in the lamplight, gave way at a run, stumbled over the kerb, steadied himself on the pavement and put his fists up again in a pathetic show of determination.

The boy's friends made no move to come to his aid, but loitered a few yards away. They uttered thin, puppy cries of encouragement. Mark heard his own companions, who held aloof after they had seen that he did not need help, shouting, 'Go on, boy!' 'Kill 'im, Markie!' 'In the guts!' He drew breath, mounted the pavement, tapped the boy's chin with a long right to steady his target and followed it with a violent left hook. The boy cried out and staggered backwards; he hung against the wall as if nailed by one shoulder to the grimy, black bricks. Mark closed in, jabbing again to the ribs with both fists. The boy flinched and gasped at each blow and Mark, filled with animal satisfaction at the jolt of his fists against thinly-covered bones, struck all the harder.

It was time for a finishing blow. Mark drew back to give himself room for another cross with the left. For the first time since the fight had begun he saw the boy's face clearly, white and tearful, screwed up in a childlike expression of fright and humiliation. Mark's rage drained from him. He, too, was on the verge of tears. He was overcome with weakness and his legs began to tremble. Behind him the thick voices of his companions were baying for the kill. He said to the boy, weakly, 'Go away.' The boy crouched against the wall, staring. 'Go away,' Mark repeated. The boy sidled away along the wall. The enemy band clattered away in retreat down the cobbled street, answering the jeers of Mark's companions with unconvincing shouts of defiance.

A sense of defeat grew in Mark as he watched them pass out of sight. Nevertheless, although he tried to compose his face into an expression of disdain at the babble of extravagant approbation which immediately assailed him, he could not repress an uneasy grin of triumph as he walked back into the hall. He had laid a claim to manhood. He stood at the bar drinking glass after glass of whisky as his fellow guests came to congratulate him; he heard his valour being extolled to all comers. Pride tightened his chest; yet within it there was a little core of pain, obstinately growing. He drank recklessly, reminding himself that it was impossible for him to get drunk, for he was a man; and the lights on the shimmering chandeliers multiplied and revolved, the floor swayed beneath him, the screeching tumult of music, talk and laughter filled his head. The feeling of loss was still there, cold and leaden. He plunged into conversation, gesticulating, laughing immoderately, afraid to stop talking; until he caught a glimpse of himself in the gilt-framed mirror behind the bar, flushed and foolish, looking very young, with Moss's henchmen patronising him and laughing at his boy's antics. He pushed his way hastily through the crowd that surrounded him, mumbling excuses, pursued by indulgent laughter and shouts of 'The kid's 'ad one too many' and 'Put two fingers down yer throat, boy!' Somewhere in the dark streets lurked a white-faced boy, a lost brother.

Powerful fingers gripped his arm. 'Feelin' all right, boy?' Moss was standing over him.

Mark said, 'I'm all right.'

'Bit of a terror on the quiet, ain't yer? Sid says yer massacred the bastard.'

Mark replied with an embarrassed little laugh.

'Well,' said Moss, 'your Uncle Moss knows what 'e's talkin' about after all, eh?'

'What do you mean?'

'What I told yer last week. Remember? Right, wasn't I? I tell yer, I know my bloody onions. Lived a sight longer than you I 'ave, boy. Chalk and cheese don't mix. Remember me tellin' yer? That's a lesson yer won't forget, boy, I'll lay. Bet yer been thinkin' about that job o' mine, eh? Well, it's still there. Say the word an' yer bloody fortune's made.'

'I'm not chalk,' said Mark, 'and he wasn't cheese. He's flesh and blood the same as me.'

Moss looked at him in surprise. 'You're bloody drunk,' he growled. 'You'll make me cry in a minute. Bring tears to my eyes, yer will. Why don't yer learn?' he said with sudden violence. 'Every chance they get they jump on yer face with both bloody boots. There's only one way.' He clenched a massive fist in front of Mark's face. 'The way you done it to-night. Don't you forget!'

'Oh, for God's sake!' Mark burst out. 'Every blow makes it worse!'

'Yer can't get away from it.'

'I'll get away from it,' Mark shouted. 'Try and stop me.'

'We ain't tryin' to stop yer. *They* won't let yer.'

'They?'

'*They* won't let yer.'

'I'll get away from it,' Mark said thickly, 'You wait and see!'

'Say yer don't know!' Moss turned away contemptuously.

Mark raved at his back. 'You wait and see! Just you wait and see!'

He was drinking again, conscious of nothing but the tinkle and glitter of upraised glasses and the flow of golden liquor. There were voices in his ears; he could not tell whose they were. Twice he was aware of Ruth at his side; at one moment a note of urgency in her voice came echoing down the corridors of his consciousness until the spreading fire of the next drink consumed him again; at another he heard her, dimly, speaking in anger, but the voice battered at dull walls and did not penetrate.

In a moment of clarity he looked round for her, but she was gone. Panic took hold of him. He had to see this girl again; he was terrified that she might have disappeared for good. He set out in search of her. He seemed to be walking on cotton-wool. Mickey appeared, very close to him. Mickey was speaking to him. Mickey was shouting, angrily, trying to make himself understood. She was gone. She had gone home. She had tried to say goodbye. Mark mumbled to himself in unintelligible despair. He had to find this girl again. In his drunkenness he wildly exaggerated his need for her; but dimly, within, he knew that the need was real, and the fear that touched him was real. He pulled himself free of Mickey's grasp and made for the door, treading frantically at the billowing floor.

Moss's red face appeared before him again, monstrously magnified over the white, stiff-winged collar, leering at him through the haze of rising suns. Mark opened his mouth to cry out for Ruth, and heard himself shout instead, 'You wait and see!'

The walls vanished and the hall became infinite in its extent. Somebody gripped his arms and the fingers seemed to sink into his flesh like heated metal into butter. The floor fell away and he dropped out of the light, treading vainly at space. As he fell through the void he heard multiple echoes of his own voice, within himself and far away in the vast halls of night. 'Wait and see!'... 'You wait and see!'... 'Just you wait and see!'

1939

1939

1

In later years Mark was able to remember little of Bella's wedding. It was mainly from the lips of others that he pieced together a recollection of the last hour or two of that night. But it was with approval that he recalled his cry, 'I'll get away from it!'

At the age of twenty-one he was able, although it meant turning a blind eye to much that had befallen him in the intervening years, to fancy that he had enjoyed considerable success in 'getting away from it'.

He was employed by a respectable firm in the City; he played cricket, spending his Saturday afternoons running about in white flannels for the honour of the firm, meeting the jolliest of good fellows at tea in the pavilion and bawling bawdy songs in the coach on the way home; he had a number of cordial acquaintances among his workmates, all undeniably Anglo-Saxon; and he had a girl.

His present girl was not the one who had been the object of his first thoughts on that distant morning when he had awakened after Bella's wedding. In fact, he was liable to flinch at the mere mention of Ruth Seelig.

For some time after the wedding he had not had the courage to seek her. Indeed, since he still led a boy's life, with games, examinations, and a hundred other interests to absorb him, he had no great urge to do so, although he permitted himself to weave his romantic, adolescent day-dreams about her until she became a familiar presence in his imagination. Then, nine months later, when Mark was in his eighteenth year and had just left school, his Aunt Bella punctually and proudly brought forth a baby boy of champion dimensions, and the family gathered once more to celebrate the achievement. Here he came face to face with Ruth for the second time; he was sheepish, she was serene; after some tactful prompting on her part, he asked her to meet him one evening, and she agreed.

Their first evening together was a nightmare for Mark. In the days beforehand his impatience made him behave like a madman at home; the whole household suffered for his ardour. Mark reached the rendezvous an hour early and was almost fainting with suspense when Ruth arrived. From that moment onward he was like a man paralysed. Throughout dinner he sat staring across the table at Ruth. She tried every opening she knew to start a conversation; finally, she ran dry and they finished their meal miserably. By the time they reached the theatre Mark was completely demoralised and did not even dare to turn his head to look at her as she sat beside him. He left her at her front gate, without carrying out his carefully-laid plan for kissing her good night, and he trudged unhappily home, having spent his whole week's wages.

In the weeks that followed he spent several evenings with her. Each was the same. He made no progress, and he lived in a daze of happiness and despair. After much persuasion, she succeeded in introducing him to her parents. They were elderly and doted on their daughter. Mr. Seelig was portly, yet tall enough to carry his bulk with dignity; he had a broad, leathery face and a thick moustache; and he spoke good but guttural English. He had come to England from Poland when he was thirteen years old, and after a youth passed in bitter poverty, during which he married and lost a first wife, had established himself as a furniture manufacturer in a small way, prospering but continuing to work at the bench himself. His second wife, Ruth's mother, was English-born, but of his own faith. She was a plump and vigorous woman, pleasant, but a trifle shrill. Between them they completely unnerved Mark. The mother, despite his obvious youth, prowled about him undisguisedly weighing him up as a matrimonial prospect. The father, who was both pious and pompous, made ponderous religious jokes and frowned at Mark's heathen incomprehension. For some months Mark continued to take Ruth out and to face the ordeal of visiting her home. He attained a state of uneasy familiarity with Ruth, but never succeeded in making any demonstration of tenderness. The strain became too much for him: the intervals between their meetings grew longer. One night they parted without settling a date for their next encounter. 'I'll ring you,' said Mark. A week passed, and he did not ring. He was unhappy, but he could not think of an excuse for having delayed. Another week went by, and it became still harder to nerve himself to telephone. Weeks became months, and Mark, reviling himself as a coward, resigned himself to having lost Ruth. She wrote to him. Had she been wiser, she would have been offhand and tactful; but she, too, was young, and her letter was excited and full of bitterness. Mark made many attempts to write a reply, but each time his courage and resource failed him; and the fatal gap in time continued to widen.

It was now two years since he had seen her, but although she filled his adolescent daydreams, he had made no move to regain her.

Nevertheless, he was a healthy young man, and Paula, the girl whom he had encountered after two years of boyish loneliness, found him an easy prey.

She was a German refugee, she was eighteen years old, she had found Mark at a charity dance into which he had wandered three months ago, she had (being dowered by misfortune with an unnatural amount of experience) understood at a glance his condition, and had lost no time in getting him into her bed; for she had plans; and now, on a sunny Monday evening towards the end of August, 1939, she was waiting for him at her window, ready to make her next move.

2

Paula lived in a furnished room in Hampstead. She opened the street door to Mark and he kissed her clumsily. He followed her up the stairs to her room. She had spent most of the day in bed. Her hair was unkempt, she wore a faded brown dressing-gown and slippers flapped on her feet. The room still smelled of the previous night, the blankets were crumpled on the divan and unwashed crockery stood on the table.

'Such a day!' she sighed. 'I went to a dance with Putzi last night and I didn't go to bed till three in the morning.' She turned her pale, peaked face up to him and smiled; for a moment she looked beautiful. 'Are you angry with me for looking so terrible?'

He mumbled, 'Silly, get dressed and we'll go out.' Content, she moved away and turned on the cold water in the sink. It was because she was so sure of herself that she had let him find her in this state. He was a submissive lover, without the wit or experience to dominate. She believed she could do as she willed with him.

'I didn't go in to work today,' she said. 'Anyway, I made enough at the dogs on Saturday. I should worry!' She gambled wildly at the greyhound tracks, usually with Mark's money. He hated the evenings they spent at the dogs. There was no feeling of pleasure or enthusiasm among the crowds as there was at horse races or football matches; only fear and greed. The noise that arose from all these thousands of people was not the surging roar of a football crowd but a clamour made up of innumerable little shouts and yelps and groans, each separate, each hostile to all the others, like the greedy crying of gulls. This was the world of something-for-nothing that Mark loathed. Paula disgusted him when she screamed encouragement at the dog she had backed, bouncing her body up and down in anguish, brandishing her clenched fists in front of her.

Mark sat primly on the edge of the armchair with his hands on his knees. He still felt self-conscious when she undressed in front of him, but he would think, with some pride, 'If the chaps at the office could see me now!'

Paula had dried herself and was brushing her hair vigorously. 'Where are we going tonight?' she asked.

'Flicks,' Mark answered. 'Let's clear the room up before we go out.'

She shrugged her shoulders. 'What does it matter?' She began to beautify herself. Shapely in a white sweater, with a gay, swinging skirt, her hair sleek and shining beneath the comb, her legs in gleaming stockings, her lips bright and neatly pouted with lipstick, she was transformed. She could put on beauty as if it were itself a garment. Now she was all poise, insolence and laughter.

'I thought of going down to Brighton next Sunday,' Mark said. 'It's a pity not to make the most of this weather.' He gathered up the breakfast things and took them over to the recessed sink.

'Why not for the whole weekend?' Paula asked. Mark, folding the blankets, searched for a reply. He was afraid to tell her that he could not afford it. He remembered suddenly and answered, 'I've got a cricket match on Saturday, for the firm.'

She pulled a face. 'Silly cricket,' she said. 'All right. So it is Sunday.'

Mark finished sweeping dust and crumbs on to the landing, put the broom away, and opened the window wide. 'Let's go,' he said. He picked up a crushed cigarette-end that his broom had missed, threw it out of the window and followed Paula out of the room.

They spent a dull evening at the cinema, had sardines on toast at the Corner House and came back to Paula's room a little before midnight. Paula lit the gas ring and prepared coffee. She looked down at Mark's face, decided that the time was ripe for what she had to say, and sat down next to him on the divan.

'Tired, darling?' She took his hand.

'A bit.' He lay back across the divan.

She leaned over him and let her hair fall forward so that it almost touched his face. She knew he liked this. 'Do you like me, dear?'

'Of course.'

'How much do you like me?'

'Oh —' He hated baby-talk. He put his arms round her shoulders and squeezed, without much enthusiasm. 'This much.'

'No. Really. How much?'

He sat up resignedly, treated her to a more prolonged hug, and nuzzled in her hair, hoping that the noises of affection which he uttered did not sound too half-hearted. 'This much.'

'Do you love me?'

'Yes.'

'Let me hear you say it.'

'I love you.'

'Then why don't we get married?'

Mark stared at the Van Gogh print on the opposite wall as if it were the portrait of Death.

'Why not? If you love me?'

Mark was too bewildered to answer. He was afraid that, if he could not think of anything else to say, he would agree out of sheer despair.

'Mark!' She gripped his shoulder. 'It would be so nice together. We could enjoy ourselves. We could have a home. A home, Mark! We could go into business.' He did not answer, and she added, with bitterness, 'Or perhaps I'm not a nice person, yes? Perhaps your family would not like me? Or do they want a dowry? Or perhaps you don't want me? A nice little foreign bit — I speak good English, don't I? — only to sleep with? Good sport? No more?'

'Oh, no!' Mark said desperately. 'I — well, it's — I wasn't thinking of marriage just yet. There's heaps of time. I mean —'

'We could wait if you want. But we could save, and buy things, and arrange things.'

'Oh, Paula, not now. Let me think. I'm in such a muddle.' He heard with gratitude the bubble and clatter of boiling liquid. He said, 'The coffee's ready', and hurried to the gas ring.

Paula watched him complacently. 'All right, dear', she said. He was in retreat at the first onset. If she timed the next correctly, she would win.

3

As Mark was leaving the house for work next morning, he noticed his mother taking up a slice of toast that he had eaten and left, folding it and, in a tired, absent-minded way, eating it. It was this that caused him to think about her more deeply than he usually did.

At forty-five, she was ageing fast, a contrast to the expensively-preserved Jenny. Her rosy cheeks were becoming loose and puffy, there were folds in the skin under her eyes, and the grey streaks were thickening in her hair.

The immediate cause of her depression, Mark knew, was the danger of war, which all the newspapers shouted daily. A deeper cause was the dull, pinched life, worse in many ways than real poverty, which she and her husband led without hope of change.

It was true that Joe, after several periods of illness, was working again, but he was not the ruddy and healthy man he had been. He was bowed and subdued as if he had accepted defeat in life, he was always coughing, and he was able to earn little.

It was true that she had the consolation of Mickey married, and happily settled with his Mill, who was expecting a baby, in a two-roomed flat not far away in Clapton.

Still, there was no more money coming each week from Mickey; and Mark, who had begun work as a warehouse clerk four years ago at twenty-eight shillings a week and was still with the same firm earning four pounds a week, was not able to contribute much. Mark knew that his parents were disappointed in him, not because he could not support them, for they were too fond of him to let the money matter, but because they had once hoped that he would compensate for their hopeless, anonymous lives by becoming (for instance, by following in Moss's footsteps) 'a success'.

Life was an endless rush for Clara. Mark could imagine her, after his departure, hurrying to finish her housework, then scrambling into her coat and making her way to the market, where she worked for five days a week in Moss's fish-shop. The money enabled her to make ends meet, and she was needed there, for Moss was fully occupied with his bookmaking business, leaving Jenny in charge of the shop. Mark knew what a strain it was for her to stand all day at the counter, driven by Jenny, besieged by the rush and clamour of women, handling and wrapping the wet, ice-cold fish. The shop was always crowded: Jenny specialised in a brand of bawdy discourtesy which brought the Cockney housewives flocking in.

Well, Mark thought as he arrived at work, there was nothing he could do for his mother just yet.

The head office of Messrs. Badgett and Dogg, Importers, was on the top floor of a grimy building which formed the end of a narrow cul-de-sac off Gracechurch Street. As Mark turned into the doorway on Tuesday morning he came up with one of his fellow clerks, a large, fat young man with a smooth pink face and fluffy fair hair. 'Morning, Leslie.' 'Mornin', Mark.' Leslie Sanders was the closest friend that Mark had among his workmates. Most of the young men who worked at Badgett and Dogg's maintained a strictly formal attitude towards each other, addressing their colleagues by their surnames even after several years' acquaintance. Mark and Leslie had got as far as Christian names; they often discussed politics together (Mark's views coincided curiously with those of the *Daily Express* and his friend's with those of the *News Chronicle*. Their workmates thought that 'it was a bit thick, talking this sort of rot in the office'); they confided in each other about women; they both read more than most of their colleagues thought was good for them; and once they had even gone together to the Tate Gallery — an escapade as the result of which Mr. Palfrey, the senior clerk, had addressed them for some time as 'our two Bow' — crushing pause — 'Heemians.'

They trotted breathlessly up four flights of stone steps and past an open door that bore the firm's name on its frosted-glass panels. There was no daylight in the narrow stone corridor except that which filtered into it through filthy skylights and from the rooms which lined it. The rooms on each side of the corridor belonged to managers of departments; through their doors came snatches of deep voices and the musty smell of old upholstery. The door at the far end of the corridor led into a general office, in which Mark and Sanders worked with four other clerks.

Violent trumpeting noises greeted them as they approached their room. 'Old Palfrey's in,' Sanders said. 'I hope we're not the last. He won't half rub it in.'

To their relief, Mr. Palfrey was alone in the office when they entered. His face was still buried in a large handkerchief which he removed in a few moments, revealing cheeks still scarlet with the effort of blowing. He wiped his nose — a veined, purple monstrosity shaped like an inverted pear, and turned a dull and monitory eye on the two clerks. 'None too soon, I must say,' were his first words.

'Oh, I say,' protested Sanders. 'We're the first in.' He opened his newspaper. 'Four minutes to go yet before starting-time.'

'That's right,' said Mr. Palfrey hollowly. 'Never give a minute to the firm. That's the way they bring 'em up nowadays. The youth of today! God save us all!'

'Here, I say,' Sanders looked up from his newspaper. 'Old Hitler's coming it a bit. Looks as if he means business over this Danzig affair.'

'Oh, I don't know,' Mark said uneasily. 'It says in my paper—'

'Of course he means business,' interrupted Mr. Palfrey in a lugubrious voice. 'What's he got to worry about? Who's to stop him? The young men of England? Caw!' He rolled his eyes up towards the cobwebbed ceiling and made noises of disgust. 'I saw some o' them young Territorials on Liverpool Street Station this morning. Just as I stood there looking at 'em the noise of a train come up from the Underground, and I turned to a porter, and I said, "God save us all, that's Kitchener's Army turning in their graves."'

Two other clerks came in and sidled towards their desks. Mr. Palfrey turned towards them. 'Good morning, your lordships,' he jeered. 'This is indeed an honour. Only one minute late. It wouldn't do to get in earlier, would it? Oh, no! Oh, dearie, dearie, no! Service? Discipline? *Esprit de corps*? *Quid pro quo*? Never heard of 'em, have you? All take and no give. Never a thought for the firm. Ah!' The last of the clerks arrived, a skinny youth with a white, sullen face, dressed in one of those suits — dark grey, with narrow trousers whose cut and colour seem to render their wearers invisible in the crowded City streets. '*Mister* Venner in person, come to give us the benefit of his services.' Venner looked as if he were about to cry. 'Well, I do declare,' exclaimed Mr. Palfrey, 'there's tears in the dear boy's eyes. Dear God! Wait till you're all in uniform. You'll learn a thing or two, you will.' Venner glared at him with hatred and scuttled to his desk.

'What does it say about the match against the West Indians?' interrupted another of the clerks irreverently, leaning over Sanders' newspaper.

Mr. Palfrey, outraged, said, 'All right, my lads. That's enough fiddle-faddle. It's the firm's time now. Put those papers away and get on with it. Strong, I want all them delivery notes checked that come up yesterday.'

They went on with their work, occasionally breaking the silence to exchange remarks about their recent holidays or the latest Test Match against the West Indians or the prospects for the football season.

The telephone bell rang. Venner took the call.

'It's for you,' he said to Mark. 'A lady.' He uttered the word 'lady' with a sick intensity that made it sound obscene.

Mark took the instrument. 'Strong here,' he said. 'Who's that? Oh!' — he was startled, and a little scared, but he raised his voice for the benefit of his companions — 'Paula?' He was gratified to hear whistling and the clucking of tongues behind him. 'Yes, dear. Yes, of course, dear. No, no,

I'm not. I'm not cross at all. Really I'm not. Yes, of course. Tonight. I hadn't forgotten. At your flat.' He was pleased that the others had heard that. 'I'm busy now. I'll have to hang up.' Private calls were not encouraged and were sometimes reported to Captain Dogg, the ferocious Junior Partner. 'Bye-bye, dear.' He hung up the receiver and went back to his table.

'At her flat, eh?' chuckled Mr. Palfrey. 'Very nice! *Very, very* nice. Bit of a lad on the quiet, eh?'

Mark said, 'Aha!' mysteriously, and went on with his work. Venner, who had not spoken since he had called Mark to the telephone, was still staring at him. He was always staring, intensely, as if he saw in every other face a challenge which he was determined to answer.

'There's another one,' said Mr. Palfrey, wagging a nicotine-stained forefinger at Venner. 'A real dark horse, he is, I'll warrant. Never says much, but look at the rings under 'is eyes. I bet he could tell us a tale or two, eh?'

'Who is it, Ven?' asked one of the clerks. 'Ann Sheridan or Hedy Lamarr?'

Sanders suddenly emitted a shriek of mirth. 'Mae West!' he spluttered. He slapped his thigh. 'Oh, lordy, lordy! just imagine!' There were howls of laughter from the other clerks. 'Here!' Sanders gasped. 'Here!' He was doubled up with laughter. He could hardly speak. 'Famous last stands!' He rolled in his chair, his face bright pink with laughter, tears of delight in his eyes.

Mr. Palfrey laughed, coughed, wiped his eyes, blew his nose and laughed again. 'Haugh! Haugh! Haugh!' The noise seemed to emerge from profound inner convulsions. 'That's good! That's rich! That's a winner if I ever heard one! Famous last stands! God save us all!' He pointed at Venner and was seized by fresh paroxysms. 'Haugh! Haugh! Haugh! Haugh! Haugh!'

Venner glared back at them. The last trace of colour drained from his face and he hid himself behind the covers of a big ledger.

Mark laughed dutifully with the others, but he was too full of his own troubles to be genuinely amused, and he turned back to his work, blindly thumbing delivery notes while he struggled with his conflicting thoughts. He was terrified of seeing Paula again; he knew that she would persist in her idea of marriage and that each time she pressed him he would become less likely to withstand her. He lacked the courage and the experience to deal with a situation like this. All his dreams of Ruth revived, exaggerated by his dilemma. For months he had promised himself that he would summon up the courage to get in touch with her again; now he could not put it off any longer. His fears and perplexities grew as he brooded over them, a burden of which, somehow, he had to relieve himself. He looked doubtfully at Sanders, and, after some hesitation, scribbled a note, folded the piece of paper and threw it across to him.

Sanders unfolded the note and read: *I want to talk to you lunch-time. Get rid of Venner.* Without raising his head, Sanders cast a brief, startled glance at Mark. Mark was looking at him with apprehension, with almost a hint of regret at what he had done. Sanders mouthed 'O.K.' and tore the note up.

A little later, Venner said, 'It's five to twelve'. The clerks took their lunch break in two shifts; first Mark, Sanders and Venner, then the other three. Venner rummaged in a drawer and produced a towel and a soap-box. 'I'm going to wash.'

'Here, I say, Ven,' Sanders called to him as he turned towards the door, 'don't wait for us. We've — ah — we've got a special call to make.'

'Oh' — Venner's voice was harsh — 'that's all right. I know you've got your little secrets.' The glitter of tears appeared in his eyes again. 'You and your pal there. Enjoy yourselves!' The door slammed behind him.

'We've upset old Ven,' Mark said as he and Sanders made their way across the road to the dingy Wine Bar which was their favourite resort.

'Oh,' Sanders answered negligently, 'doolally taps, he is. I mean, you and me, we like a bit of serious conversation, don't we? We don't have to put up with him *all* the time.'

'That's true.' Mark was gratified at the implication of intimacy. 'I mean, when you were talking about Beverley Nichols yesterday he didn't know which way to look. I bet he's never read a single one of his books.'

'I bet he's never even heard of him!' cried Sanders.

They had a glass of cheap sherry each, and nibbled at withered little sausages on strips of toast. Their meagre lunch concluded, they strolled in the crowded streets, enjoying the dust-laden sunlight. They skirted the walls of the Tower and made their way down to the waterfront promenade, where they sat on the barrels of a couple of ancient cannon. There was a period of silence, passed in apparent meditation as they watched the olive surface of the river swirl and sparkle; a ritual prelude to confession.

At last Mark spoke. 'Look, Leslie!'

Sanders screwed his face up in an expression of intense sympathy and said, 'Ah!'

Mark hesitated again. It was a new experience for him to confide in someone. His instinct had told him that to do so would bring relief (which, rather than good advice, was what he sought) but each time he nerved himself to speak, the carefully-marshalled words broke ranks and fled in panic from his mind. 'It's about a chap I know.'

'Ah!' echoed Sanders, nodding impressively to show that he understood all. 'Yes?'

'Well,' Mark went on, 'this chap's been in love with a girl. He stopped seeing her. I guess he lost his nerve.' His breath kept failing him, and he spoke in jerks. 'Then he got mixed up with another. Pretty deep. You know.'

'Ah!' Sanders compressed his lips, strove to look sapient, and continued to nod.

'Well, now the second one's on at him to get married. He's got her and he doesn't want her. He wants the other one and he hasn't got her.' He paused. This was all so inadequate. How could he explain that, despite Paula's faults, there were moments in her arms when he was so overwhelmed with gratitude for her tenderness that he became as helpless and trusting as a child, and that his greatest fear was of what might happen in one of these moments? How could he speak to anyone about Ruth, and of his despair at the thought of abandoning all hope of her? 'Well, I'm not sure — you know — what to tell him.'

'Ah!' Sanders sighed as a ship slid by, silent and purposeful, its hull towering cleanly out of the water, its superstructure intricate and exciting. His dreams were of the sea. Mark's secret imagination was elsewhere, attracted by the murmur of aero-engines which, throughout this week, was never absent from the sky. Each groped inwardly after a vision, of a life that was whole and uncomplicated, lit with beauty and filled with the promise of peril and achievement. 'I say' — Sanders communicated a discovery — 'life's a proper blooming problem, isn't it?'

'It's a proper mess-up. I know that.'

'Certainly is!' Sanders was playing for time. The moment called for a display of manly assurance. 'Here,' he announced, 'I'll tell you what I'd do. Go and pop the question to the first one. Straight away. No nonsense. No second thoughts. Right away.' He became enthusiastic. 'Don't give her time to think. Sweep her off her feet. They like a bit of cheek. You take it from me!'

'Easier said than done.'

'No sooner said than done, you mean.' Sanders' own experience was slight; his courtship of a young lady at his tennis club was entirely respectable. He was, he felt, enlarging his own knowledge of life as well as establishing himself as a man of the world. He threw himself into the part for all he was worth. 'Look, ring her up now. While the iron's hot. It is you, isn't it? Go on. Right away. I'll come with you.'

'Here!' Mark was confused. 'Hold on a minute.'

'Hold on, nothing. You know what they say. He who hesitates. Faint heart never won fair lady. Come on.' He grasped Mark's arm. 'You'll thank me for this.'

Mark, dazed, permitted himself to be led to the nearest telephone box. He was willing to be urged, for he had been seeking the courage to do this for a long time. But, as he stood in the booth, fumbling with his notebook to find the telephone number of Ruth's home, clumsily pressing the pennies into the slot, and dialling, he grew faint with panic. His feelings were those of a soldier going into the attack, a mixture of bravado, fright and compulsion. As he listened to the telephone bell ringing at the other end of the line the bravado cooled, the fright increased, and he forgot utterly what he had meant to say if his call was answered. Sanders' face was at the window, displaying an imbecilic grin of encouragement. The soft ringing tone continued in his ear. Sanders was raising his eyebrows and waggling his hands in lunatic gestures of enquiry. The bell continued to ring. Mark hung up the receiver, and left the booth, weak with disappointment and relief. 'There's no reply,' he said. 'I'll have to try again later.'

4

'That's West Pier,' Mark mumbled sleepily; 'the other one is Palace Pier.' He rolled over again and relaxed, face downwards, his left cheek resting on the hot pebbles.

Paula was lying on her back, arched up blissfully to meet the sun. Her eyes were shut. 'So many people,' she muttered. 'It is beautiful.'

Mark ceased to listen to her talk and withdrew into a half-sleep. He was tired. They had spent the whole morning wandering about the crowded Brighton streets so that Paula might look at the displays in the shop windows. They had had to queue for ices, for lemonades and for a greasy fish lunch; and afterwards, when he had longed for rest, they had wandered along the promenade so that Paula might admire the dresses and jewellery she saw.

He crossed his arms under his chin, and propped his head up. The sunshine beat at his closed lids and sent veils of colour swirling up before him. He felt that he could sprawl here, drugged and inert, for ever, listening to the crash of shoes on the pebbles, the noise of the crowds, and the whisper of aero-engines in the flawless sky. He opened his eyes and, with his arms folded like a mask in front of his face, looked surreptitiously at the girls hurrying by in their bathing costumes, long-legged and gleaming wet. Paula's moist hand was inside his shirt, kneading at his back. He moved one of his arms and let it fall across her body, apathetically. Paula mistook the purpose of his sudden movement and wriggled against him. She said, sleepily, 'Kiss me, Mark dear'.

Her voice aroused Mark from his torpor. He removed the other arm from before his eyes and blinked at the dazzling sunlight. 'Not in front of all these people,' he protested.

She made a moaning noise of derision. 'You silly boy,' she murmured. 'Why are you always fearing other people?' She pressed herself close against him and pulled a sheet of newspaper over their heads. 'Now,' she demanded, 'no one can see us.' In the tiny tent that the paper made the heat was stifling; black patches of sweat spread on the paper where it touched their skins. Mark kissed her and turned his head quickly away so that his face was in the sunlight once more; he breathed the fresh air gratefully.

Her voice invaded his thoughts again. 'Poor boy, you are tired after your cricket yesterday.'

He grunted.

'Did you get back to town very late?'

He yawned, and answered, 'Yes; the other lot invited us to stay for supper. It turned into quite a party.'

'You had a nice day, yes?'

'Very nice,' he lied. He had not stayed for the party; and yesterday had been a terrible day. In the morning he had made the latest of several attempts to telephone Ruth, but again there was no reply. Until midday came, and the weekly liberation, the clerks had passed the time by baiting Venner, and when Mark — already depressed by his own problems — was provoked by their fatuities into intervening on the victim's behalf, Venner had turned on him with a shrill, 'I don't need your pity, thank you!'

The afternoon's cricket, instead of bringing relief, had seemed like some endless and unpleasant dream, of which he could remember nothing but the heat and fatigue, the indifference that weighted his limbs as he trotted apathetically after a soaring ball, the dazed remoteness with which he had seen his wicket go flying, the obsession that he must escape and resume his search for Ruth before his courage failed him, and the frantic impatience that this feeling generated in him.

At the close of the game he had mumbled his excuses and fled back to Town. His fit of coward's courage had driven him to Ruth's home in Willesden, where, sick with suspense, he had stood on the doorstep for more than an hour, stupidly ringing the bell long after he had realised that the house was empty. Half-dead with disappointment and fatigue, he had plodded home to bed.

The movement of Paula's hot little hand against the back of his neck recalled him to his surroundings. 'This is so nice,' she sighed.

'How sleepy this sunshine makes you feel,' he said; 'it melts all your troubles away. I wish we didn't have to go back.'

'If only we could be together all the time. Mark'— she tugged at his ear — 'why not?'

Mark did not reply.

'You know, you need someone like me. If you married me, you could go a long way. You wouldn't have to stay in that silly office working for next to nothing. There are so many easy ways of making money, and so many good things to enjoy.'

He sat up. 'That's just the trouble!'

'I don't understand, dear. What's wrong with it? Why do I make you angry?'

'Oh' — he searched for words — 'I don't know. Being smart. Always knowing the easy way. You — you always have the laugh of other people. I feel such a fool with you. It makes me angry. You're too clever for me, you and — I don't know — all you people who live by your wits.'

'When they drive you across a frontier, they don't let you take anything with you, except your wits.' She lay back and looked up into the sky.

There was a crash of pebbles as he scrambled to his feet. 'Let's go and get a cup of tea. I'm dying with thirst.' Before she could answer, he was stumbling away from her towards the promenade steps, and she ran to catch up with him.

One of the loungers at the rails was shouting and waving, apparently at someone near them on the beach. Mark paid little heed; Paula, as was her way, looked about her curiously. They walked, lurching on the ridged pebbles, towards the steps.

'I think he is calling us,' Paula said.

'Eh?' said Mark stupidly. He looked up at the promenade. Sid Strong was hanging over the rails, waving wildly and shouting, 'Oy!'

Mark's heart sank; he was doubly ashamed — for Paula to learn that the hideous little man with the huge nose and the receding chin was an uncle of his, and for Sid to be able to tell the family that he had seen his nephew at Brighton with a girl. There was no avoiding Sid now; he was pushing his way towards the head of the steps, and for the first time Mark saw that he, too, had a woman with him.

They were face to face, on the promenade, and Mark was mumbling introductions. Sid looked more like a music-hall comic than ever. He wore a dazzlingly light grey trilby hat with a big brim that was turned down over his little darting eyes. His tweed jacket, which had swooping, knife-edged shoulders and hung almost to his knees, was woven of a fabric which looked light grey from afar, but on closer inspection was seen to be shot with every colour in the spectrum. A yellow sports shirt and tie, brown gaberdine trousers and shoes of elaborately-patterned black-and-white patent leather completed his attire. Mark could not take his eyes from the girl whose arm Sid gripped proprietorially. She was tall and red-haired, with a beautiful figure and lovely legs. She was expensively dressed and stood docilely in Sid's grasp.

'What are you doing down here?' Mark asked lamely.

'Oh, I dunno,' Sid answered. 'Bits an' pieces. Business an' pleasure. Done all right on the races.' He turned to the red-haired girl. 'Didn' we, gel?' He released his grip on her arm. 'You done all right this trip, eh, June?' He explained: 'Every 'orse I backed, I put a bit on for 'er. She 'asn' 'alf cleaned up.'

While he talked he was inspecting Paula, eyeing her up and down as frankly as if she were a horse in the paddock. She seemed to Mark to be showing no resentment. There was no artificiality in the smile she gave Sid, and every few moments she found pretexts to turn and look about her, as if to show herself to him like a model in a dress parade. The way in which Sid and the two women grouped together, ignoring him, reminded Mark of moments in his childhood when his parents, walking with him, encountered friends; and he would stand, tiny and unheeded, on the fringes of the group, tugging at his mother's dress to try to win back her attention. He felt the same humiliation now.

'Come down 'ere often?' It was to Paula that Sid addressed the question. 'We do. June likes the place.' He jerked his thumb at the hotel across the road. 'Over there we stay. Y'oughter see the room. Talk abaht the royal suite. She' — he indicated his girl — 'she loves it. Don't yer, gel? Looks a bit of all right 'erself, she does, too, on a satin bedspread. Eh?' He patted her buttocks affectionately.

Mark could not bear to look at the girl, but Paula was laughing delightedly.

Sid poked a finger in Mark's ribs. 'You're a bit of a devil, ain't yer, in yer own little way? Our little Mark! Quietest boy in the family! An' I catch 'im dahn Brighton wiv a tart! Eh?' Mark muttered, like a small boy making excuses, 'We're only down for the day.'

'Git aht of it!' jeered Sid. 'Lovely cob like that!'

Mark was too confused to protest. He said, 'We've got to be going,' and tried to take Paula's arm, but she drew away from him and laughed. 'He's so shy, poor boy. You won't give him away, will you?'

Sid pulled a face and passed his thumb in front of him in a semicircular motion of reassurance. 'S'all right, gel. Yer know the old saying. Only God an' me knows, an' I won't split. 'Ere,' he said suddenly, 'we'll all die o' sunstroke out 'ere. Come over the road an' 'ave a drink. Bar's still open for a bit.'

They hurried across the road, dodging traffic, Sid holding the two women each by an arm, Mark following.

As they walked into the tall, cool lounge Mark tried to draw Paula back so that he could speak with her, but again she brushed him aside and padded across the thick carpet after Sid, her face upturned in ecstasy as if she were entering a temple to worship. She walked archly and sleekly. Mark watched her as she sank into a deep armchair, dangling her arms contentedly over the sides.

She said, looking at Sid with shining eyes, 'Oh, there is so much life in this town that I have never seen. The races. It must be so exciting. And the dancing. And the bars. And all those lovely shops. You are enjoying all these things, I suppose. Oh, if I had money!'

Sid shrugged his shoulders. 'Well, it's there all round yer. All yer got to do is 'elp yerself.'

'You see!' Paula said to Mark.

'Oy! George!' Sid summoned a waiter and ordered Martinis. The drinks were served. Sid raised his glass. 'Well,' he grinned at Paula, 'Through me teeth, past me gums; look out, belly, 'ere it comes! Good luck, gels!'

The women raised their glasses in admiring response and resumed their chatter about dresses.

Mark remembered a piece of family gossip he had heard about Sid: 'I hear you're taking a long holiday.'

'Ah. Ireland. Before they start this conscription lark.'

'But they wouldn't — I mean — they only take fit men. You wouldn't have to—'

'What d'yer mean?' It was the first time Mark had ever seen Sid flush. 'I'm a fit man. 'Ere, June! Am I a fit man? Go on. Tell 'im.'

June rolled her eyes. 'I'll say!' she murmured.

'What about Granddad?'

'Oh, 'im? I'll see 'im all right, I will. I tell you, though, 'e don't deserve it. I told 'im I was goin'. I wanted 'im to move down to Mossy's new place at Torquay. Laughed in me face, 'e did. Know what 'e done?' Sid became indignant. ''E gives me a look. Then 'e spits on the floor, an' 'e says to me, "Come 'ere, Sid." I goes over. 'E points at the spit. "Look at this," 'e says. "'Ave a good look." I looks. 'E says, "Sid, if that grew up it'd be twice the man you are." Then 'e thumps 'is chest, an' 'e says in that growl of 'is, like an old bear, "When I was young," 'e says, "no two men in the market'd dare fight Jacob Strong. And this is my son! My son!" 'e says. What can yer do wiv an old loony like that?' He turned away and touched Paula's arm. 'What yer doin' to-night, Poll, gel? We're goin' dahn Sherry's, dancing. Like to bring this bloke o' yours?'

Mark stood up. 'We're catching an early train. We want to miss the crowds.'

Paula looked at him with contempt. 'There's plenty of time. Sit down and relax.'

'You can please yourself.' Mark experienced a wild moment of anger, and of hope that the break might come now. 'Stay if you like. I'm going.'

She followed him.

5

'Poland Invaded,' ran the headlines. 'Conscription for All.' The office buzzed with a subdued and interrogative chattering. The clerks, startled by the news out of the complacency into which the lovely summer had lulled them, were excited, bewildered and faintly frightened.

'I reckon this is it, all right,' said one of the clerks. 'I don't know,' said another. 'So long as they haven't actually declared war, they can still call it off.' He turned to Mark. 'Don't you think so?'

'Oh, shut up,' said Mark. 'I can't hear.' He sat on the edge of a desk with the telephone receiver to his ear, his face rigid with expectancy. The threat of war, the agitation around him, these were held at bay on the outer ramparts of his consciousness; within, he was absorbed by matters of much more immediate importance. At three o'clock that morning he had awakened from his sleep, cried, 'Good Lord, of course!' — jumped out of bed, rummaged in an old jacket and found what he was looking for — a creased and dirty piece of paper on which was written the telephone number of the office at which Ruth had worked. He had lain awake for the rest of the night trembling with impatience and now — his breath was icy and hard to control — he was making the call. Conditions were favourable. The dreaded Captain Dogg had departed yesterday, amid deferential farewells, to join his Territorial regiment. Mr. Palfrey was unaccountably late. Mark's call was answered. He expelled a long, trembling breath, gripped the receiver harder to stop his hand shaking, and asked for an extension number.

'Hallo. Extension 324? Is Miss Seelig there?'

An interminable second; then a woman's voice, high-pitched and (so it seemed to him) intolerably silly in tone: 'No. She's not in.'

Another pause. He could not summon speech, and was on the point of hanging up the receiver. He heard his own voice, unnaturally loud and harsh. 'Does she still work there?'

'Oh, yes,' the shrill and cheerful voice replied. 'I should jolly well say so. She's on holiday. She'll be back next week.'

'Oh,' He sagged with relief. He managed to say, 'Thank you,' and was about to hang up.

'Here,' the voice recalled him urgently. 'I say. Can I help you? This is Dolly. I'm Ruth's friend. Dolly French. I say —' a confidential giggle came to his ears — 'which one are you?'

He was assailed by a new wave of terror. 'Which one are you?' It had never occurred to him that Ruth would probably have found fresh attachments in the last couple of years.

The office door banged behind him. He looked over his shoulder. The voice of Mr. Palfrey boomed through the room. 'On parade there, on parade! Sharply now! Swing your arms to the shoulders! Step lively! Everybody on parade! Ha! Ha! Haugh! Haugh! Haugh!' It looked as if Mr. Palfrey, without waiting for the statesmen, had declared war privately, for already he carried a gas mask and steel helmet slung on his back, and his air raid warden's armlet was pinned to his right sleeve. He strutted about the office, his face more bloated and purple than ever, shouting, 'Git on parade, there! Hep, right, hep, right, hep!' and rousing his subordinates with thumps on the back and digs in the ribs.

'I say,' the girl's voice came faintly over the telephone line, 'you haven't fainted or something, have you? Trust me to say the wrong thing. Here, who *are* you? Come on, be a sport.'

Mr. Palfrey was at his elbow. He dealt Mark a mighty blow on the back and screamed, 'Wheeeeeeeee...' He was evidently imitating some kind of projectile. He put his mouth to Mark's ear and bellowed, 'Ker-RASH!'

'Hallo,' Mark was shouting. 'Oh, damn! Shut up! Look, leave me alone for a minute, will you? No! Hallo! Hold on. I say, hallo!'

'You must be Geoffrey,' said the girl on the telephone, giggling and whispering asides to someone else. 'She said you were excitable.'

'No; I'm not Geoffrey,' Mark shouted. 'Listen, what day...?'

'Hallo, hallo!' roared Mr. Palfrey. 'Geoffrey? Who's Geoffrey? Aha! The plot thickens!' He returned to his own affairs with another prolonged, 'Wheeeeeeeeeee — Kerrrr-ASH!'

'Oh, hell!' Mark moaned. 'I'll ring again. Goodbye.' He stepped over Mr. Palfrey, who was crawling across the floor beneath an imaginary hail of bullets, and returned to his desk.

It became quite clear, as the morning went on, that this was a great day for Mr. Palfrey. Between the more frantic manifestations of his martial ardour he lectured, with a weighty and infuriating benevolence, on his extensive experiences in the last war and on the prospects in the one to come. He reminded his listeners at uncomfortably frequent intervals that they would all be in uniform within a few days, and whipped himself up into deafening and spluttering convulsions of mirth as he prophesied what babes, what ninnies, what hopeless, listless and spineless softies they would prove to be. It became clear that, until today, November 10th, 1918, had been the last happy day of Mr. Palfrey's life. He stamped and tramped up and down the room, sloping arms with the window pole. 'The good ol' slope!' he enthused. He inflated his cheeks and thundered, 'Slo-hope... HIPE!' He rushed back to his desk, picked up a penholder and took a new nib from a box. 'Fix!' he screamed...

'Baynits!' — and with a great flourish of both hands he planted the nib in the holder. He jumped to his feet, holding the pen with both hands in an offensive position, and began to prance about, snarling and growling and pulling a succession of horrible faces. 'On guard! Lunge! Withdraw! In! Out! On guard! Ah, the good ol' cold steel!' He bared his tobacco-stained teeth, yelled 'Charge!', hurled himself across the room and plunged the nib into Venner.

Venner screamed, checked himself, and flapped a hand feebly at Mr. Palfrey. 'Oh, *go* away!'

Mr. Palfrey mocked Venner's squeal. 'Go away!' He flounced from desk to desk, simpering horribly and fluttering his finger-tips effeminately. 'Go away! Boo-hoo. Ickle dearie-wearie-me says go away.' His caperings brought him back to Venner's side. 'Ho! Ho! I can just see you in the Army. Brigade of Guards, eh? Fine specimen of a man!' He dug his fingers into Venner's arm. 'The ol' medical inspection, eh? Muscles, nil.' He poked viciously at Venner's stomach. 'Guts, nil.'

Venner was trembling, staring at the papers on his desk as if afraid to move his head, his mouth slackly open.

Mr. Palfrey bent forward and thrust his face close to Venner's. 'Blood, my lad! Buckets of blood! Fancy it? Wake up in the night and see a big fat rat squattin' on your chest. Like the idea? See arms and legs blown off and guts hangin' out. Think you'll get used to it?'

Venner did not look up. He was shaking from head to foot. 'Leave me alone,' he muttered. 'I don't feel well. All this excitement.'

Mr. Palfrey threw his head back, uttered a sickening shout of laughter and smote his own belly ecstatically with both hands. 'Haugh! Excitement! God save us all, he says excitement.' He leaned forward again and asked, with pretended deference, 'Pardon me, my lord, but did I hear you say excitement?'

Venner managed to utter a choking noise of assent.

'You'll get excitement,' snarled Mr. Palfrey. He snatched up an ebony ruler and began to hammer on the desk, reinforcing the clattering din by shouting, 'Rat-tat-tat-tat-tat-tat-tat-tat. Ha! Ha! The ol' machine-gun!' His face was darkly flushed. In years of bullying he had never been able to go as far as this; but now, it seemed, he had sniffed blood. He began to batter with the ruler at Venner's bony shoulders. 'Rat-tat-tat-tat-tat-tat.'

Venner made a noise like a long, shuddering snore, and began to cry.

The other clerks, out of whom Mr. Palfrey's antics had wrung an unhappy laughter that arose more from their nervous state than from amusement, lapsed into an embarrassed silence. They opened big ledgers, rummaged pointlessly in cupboards and drawers, looked everywhere but towards Venner.

The silence — the absence of Mr. Palfrey's voice — was itself a positive, sensible presence in the room. From Venner's desk there came only a soft sniffing and an unintelligible, self-pitying mumble.

The strident voice assaulted the silence again. 'Can't take a joke, eh?'

Venner continued to sob.

'Eh? Answer me! Can't you take a joke?'

'Give it a rest, will you?' Mark, who all this time had been trying in vain to concentrate on his own worries, spoke as much out of exasperation as out of pity for Venner.

Mr. Palfrey was in fighting fettle by now. There was a vein of hysteria, born of all the resentments and frustrations of twenty dull years of peace, becoming increasingly apparent in his ponderous tomfoolery. The subconscious anger and hatred that he felt towards these young men took hold of him as he turned on Mark. 'Oh? Listen to Lord Muck giving orders!'

'I'm not giving orders. We've had enough, that's all.'

'We? We've had enough? And who appointed you spokesman of public opinion. I didn't hear anyone else object. I've got two ears, you know. One on each side. I wash 'em every day. No wax in 'em, you know. Who are you, eh? You're not exactly backward in coming forward, are you?' Mr. Palfrey was seized by an inspiration. Here was a victim whom he could isolate more easily than he had Venner. 'Your kind never are.'

Mark's face, pale and blank, told Mr. Palfrey that he had scored. 'Are they?' he added, with relish.

Mark turned away and took Venner's arm. 'Come on, Ven, come and wash your face and forget about it. Don't you worry about him.'

Venner pulled himself free of Mark's grip. 'Ha!' he shrilled. 'You didn't like that, did you? Don't you suck up to me, just because he's turned on you.' He was shaking violently again. 'You think I can't guess who's been behind it all? You think I don't know who's been laughing at me behind my back, and talking, and making trouble? You,' he gasped. 'It's always one of *you*! Whenever there's one of your lot —' He could not go on, and ended helplessly with a long, blubbering sigh.

Mark looked about him, overwhelmed. He did not mind Venner speaking like this, nor even Palfrey; but the others — they were his friends, his court of appeal. He looked at them beseechingly, but they huddled in embarrassed silence over their work; and in his inflamed imagination they were all united against him. Even the silence, to him, was a kind of speech between them; and into each scuffle of papers, each furtive scratch of a pen, he read a taunt against him, being communicated from one of them to another. He went back to his desk. Venner and Palfrey returned to their work, in silence.

6

Mark went to his room as soon as he reached home, took his shoes off and lay on his bed. He remained there all the afternoon, exhausted, incapable of thought. He sank into a half-sleep and awoke sufficiently restored to think. He brooded over all his relationships, with Paula, with Ruth, with the clerks at the office; he searched his memory for actions, gestures, remarks, facial expressions that might reveal what all these people thought of him; his imagination, fed with scraps of recollection, began to weave angry fantasies. His body tingled with an inexplicable energy; the blood beat in his head; he had to force his breathing. There was no one against whom he could direct this profound and mysterious rage. The fit passed, and he sprawled for a while in a blank torpor.

Now that his anger had passed, he was able to think, calmly and wearily. The imminence — the certainty — of war enabled him to take stock of his life; something we are unable to do in normal times, when the days flow past us silent and unnoticed, and we cannot discern the process of change, of fading hope, of defeat.

With the sudden shutting of a door on one stage of his life, he was able to see how he had been drifting since he had left school. His dreams were still there, somewhere at the back of his mind, but life had turned out to be merely a succession of things happening to him, instead of a succession of things that he did. It slipped past him; he was unable to take hold, to direct his own existence.

'Who can?' he asked himself defensively, and consoled himself that it was the same for everyone. He had seen it happening to his elders, this gradual decline from youthful hope into comfortable passivity, a lifelong waiting for death. He had said, like all young people, 'Yes; but it will not happen to me.' It was happening to him: no glory, only a shabby job, a shabby love affair, humiliations. Lying on his bed, he realised that life, the cheat, might still be cheated. He made his plans.

The patch of sunlight on the floor grew smaller. The triumphant shrilling of the birds faded into the noises of the city. The lustre had already faded from the evening when he rose stiffly, went to the kitchen and tried to eat. He felt sick at the sight of food. He succeeded in swallowing a cup of tea and a piece of dry toast. His head swimming, he went back to bed. As he lay down, he remembered that he was supposed to spend the evening with Paula. He crossed the room uncertainly to the window, let the blind down and returned to the bed. Swaying with weariness, he dragged off his clothes, slid in between the sheets and fell asleep.

He awoke late the next morning. The tension was gone and he ate a good breakfast. He listened to the declaration of war on the radio. When, a few minutes later, the air raid sirens sent the family stumbling downstairs to the cellar, he went out on to the front steps to see what would happen, and sat unperturbed on the balustrade enjoying the sunshine.

The day passed serenely. Joe and the young man who lived downstairs were busy piling earth on the Anderson shelter in the back garden. Clara concealed her agitation and hurried from one household task to another. Mark, unusually sociable, sunned himself on the front steps and talked with the neighbours. Later, he helped with the work in the garden, and when this was completed he settled himself on the sofa in the parlour and read a detective story. He went to bed early and again he slept well.

On Monday morning he left the house at the usual time, and boarded a bus, humming to himself and smiling secretly out of the window. Instead of going to work, however, he travelled to Kingsway, where he left the bus and walked briskly for several blocks until he came to his destination; the Air Ministry building. He was surprised to find a long queue already waiting.

The building occupied most of the frontage of a block. The queue was extending ceaselessly along the buttressed grey walls, restless but subdued. Some of the recruits looked so young that they must have been schoolboys, their caps left at home for once. Jostling against them were students with masses of shaggy hair and purple scarves; and sleek-haired clerks, ill at ease, as if they expected their employers to appear suddenly and berate them for their truancy; and burly young businessmen in pork-pie hats; and a few young gentlemen of fashion. Some of them stamped on the pavement as if to keep themselves warm, although the morning was radiant. Some leaned against the wall and kicked at it impatiently with their heels. Some looked at the photographic displays in the windows. Some talked, shyly or with exaggerated assertiveness.

Mark hurried to the end of the line and took up his place. He felt conspicuous for a moment, and alone; then others arrived, the queue extended behind him, and he began to shuffle forward. A young man in front of him engaged him in conversation. He was alone no more, but one of many, one of the hundreds of nervous, eager boys who were moving slowly, in the sunshine, towards a dark doorway. As he walked up the steps into the doorway he felt as if he were entering a sanctuary. Paula, Palfrey and all his problems were left behind. Ahead was the chance to belong, the promise, at last, of living gloriously. He wondered: for how long? To a clerk sitting behind a desk he said, 'Aircrews, please, for the duration.'

1940

1940

1

The Hurricanes were ranged in the sky in a starboard echelon, like a staircase to the sun. Each machine swayed gently as it slid through the air at three hundred miles an hour, like a boat idling on a smooth swell.

Mark moved the control column slightly to the right and looked out through the perspex, over the leading edge of the right wing. Below, in long, loose lines, aircraft were swimming slowly across the squadron's path; the outlines of their silver shapes were rounded and fishlike — Heinkels.

The earphones crackled: 'Going down!'

He gave a last, quick glance up into the sun's glare, where the Messerschmitts were swarming like midges. Well, the Boss knew what he was doing: and the Spits were on top to handle any trouble that broke up there. His gloved finger pushed the gun button to the 'Fire' position.

One by one the Hurricanes rolled over, showed their bellies to the sun and dropped away, falling like projectiles upon the German bombers.

Mark was crouched over instruments and controls, the living heart of his machine, leaving his flesh to absorb the wrenching speed of the dive, the harsh, obliterating roar of the engine. His hands and feet, trained and sure, looked after the controls without bothering his brain; his mind was concentrated behind his eyes, focused on the Heinkels. The German machines grew larger, slowly for a second or two as if they were travelling up through the sky within an invisible lift-shaft, then more and more quickly until for an annihilating instant one of them occupied the whole of his field of vision. His finger pressed the gun-button, and the falling Hurricane trembled to the vibration of the eight machine-guns in its wings. They had passed through the German formation, and there was only empty sky below, coloured glimpses of the Kent countryside shifting beneath the veils of wispy cloud. The Hurricanes strained protestingly out of their dive, closed in and shot up again in a wide climbing turn, this time coming in at the Heinkels from abeam. Mark saw a black stain of smoke leave the Heinkel formation and grow vertically down towards the earth, with a broken shape, half-hidden by flames, at its base. Then the enemy aircraft were expanding magically into his sights again, and he was in the midst of a confusion of machines, swerving and climbing and plunging, saved from collision a score of times by inexplicable instinct, guns shaking the Hurricane as one target after another flashed past.

He found himself above the fight for a moment, alone in an expanse of unspoiled sky. A Heinkel blew up beneath him, crumbling slowly and vanishing in a great blossom of smoke. A Hurricane, its destroyer, came up through the smoke and turned alongside him. It was his friend, Davy. They waved to each other and Davy held up a triumphant thumb after pointing at his victim. Then they went down together.

Mark closed in on a Heinkel from below and opened fire at two hundred yards. He saw the belly gun of the enemy machine answering. Obsessed, unable to feel anything but the urge to kill, he drew in; a hundred yards, fifty. He was still firing. The blister beneath the belly of the Heinkel suddenly came apart and the tiny figure of the German gunner went whirling down through the sky, with fragments of metal swooping and tumbling after it. He slammed stick and rudder to the right, and raking the Heinkel with a last burst, sent his Hurricane screeching away in a tight turn, just as it seemed that he must fly on into the German machine. He came round again. The Heinkel's starboard engine was burning, unwinding a long streamer of black smoke across the sky. The Heinkel went down in a gentle dive. Before he could go after it, he found himself engaged by another bomber abeam and fell away past its tail to avoid its fire. He climbed again, and was just able to notice another Hurricane going after the crippled enemy which he had been forced to abandon. He came round to deliver a stern attack; a moment later, his guns empty, he dived clear of the battle. He went down through the cloud before he levelled off, set a course for base and climbed again through the cloud.

In a few seconds he had travelled miles. The formations of Heinkels had changed course and were dwindling back towards the coast, driven away from their target. A few fighters still whirled like mosquitoes over them. Otherwise there was nothing in the sky.

A black dot appeared in the white-streaked sky to starboard and grew as another machine approached head-on. He watched it with anxiety, and relaxed gratefully as the silhouette of a Hurricane became clear. The other machine drew alongside. He recognised 'Bones' Gascoyne, his face hidden by his helmet and the snout of his oxygen mask but his tall, stooping body unmistakable.

Bones' voice came over the radio-telephone: 'Seen Davy?'

Mark shook his head.

They circled over their base and came in to land. Four Hurricanes were already drawn up around the perimeter of the field. They taxied in and climbed out of their cockpits. Mark felt numbed as he stepped clumsily down; for a moment he could not feel the ground through the soles of his boots.

Davy came to greet them: 'We got three,' he said, 'and a couple of maybes. I saw Rossiter go down. We're waiting for the others to come in.'

When the Intelligence Officer had finished with them they sprawled on the grass beneath the wings of their machines, while a horde of armourers and mechanics swarmed over the Hurricanes, servicing them in readiness for the next flight. In these last days of September, 1940, it was not worth while going back to the dispersal hut. Business was still far too brisk, as it had been throughout the last month.

Mark lay sleepily in the sun, with his hands under the back of his head, listening to the rumble of engines, the quiet murmur of talk and the singing of birds. The sound of dance music played on a gramophone came from the dispersal hut. An armourer, nearby, defied the noise and raucously sang *Begin the Beguine*. Mark enjoyed a remote feeling of satisfaction, and a faint relief, as the other five Hurricanes of the squadron came whining overhead, one by one, and drifted quietly to earth.

It was good to lie in the scent of the warm grass, refusing thought, body limp and moulded to the earth, letting the fatigue and the strain drain away. He was conscious of no fear that had to be fought off; not fear, that is, of the mean and paralysing kind; his discovery of this fact had brought him great joy; but there was, all the time, a sensation of suspense that could scarcely be analysed, a sublime terror, perhaps, that only served to sharpen his senses, to increase the intoxication of the dive each time he attacked, to visit him as he sat in the cockpit, before the take-off, with a scared, exultant pang, to endow him when he was on the ground, and among his comrades with an exuberance which he had never before possessed.

He lay in a stupor, heedless of time, until the clouds crept across the sun and a cold wind came from the sea to rouse him. He sat up, shivering. He accepted this life; he enjoyed it; but he did not want to fly again for a little while. There had been too much of it in this last month; too much speed, too much strain, too much battle, too little rest. Nevertheless, when the 'Scramble!' came again he felt no resentment.

Only when he had heaved himself up into the cockpit, secured himself, and was waiting to move off did the cold pang come for a second: then the engine grunted, roared, the propeller blades quickened, power tugged at the wheels and he was moving across the grass again, the other Hurricanes trundling alongside; and he was wholly absorbed in the machine which functioned in such subtle response to his hands and feet.

The low rumble of engines swelled into a single, pure, blaring note that reached every corner of the airfield. Flight by flight the squadron lifted from the ground and climbed in wide, deliberate circles round their base until, tiny toys high up in the pale blue sky, they turned north-east and flew to meet the enemy.

2

A new life had begun for Mark in uniform, an ever-intensifying round of mental and physical endeavour. Mathematics, meteorology, navigation, aerodynamics, engineering, gunnery: every day of his early training brought a fresh strain, a fresh trial, with rejection as the price of failure and mounting confidence as the reward of success. There is nothing more beautiful than the discovery in ourselves of our full human potentialities, and this is what happened to Mark in the reckless university of war. At the beginning he had been terrified of his own weaknesses; he had wondered if his inherited over-sensitiveness, his hesitancy and his fear of people might unfit him for flying. He had done battle with his doubts, daily, crouching over his gloves in the boxing ring, lolling in classroom or engineering shed, sprawling triumphantly behind a rifle on the range; the prize was self-respect, and he pursued it doggedly.

Then came the ineffable exaltation of flight, the vain but glorious ascent towards the sun, the courtship with the clouds; day after day spent amid the din of engines and the intoxicating reek of exhaust fumes. Dawdling about the sky in a slow trainer, progressing to more powerful machines, plunging into the controlled insanity of aerobatics, watchfully absorbing tactics and formation flying, the first flight in a Hurricane; a trial flight in a Spitfire, with Mark as nervous as a bride at the controls, remembering the candidate before him who had overturned in landing; the daily scrutiny of the notice boards, incredulous and joyful, as he saw against his name, 'Passed', 'Passed', 'Passed'; and the final *brevet* of manhood, the posting to Fighter Command.

Throughout this moral steeplechase he was kept too busy to think of his former emotional problems. He was out of Paula's reach, and he rarely had time to think of Ruth. When he had arrived as a recruit at the Air Force depot he had tried to compose a letter to Ruth. After he had prepared several long drafts, he finally wrote, 'Just a line to let you know I'm in the Raf. Address as above. All the best, Mark.' She had replied, 'Good luck. Let's hear from you sometime.' He had judged this to be an unenthusiastic response, had thought miserably of the Geoffrey of whom he had heard on the telephone, and had not written since.

He formed no deep friendships during his training; life was too swiftly changing; people were always coming and going. But he had come to mingle with young men of a kind he had never before known, cheerful, courageous and superbly poised. They accepted him without question, just as they accepted the Australians and Canadians who had come to fight, the Indians, the coloured Jamaicans, the beaming Czechs and the suicidally-daring Poles. Nevertheless, he remained more reserved than most of them, and on arrival at a new training centre, he usually displayed for some days the stealthy caution of a new boy at school.

In August, 1940, he came to the squadron, which, from its base in Essex, was already flying a dozen times a day to meet the German air onslaught. Although the squadron was hard-pressed, he was kept out of the fighting for some days, practising formations and learning the latest battle tactics. It was at this period that he met Davy Collins, who had been ordered to put him through his paces in air fighting. Davy took him up and knocked all the false confidence out of him with a dazzling display of skill. When they landed, and Mark climbed dejectedly out of his machine, Davy thumped him on the back and said, 'You'll do, cocky,' leaving him weak with relief. At lunch-time, Mark entered the large dining-hall, was served at the buffet, and stood holding his plates, uncertain where to sit. The room resounded with the hubbub of a hundred conversations and the clatter of crockery. Men hurried to and fro with their plates and Mark felt lonely for the first time in months. Then he saw Davy, at the far end of the room, standing up and waving his fork, and shouting, 'Hey! Hey, you! Blue-eyes!' Mark went over to Davy's table. Davy gave him a casual, sidelong glance, pointed at the vacant chair next to him, said, 'Sit down and dig in. Your grub's getting cold,' and went on forking food into his mouth. Mark sat down, and a tall, gaunt flying officer sitting across the table said, 'Hallo. I've been hearing about you. My name's Gascoyne.' Davy looked up, grunted,

'Bones,' and bent to his food again. That was how their friendship, cemented in battle a few days later, had begun.

3

Superficially, Mark's two friends were utterly dissimilar. Bones — Christopher Gascoyne — was a twenty-seven-year-old barrister, fond of books, conversation and music; Davy was twenty-one, wealthy, red-headed and handsome. He had come straight from Cambridge; he was in love with speed, noise and women. Bones liked to spend his spare time in his bedroom, puffing at his pipe and talking or playing his portable gramophone; Davy received invitations to parties by every post and was always wanted on the telephone. Yet each possessed, latently, the other's best qualities. Bones, normally thoughtful and deliberate, could be as reckless as Davy in the air or on the ground. Mark remembered one occasion when the three of them had gone to a party at a big house in the district. They had been standing on a balcony, sipping drinks and looking down on to a paved terrace. The talk had turned, absurdly, as such conversations do, to the legendary immortality of cats. Davy had quoted stories he had heard of cats falling from high buildings and walking away unhurt; and Bones had replied, 'It's all a matter of keeping the muscles relaxed. Look!' And he had vaulted over the balcony and dropped fifteen feet to the pavement. He had returned, shaken but unhurt, swallowed another drink and said, 'I can't imagine why I didn't break my leg.' Davy, on the other hand, despite the indifference that he affected towards his friend's interests, was one of the few members of the squadron who had the intellectual capacity to keep up with Bones. In arguments, when Mark could only make an uneasy comment from time to time, Davy would match himself against Bones with dexterity and gusto. They both had a tortuous sense of humour that expressed itself in fragmentary and mysterious remarks which few other people could understand. Davy had come to derive, in his own secretive fashion, satisfaction from the concerts to which he and Mark were persuaded by Bones from time to time. Recently, coming away from an orchestral concert at which they had heard the Beethoven Violin Concerto, Bones had asked them, 'What did you think of it?' Mark had replied dutifully, 'Fine!' Davy had said, 'Nice bit of homework that soloist, wasn't she?' But for days afterwards he had walked about whistling to himself the sweet and sprightly melodies of the final movement. Bones and Davy both had the same unbounded capacity to enjoy life and the same curiosity about everything under the sun. They flew off on their own whenever they could, and fought as if one brain directed the two of them, roaring into the enemy like twin Lucifers.

In their company, Mark became aware of a complete honesty of spirit which baffled him at first. Their own behaviour possessed a strange transparency, as if they were men with nothing to hide, and they had a disconcerting gift of seeing into others.

At the end of September the squadron, which had fought hard for two months and suffered heavy losses, was relieved, and settled down to a more restful life on an airfield further north. The pilots had little to do but chase an occasional German intruder away from the port areas of the Humber, and to train replacements. They learned that leave was to begin again, although on a limited scale, and that more weekend passes would be permitted.

One afternoon a few weeks after the move, Mark was sitting in a dispersal hut writing a letter to Mickey. A number of pilots who, with Mark, were on duty that day were warming themselves at the barrel stove. So far there had been nothing to do, except a two-man patrol to hunt a single enemy raider; Bones and Davy, always eager for this kind of job, had gone.

'Keep a hold on that temper of yours,' Mark wrote, 'and you'll be all right.' Mark smiled. It was a novel experience to be in a position to give advice to his older brother. Mickey was in a Fusilier battalion on the Kent coast, manning trenches against the still-expected invasion. On his first day with the battalion an N.C.O. had told him to take his hands out of his pockets. Mickey had answered, 'Didn't your Mum ever teach you to say "Please"?' This pleasantry had earned him seven days' C.B. On several subsequent occasions his truculence had got him into trouble, but a week ago he had written bewilderedly to Mark: 'They've just give me a stripe. Me a lance-corporal! Daft isn't the word for it.'

The faint, nagging hum of distant aircraft filtered through the grey-ribbed roof of cloud that covered the countryside. The east wind carried it across the airfield to the dispersal hut, and the pilots stirred in their deep, battered armchairs. Mark screwed the cap back on to his fountain-pen and closed his writing case. The Boss, their squadron leader, who had been standing at the window like a sentinel, said, 'They're coming this way'.

He opened the door and the cold October wind blustered triumphantly into the hut, routing the warmth and awakening even the two pilots who had been sleeping on the bunks built into one corner of the room.

'They haven't picked him up yet,' said Mark.

The Boss raised a cautionary hand. 'Quiet!'

The pilots, grouped outside the doorway of the hut, listened intently and comprehendingly, as if to music. The thin, droning sound gradually grew louder, coming to them in a series of sudden, loud down-beats like the probing of a giant dentist's drill. Somewhere beyond it, hardly audible as yet, there was a deep, steady rumble. The even roar increased in volume, as if overtaking the other noise. Until now these sounds had been moving steadily towards them, but when they were almost overhead they began to swing and shift bewilderingly about the sky. The pilots on the ground, however, knew what was happening above the clouds. They heard the thunder of Rolls-Royce engines smother the noise of the intruder; new notes began to drive earthward through the grey pall — higher and louder notes, as if the engines were speaking — now in anger, now in protest, now straining, now exulting; a new sound was heard, the dull blast of machine-guns and the quick pop of cannon; and, suddenly, there grew out of the roar of the battle a long, rising moan, growing louder and shriller.

'There he goes,' shouted one of the pilots, pointing. The tiny shape of an aeroplane came boring down out of the greyness. The moan of its falling swelled to a grating shriek; it disappeared behind the trees, the earth jerked beneath their feet, a dark dome of smoke rolled up over the treetops and the loud, dull, sickening *whoof* of the explosion reached their ears.

The victors came into sight, two Hurricanes, descending through the haze. They made a wide circuit of the field, scudding through the misty undersides of the clouds, disappearing for seconds at a time behind streaks of dark grey vapour, their engines' song, unchallenged now, swelling victoriously. They came racing in, low over the heads of the watching pilots, settled to the ground with a last surging roar, taxied over the grass and came swaying slowly and contentedly back towards the dispersal hut.

The pilot of the leading machine pulled back his cockpit cover, raised his goggles and dragged the helmet from his head, releasing a mass of shaggy, fair hair. It was Bones. He heaved himself up on to the coaming and called to Mark. 'The pilot bailed out. Is he down yet?'

Mark looked up into the sky and saw the parachute sailing slowly down through the mist about a mile away. 'He's dropping right in on the station,' he shouted back. 'There's a lorry starting off from H.Q. It must be going to pick him up.' Davy had taxied his machine up to the edge of the perimeter road and had hurried across to his car, a red Bentley, which was parked nearby. He beckoned to Bones and Mark. 'They'll have him in the guard-room by the time we get down there. Coming to have a look?'

Mark replied, 'I can't.' He was still on duty. 'I'll wait for you here.'

Mark returned to the hut, and Bones and Davy drove off to see their prisoner.

They were back in less than ten minutes.

'Whew!' exclaimed Davy as he dropped into an armchair and flung his legs wide apart. 'What a stinker!'

'Blond beast?' asked the Boss.

'No. Nasty little tyke. Black hair, beady eyes, chin like Joe Goebbels. Full of hate; you should have seen him; huddled in a corner. He looked as if he'd scratch if we came too near. Still,' he added triumphantly, 'look what I've got. Souvenir.' He produced a German automatic pistol and banged it down on the table.

'How'd you get hold of it?' asked Mark.

'Don't ask bloody silly questions. Here' — Davy turned to one of the other pilots — 'give us a pack of cards, Mike. Thanks.' He shuffled the cards. 'We'll cut for it. Aces high. Take a card.'

'Leave me out,' protested Mark. 'It's between you two. You knocked him down.'

'Idiot,' said Bones, 'take a card.'

Mark's card was the highest of the three. He took the pistol and put it in his greatcoat pocket. 'Well,' he grinned, 'I can blow my brains out any time I like now, by courtesy of you two blokes.'

'Sounds like a mean little devil, that German,' said one of the pilots as Mark returned to his chair. 'We'll have a tough time if they're all as stubborn as that.'

'Oh, I don't know,' said Bones. 'It was only a front. He was scared stiff.'

'What? Of you? It didn't sound like it, from what Davy said.'

'Not of us. Of everything that had gone wrong. All the things in his book of rules that hadn't come true. The poor little wretch hasn't the faintest idea what it's all about. Now that he's got no one to tell him the answers, he's in the dark, and all he can do is pull faces and make defiant noises like a terrified kid.'

'And you think they're all like that?' asked Mark.

'The Germans? I think most people are — a part of them, anyway. Most people imagine that the world's beyond their control, and they're frightened of it like children afraid of the dark. What they don't understand, they fear. And fear generates hatred. This Jerry was full of it.'

'Loaded!' said Davy.

'The trouble is,' Bones went on, 'this kind of sick hatred isn't fundamentally at anything, or against anything. It's just a kind of explosive force — distilled fear bottled up under high pressure inside people — and Heaven help whoever comes along to touch it off. You see it in neurotic individuals, don't you? You never know who they'll turn on.'

The Boss tapped his pipe out against the stove. 'You take a pretty gloomy view of people, don't you? I mean, if it's human nature, we shall go on like this for ever, carving each other up.'

'Why? Human nature changes. It's changed a lot during the last thirty centuries. To start with, there are plenty of people who aren't frightened, right now. They're the ones I put my money on. After all, when you have a set-up in which people have always had to fight for their livings like dogs for bones, with everyone else a potential enemy — and nations fighting each other for more or less the same reason — you're bound to have the world careering along like a bus out of control. And then all the passengers rave and struggle and make things worse because they don't know why it's that way. That's why fear rules us just as much as it rules the beasts of the jungle.

'It's just possible that one day we'll come of age, and work together to share the good things instead of scrabbling for them. I don't see why trust shouldn't take the place of fear. And what there'll be left then to fight about I really can't imagine.'

'Pipe dreams, you old Bolshie,' grunted the Boss.

Davy stretched himself hugely, and emitted a sceptical groan. 'Boy, am I sleepy!' he said. 'I don't know whether it's this stove or your sermon. Why don't you all relax. Have a good time! Let the world look after itself! It's only an aggregation of bloody fools who don't deserve any more than they get. Why worry about 'em? You'll be dead before you've got it sorted out, anyway.'

Bones laughed. 'Life's too short for chess,' he quoted.

'Good old Byron. My hero, that chap — wine, wit and women.'

'Ah!' said the Boss. 'Women! Now that we're back on the subject, have you heard this one?' They all drew their chairs closer to the stove and settled down to a round of dirty jokes.

In later years they were to talk, and laugh, many times about this moment. Yet when she asked, 'How did you feel when you first caught sight of me?' and he answered, 'Wonderful!' he was lying, for in that first second of recognition there was only blind panic, a shock sudden and scalding as the impact of boiling water.

'The whole day,' he would say, 'felt like a dream, even without my knowing what it was going to lead up to. I suppose that in the last couple of months, with my friends being killed one after another, I had unconsciously abandoned the idea that I would ever come back to the real world. And then, all of a sudden, everything had gone quiet. I was alive. I had a nine-day leave. And I was in a train, one of those dirty, crawling old London and North-Eastern trains, on my way back into a life I'd almost forgotten.'

He sat numbly, somehow sceptical of the reality of all that he felt and saw, in the corner seat of an empty carriage, looking out of a grimy window as the sooty panorama of East London crept by. Ochreous patches of desolation pocked the grey pattern of streets which stretched away into the mist. Wet roofs gleamed darkly, their uniformity broken by blotches of utter blackness where blasts had stripped the slates away. Close to the railway line reared a bombed factory, its gaping walls revealing the twisted girders like bones laid bare by a wound. At one place lay heaped the rubble of a building so completely demolished that it resembled nothing so much as an abandoned brickyard. At another a dirty column of smoke still crawled up into the sky and fire engines lined a shattered street. Yet, in the little back-yards that streamed past, washing fluttered defiantly on the clothes-lines, the windows of the houses were still freshly curtained (except where, for a mile at a time, they had been smashed by blast), dirty children — he had imagined that they had all been evacuated — climbed the walls to wave and scream at the train; and in the streets moved women with shopping baskets, workmen on bicycles and little red bakers' vans, as if nothing out of the ordinary had ever happened in the world.

There came to him the vision, inchoate but overwhelming, of the plodding invincibility of the human kind. People died and the products of their toil were destroyed; but life, it seemed, was indestructible. It was this feeling which fortified him against the scenes of appalling ruin which met his eyes as he left the station. The familiar City streets — he was only a few hundred yards from the building in which he had once worked — were hardly distinguishable. The broken buildings which had looked merely ugly from the train were terrifying when they towered above him. Yet here were the people, hurrying about their work, the same crowds of typists, clerks, messengers, travellers that he had left behind in 1939, swarming on the pavements and scampering across the streets between the lines of vehicles; some chattering, some preoccupied, some bullying their way through the throng, some ducking and dodging and huntedly imploring every passer-by to excuse them. People lived on. And this grey, teeming world which at first had seemed so unreal to him, a dream into which he was wandering, gradually assumed reality, and it was the past, the battle, which became a dream.

Bewilderment turned to pleasure. The feeling that he was himself alive flowed back into him. He looked forward with relief and tenderness to seeing his parents. Like an excited schoolboy, he began to hurry, impatient to see his home again.

He was shocked, when he saw his mother and father, at the change which had come over them in the last year.

His father's face was yellow, the ruddiness of the cheeks replaced by veined purple patches under the cheek-bones. He looked smaller, for he was growing fat, and his hair was receding. Since the outbreak of war, when his own business had come to a standstill, he had been working as a cutter in a big clothing factory. The job had its advantages. He was well paid, he was glad to be making uniforms now that both his sons were in the Forces, and he had come to enjoy the company of his fellow workers, especially since he was honoured by them as the father of a fighter pilot. But it had grieved him to lose his independence, and the work placed a great strain on him, keeping him standing all day wielding the great power-driven blade with which he cut out piles of cloth at a time.

Clara's hair was greyer, her face losing its firmness. She had both her sons to worry about, now that Mickey was in the infantry. In addition to her daily burden of work in the house and at the shop, she now had to hurry home every evening to cook a meal before the nightly air-raid warning sounded.

She was crying silently as she put her arms about her son, and she covered his face quietly with kisses. Mark was embarrassed by her emotion, but he held her close. He felt sorry for her and angry that she should have had to suffer. His father hovered awkwardly about them, offering Mark a fatuous grin every time their eyes met. He shook his son's hand heartily and assailed him with brisk and stupid greetings that sounded as if they had been painfully rehearsed. He took Mark's greatcoat from him. 'Swagger, eh?' He held the coat up for Clara to admire. 'A lovely job. A lovely bit of cloth. Feel the weight of it.'

They were in the dining-room, Mark sprawling in an armchair by the gas fire. He took the glass of whisky that his father poured for him and raised it to his mother's toast; 'Please God it will soon be over and you and Mickey home.' They questioned him anxiously about his life in the squadron — about his friends, the food, the comfort, his experiences in the air. He answered vaguely and evasively, and turned the conversation by asking for news of the family. They told him how Mill, who had been evacuated to the country, was getting on, how much her baby weighed, how old Jacob had refused to budge from his East End house and lived like a hermit under the bombs, amid a desert of rubble; they read him a letter from Jenny, who was living the life of a *grande dame* at Torquay and who boasted of her cleverness in securing exemption for her son from military service by buying a farm and registering him as its owner. They talked, deprecatingly, about their own discomforts. They no longer went each night to the Underground stations. Joe said, 'It was too much for your mother. We go downstairs at nights now, when the sirens sound, and we sleep under the stairs. We've got a bed fixed up there, and a stove. You'll stay down there to-night with us, won't you?' Mark had no intention of sleeping anywhere but in his own bedroom, but he did not contradict his father. The district had been badly hit by the bombing. Joe said — not without pride, 'One hit the factory; it was during the last daylight raid. I was working when it happened. It felt like an earthquake. I was thrown right to the other side of the room, and the windows came in. We never stopped work, though. Some people on the top floor were hurt. It was only a small bomb.' The parish church had been burned down and several neighbouring streets demolished. A mile away, along the Stoke Newington Road, a parachute-mine had caused an entire block of flats to collapse into the communal shelter underneath, killing hundreds of people.

There were more drinks, and lunch, a rich and heavy meal which Clara must have laboured for days to prepare. Afterwards Mark went back to his chair by the fire, bored now and ill at ease. The sense of reunion had worn off. His obligations were fulfilled. He could think of nothing more to talk about. The constraint that had kept him apart from them in the old days returned, the long silences, the three of them sitting stiffly in their chairs avoiding each others' eyes. He said, 'I've got to go out. I've a number of calls to make.' He did not relish going out into the cold; he would have preferred to sprawl lethargically by the fire. He had nowhere to go, no idea of how he might pass the rest of the day. He knew that he would only wander aimlessly and tire himself out; but he had to escape from their smothering attentiveness, from the anxiety and adoration and horrible humility with which they sat forward on their chairs and looked at him. He hardened his heart against his mother's aggrieved 'So soon?' and left them.

In the streets he moved at random. At each corner, at each bus stop, his direction was decided by the mental toss of a coin. There was little to do. The cinemas were open and the West End theatres, closed in the evenings, advertised matinées. The pavements were thronged with shoppers, but their bustle had none of the gaiety of peacetime Saturday afternoons. Mark, depressed and impatient himself, looked into the faces of the people he passed and saw fear and exhaustion written there. Sometimes his scrutiny brought stares in return, but in each face there was respect at the sight of his uniform, and smiles from the women. When a young soldier saluted him his peace of mind was restored.

Wandering thus, sightseeing and daydreaming, he found himself in Rosebery Avenue. He looked at his watch. It was only just after three o'clock. He entered a little cafe and ordered a cup of tea, in order to rest his aching feet and waste a little more time. The tea was stewed and unsweetened, the cup dirty, the marble table-top wet with slop. Disgust and impatience drove him out into the street and he walked on to the corner of Tottenham Court Road, where there was a cinema that might offer a couple of hours of refuge; but the film advertised at the cinema was so stupid that he could not persuade himself to endure it. He stood in the palatial lobby wondering which way to turn next.

At this moment it occurred to him that Paula was in town. He wondered guiltily how he had come to forget her so completely. It was months since he had written to her. At the beginning of the war she had been interned, but she had soon been freed. Like a cork bobbing in the flooded gutter, into sewer and river and sea, she had the gift of survival. He had written dutifully while she was in the camp, and had sent a statement of evidence on her behalf, but after her return to London, with the sense of obligation towards her removed, his letters had become less frequent and — since the beginning of the air battle in August — had stopped altogether. The idea of seeing her again brought him no pleasure; he dreaded renewing an entanglement from which he had escaped with relief. On the other hand, his loneliness, the lingering notion that he had a duty to her, and the desire to show himself off to her in his uniform all urged him towards a reunion. His caution intervened in the debate and reminded him that by this time she would almost certainly be involved with someone else. There was — his vanity made him flinch at the thought — the risk of a snub. He decided to postpone the task of telephoning her until he had passed an hour in Charing Cross Road buying some books to take back to the squadron.

He crossed the road, walking at the laggard and reluctant pace that marks bored people in busy streets. As he crossed to the opposite pavement he leaped and dodged in front of impatient cars, feeling persecuted and undignified. Charing Cross Road was as frowsy and raucous as ever, and he reached the big bookshop that was his objective with relief at the sanctuary that its crowded quietness offered him. Nobody here looked into his face to accuse him of being alone or of having nothing to do; here he could escape from the prison of his own thoughts. Each person was contentedly alone amidst the throng, intent, absorbed in the choice of a book. Relaxed, he passed from counter to counter. He bought some Penguins and an impressive-looking book on War Aims, and moved on, shuffling sideways beneath a shelf of reprints, his head craned back, the index finger of his right hand touching the spine of each book as he read the titles, lips parted, lulled, off his guard. He bumped into someone on his right, mumbled an absent-minded apology, looked confusedly about him — and felt the fear jolt through him, paralysing, like an electric shock.

The murmuring quiet of the bookshop was lost in the sudden roaring that filled his ears; he did not dare to look again, and he looked again. She was standing, smiling, a foot from him. He wanted to turn and stumble out of the shop in panic; his mouth was parched and gummy, and although he had opened it to speak he could only utter croaking noises. He had spoken her name a thousand times to himself and now his stunned memory could not summon it to his lips.

She smiled. She seemed cool, faintly pleased at the encounter, yet neither surprised nor greatly impressed.

'Ruth,' she said. 'Ruth Seelig. Don't say you've forgotten me, Mark?'

He blushed. The heat inside his clothes was intolerable. He made more ridiculous noises and found his voice at last. He had lost all control over what he was saying and listened, in panic and disgust, to his own idiotic words, as if someone else were speaking.

'Hallo... I... how do you do... it's, ah —' He licked his lips. 'It *is* a long time, isn't it?'

'Yes.' She put down the book that she had been handling. 'I'm fighting against the temptation to say what a small world it is.'

He forced his face into a silly grin. 'How are you? I mean, how are you keeping? I... ahm... are your parents quite well? Ahm, it — it must be terrible in these raids. Do you sleep at home every night or do you go to a shelter?' He was completely out of breath by now. 'Ahm...'

There was a little light of mockery in her eyes. 'Well, I don't have to ask you any questions, do I? Your uniform tells the story. You do look grand. What are you in? Fighters?'

'Yes.' The pride flowed back into him. It was as if she had held out a hand to steady him. 'Hurricanes.'

'Oh, my, that sounds wonderful, doesn't it? Hurricanes! Have you shot down any German 'planes?'

This was a familiar cue; he could play the modest, offhand fighter pilot with confidence. He shrugged his shoulders. 'It's difficult not to, you know. There's nothing to it really. Our chaps more or less queue up for the chance.'

There was a silence. He strove desperately to think of something to say. Experience had taught him how demoralising these silences were to him, how each successive second made it harder for him to speak out. He blurted: 'Working? Ahm... are you working?'

His shyness had infected her. She looked away at the shelf and fumbled with another book. 'Yes.'

The silence came between them again.

This time she tried. 'Are you on leave?'

It was no use. He could only think of: 'Ah — a week — nine days, that is.'

'Oh.'

Now they had both taken up books and were holding them at waist level, fingering the pages blindly. Somebody came between them and said, 'Excuse me.' Mark took a deep breath, put his book clown and gabbled desperately. 'Well, ah — I've got to be running. Got an appointment. I've got an appointment. I, ahm... been nice seeing you. See you again soon. I, ahm... you know how it is. Got to hurry. Goodbye. I — yah —'

He fled.

Outside, on the pavement, he realised that he felt sick and that his heart was thumping as if he had been running. He wiped his face with his handkerchief and regained his breath. His mind began to function again; he was filled with shame and regret.

He stood in the gutter like a shamefaced mendicant, facing the shop; ignoring the people who streamed past him and bumped into him. He was afraid she would come out and see him, but he could not persuade himself to move away. How often he had longed for such an encounter! It had come and he had thrown his chance away. He reviled himself as a coward, told himself that his whole life could have been changed if he had been able for one moment to show himself a man, ordered himself to go back into the shop, and refused to obey.

He began to walk away, full of wild ideas about getting drunk, or picking up a girl, or telephoning Paula. He changed his mind and decided to wait for Ruth. He took up his stand opposite the corner of the shop's frontage and watched the door. The time went by slowly; he passed it in preparing excuses for confronting her again, in mentally rehearsing remarks which this time would prevent the conversation from drying up, and in speculating about what might happen. He realised, with a flash of terror, that he had not even noticed what she had looked like, although they had been standing face to face. Perhaps she had already walked out of the shop without his having recognised her! Perhaps — ten minutes had passed and there was no sign of her — perhaps there was another door! He explored, and found that there was one in the side street on whose corner the shop stood. He took up a position on the kerb from which he could see both entrances, miserable that he might have missed her, but determined to wait for another five minutes. The five minutes passed. He would wait for one more minute, he decided, and began to count out the sixty seconds. Somebody bumped into him as he reached the sixteenth, and he made up his mind to start again. A girl had been standing near him on the street corner, smoking a cigarette and watching him speculatively. It was a little while before he realised what she was doing there. He watched her nervously, ready to flee if she moved to accost him; he had terrible visions of Ruth walking out of the shop just as this creature stood speaking to him. The girl, seeing him hovering nearby and continually looking at her, decided at last that he was willing but timid; she smiled and approached him; he turned pale and bolted into the roadway. He had a chaotic impression of engines roaring around him like the beasts of the jungle and of vehicles looming on every side. There were voices raised in anger and, miraculously, he found himself on the opposite pavement, breathless again.

It was better, in any case, he said to himself, to wait on this side; less obvious. Again he wondered if he had missed her while his back was turned and again he resolved to wait for another five minutes. The minutes marched away and hope went with them; then she appeared.

She walked towards Cambridge Circus and he followed, keeping on the other side of the road, cunningly and confidently, like a hunter. He felt as if he had just drunk a first glass of brandy, or had awakened on a spring morning, happy and exalted. He quickened his pace, crossed the road ahead of her and walked back to meet her.

Once more they were face to face. She went past him for a step or two, then hesitated, startled. He hurried up to her.

'Hallo. Fancy meeting you again.'

She looked at him quizzically. 'Fancy!'

She was beautiful. She looked scarcely older than she had five years ago, except that there was less eagerness and more repose in her countenance. Her skin was as fresh and creamy as ever, her hair still lustrous and falling almost to her shoulders. The swagger coat that she wore added a touch of challenge to the attitude in which she faced him, hands in pockets, leaning impudently backwards.

He recited his explanation like a set piece. 'Yes, strange, isn't it. It really is a small world. I'd just finished my business and I was on my way back.'

'Where to?'

'Oh...' he was not prepared for this...'to get some tea. I thought the Corner House. Where are you going?'

'Home. For tea. I was just going to the Tube. Would you like to come?'

The shyness returned. He gaped. She said quickly, 'Of course you will!'

He mumbled, 'It seems an awful cheek. What will your people say?'

'They'll be delighted. Please come. There really is so much to talk about.' She laughed. 'Once we succeed in getting started!'

In the Underground Station he asked, 'Where shall I book to? Are you still living at Willesden?'

'Yes. We're still there.'

He unbuttoned his greatcoat to reach for his small change, and blushed with pleasure as she cried, 'Oh, that lovely tunic! And wings! Don't button your coat up. I want to hold your arm and let people see you and pretend you're my property.'

In the train the noise made it difficult to speak. They sat side by side; Mark, overcome by another wave of shyness, could think of little to say, and hardly dared to look boldly at her.

At last, he shouted, in clumsy gallantry, 'Bit of luck, wasn't it, your being available?'

'Why?'

'Well, pretty girl like you, Saturday evening. I should have thought there'd have already been some lucky chap who was booked to keep you company.'

She giggled. He could not hear her reply.

'What?' he roared.

'There was,' she shouted back. 'Poor devil. I've got him on my conscience. I was just on my way to meet him. He's probably still waiting for me at Piccadilly Circus!'

They drew closer together and laughed. He put his arm about her shoulders. Within the shelter of his arm he could feel her, still laughing.

5

'You'll like Bones and Davy,' Mark said to Ruth as their bus passed Aldgate Pump, 'they're coming down to town Saturday evening. They'll be staying at Bones' place. We can meet them on Sunday, and I'll be able to go back to the station with them on Sunday evening. Wait till you see Davy's car. It's a beauty! Ah' — he touched Ruth's arm and rose — 'we're coming into Whitechapel Road. This is where we get off. My granddad lives off down to the left, here.'

Ruth followed Mark off the bus, depressed at the reminder that the end of his leave was approaching, and at the formal way in which he held her arm.

Four days of Mark's leave had gone by. They had spent most of the time together. They had visited each other's homes almost daily. They had exchanged long confessions with each other, together with a host of explanations and excuses, about the last few years. Tomorrow they were going to Torquay together to spend a couple of days with Jenny. Yet their courtship had not deepened emotionally; their relationship was still unstable; the intimacy between them was still laboured and self-conscious. Somehow, Mark could never gain ground. One night, after walking happily hand-in-hand for hours in the darkness, with the enemy bombers droning in the sky above them, they would feel wonderfully close together and would kiss fiercely before parting. The next day they would hasten to their meeting, each confident that the barriers of reserve had been finally thrown down; but, once they were together, either Mark would be afflicted with shyness or Ruth would find herself unaccountably remote and unresponsive.

Mark could not reconcile the immense tenderness he felt for Ruth with the memory of his dismal adventure with Paula. To approach her as a woman, even to think of her in terms of his past experience, would be an insult. His humility kept him at arm's length; yet he longed for her. Ruth, in turn, was imprisoned by her inexperience and by her passive, placid nature; and although she was already able to dominate Mark with her soft, maternal assurance, although she walked at his side with a possessive, confident demeanour, she suffered at the thought that they might part at the end of the week with their future still undecided.

The little alley in which Jacob Strong lived, once so inconspicuous amid the stone jungle of Whitechapel, was not difficult to find now. It was visible from a mile away, for its dozen houses were almost the only buildings intact in a plain of desolation.

Mark and Ruth walked among the ruins, saying little, remote from each other, beneath the walls which reared like crumbling Stonehenges against the clouds, looking through empty windows at the white sky.

Jacob welcomed them on his front doorstep. 'Hah!' He looked smaller and shrivelled, but his grunt was as chesty and strong as ever, and the silver hairs sprouted more profusely than before from every visible part of his body. He wore no jacket over his filthy shirt, and the flies of his trousers were partially unbuttoned. 'If it ain't the little game-cock 'isself!' He shook Mark's hand violently, pushed back his cap, scratched his head and peered at Ruth through his gold-rimmed spectacles. 'Brought 'is bloody bes' gel wiv 'im, eh?' He inspected Ruth. 'Smart little piece, an' all!' He stepped back and glared at them both. 'Well, don't stand there dillyin' on the doorstep. Come in!' His voice was surly, yet there was pleasure in it.

The electric light was on in the little front room. The broken window was boarded up. There was scarcely space to move in the room. The piles of scrap iron in every corner seemed to have grown with the years. There was a great heap of broken boots against one wall, half-covered by a torn and mildewed mattress. Against another wall were stacked chipped and battered pots and pans, an old-fashioned gramophone with a huge horn and its broken spring hanging loose, several Victorian pictures with their glass cracked and the gilt almost worn from their frames, a fire bucket and a stirrup pump. The whole room smelt of rust and decay.

Jacob wiped the dust from a couple of chairs and capered about his guests like an old goblin. 'On 'oliday, are yer? 'Baht bloody time, I reckon, too! It don't do to fly them things abaht too long, do it? Ah long they give yer?'

'Nine days. You're looking well, Grandad. Mum sends her love. She's sorry she can't come down more often. It's the raids. She doesn't have a minute.'

'That's all right, bless 'er. She's bin a good daughter to me, 'as your Mum. She's the bes' one 'as looked arter me since my ol' missus went.'

'Why don't you go and live with her and Dad? It can't be very nice here on your own. They've got my old room empty. Or you could go down to Torquay with Aunt Jin. There's one thing about her and Moss, they will make you welcome. I'll tell you what. I'm going down to see them tomorrow, with Ruth. Shall I talk to them about it?'

'You're a good lad, you are,' Jacob said. 'Look well in that rig, you do. Proper slap-up gent' — he turned to Ruth — 'ain' 'e? I likes a young feller as likes a fight. Look 'ere, boy! I've lived in Whitechapel all my life, I 'ave. It ain't a pretty place, but it suits me, see? You reckon you're gonna ketch me gittin' aht of it jest on accahnt o' them' — he pointed at the sky, glanced apprehensively at Ruth and took the plunge — 'them *scheissers*? Oho, ketch me!'

'But you're right in the thick of it here,' Ruth said. 'It must be terrible at nights. Do you go to the shelter?'

'Shelter?' Jacob leaned forward and poked a knobbly finger at her. 'At my time o' life? Listen to me, missy. My ol' missus is waitin' for me, I don't know where, but she is, bless 'er little 'eart. I ain't pertikler whether I goes ter-night or ter-morrer night. Bleed'n' bombs! Bleed'n' land-mines! Hah! My bed's a warm ol' bug-'ole, I can tell yer. It's better'n sittin' in some ol' shelter wiv a draught up yer ear-'ole.' He indicated the stirrup pump. 'An' I'll tell yer what else. Many a night I don't git ter bed at all. Busy man, I am, when they start droppin' them there fire-bombs. Fire-bombs! Caw, some bloody fire-bombs! I could piddle on 'em!'

Ruth and Mark, who had both been brought up in the genteel tradition and who had not yet dared any frankness of speech in each other's company, both felt stiff and embarrassed.

'The bleeders broke my winder.' Jacob spoke as if the deed had been done by a band of small boys. 'Bloody bomb comes dahn. Bang!' He leaped mimetically into the air, with outflung arms. 'Bits o' glass all over the place. Blew me up in the air it did. I come dahn' — he beamed at Ruth — 'right on my arse.'

Mark looked at Ruth in apology and found that she was on the verge of smiling. He, too, dared a tentative smile. They were still watching each other when the old man spoke again. 'Hah! I done it right in my poor ol' trousis. Like a little babe!'

They both gave way to shouts of laughter and, still looking at each other, continued to laugh happily, feeling that the old man's words had broken down one more barrier of restraint between them.

''Ere?' Jacob grinned at them innocently. 'What's up? 'Ave I said some'ink funny? 'Ere, come 'ere.' His little eyes gleamed with eagerness as he beckoned them close and asked hoarsely, ''Ere, tell the ol' codger. You two walkin' out steady?'

'Well?' Mark looked hesitantly at Ruth. 'We're friends, you know.'

'Friends?' the old man wheezed, peering at them in wonderment. 'Wossat mean, I'd like ter know? Friends? Ever 'ear a nice young feller talk the like of you before? What I arst was, *are* you goin' *steady*? Understand the King's bleed'n' English, don't yer?'

Mark did not know how to answer. He had been asking himself the same question for days. Ruth sat watching him, and he could not guess what she wanted him to say.

It was she who spoke. 'Yes, we are.' She averted her head, blushing, as Mark looked at her in happy surprise.

6

Mark hired a car for the trip to Torquay. They left London on Thursday morning, pursued by sleet and a cold wind. Mellow sunshine welcomed them as they drove down through Devon. They arrived at Torquay just as dusk was creeping in from the sea.

Jenny's house was on the outskirts of the town, hidden in its own grounds behind high walls. It was one of those architecturally inexplicable relics of the middle nineteenth century in which Britain is so rich. It sprouted glass conservatories in unaccountable places; it had a tower that could only have been an afterthought; the deep porch was laid with a hideous mosaic. Yet it gave a comfortable and inviting impression.

A maid admitted them and Jenny came into the hall to greet them. She startled Ruth by kissing her, and, after squeezing Mark's arms and shoulders as if he were an animal up for sale, told him that he was looking well. She displayed herself to him, holding her hands out from her sides and looking over her shoulder. 'What do you think of me?' she demanded. 'Have I changed?'

She glittered with an artificial youth that destroyed its own illusion. The enamelled smoothness of her skin was too tight to be natural. The firmness of her bosom beneath the expensive dress proclaimed itself a lie. Her fair hair gleamed as unconvincingly as rolled gold. Mark remembered his mother, grey and sagging, trudging down the stairs in an apron of sackcloth to scrub the doorstep.

Her voice hardened when he did not respond with the expected compliment. 'I'll show you to your rooms. I expect you'll want to freshen up.'

She was waiting for them in the hall when they came down, and she said, 'Come inside. Aubrey's here, and some company. There's time for a drink before dinner.'

They followed her into a large room, which, with its high ceiling supported by narrow pillars rising against the walls, its French windows at the rear, its old, comfortable-looking furniture upholstered in a silver-grey that matched the thick carpet, bore witness to another taste than Jenny's.

'Well, well, well. Blow me down and call me Cocky!' Aubrey met them boisterously. At nineteen he was tall and, in a florid way, handsome, with waved, glossy hair, a ruddy complexion, and a black suit with wide lapels and thin white stripes that showed off his broad shoulders and gigolo's hips. Ruth commented later that he had the repellent good looks of an Irish tenor. 'If it isn't the old sunbeam-chaser in person! How ya doing, big boy? Still saving our skins in your Spitfire?'

'Hurricane. How are you keeping' — Mark put as much irony into his last word as he could — 'farmer?'

Aubrey looked down at his white, well-kept hands and showed his teeth in a grin that could have been used in a dentifrice advertisement. 'Herh! Herh!' He jolted Mark in the ribs with his fist. 'You slay me, big boy. You slay me!' He took Mark by the arm. 'Meet Wilf and Tony. Friends of the family.' Wilf and Tony were middle-aged Army officers who perched one on each arm of the chair in which Jenny was sitting. Wilf was a piggy little man with a red nose who looked as if he had been designed for the front of a Toby jug. Tony was lank and dyspeptic in appearance, like a tired and irritable schoolmaster. They wore dress uniforms with Sam Browne belts; on their collars were the insignia of one of the supply services.

'How do, ol' man!' It was Wilf who spoke. The words seemed to ooze up from his throat. 'Jolly ol' spot of leave, eh?'

'Yes.' Mark accepted a drink from Aubrey.

'All the luck, you jolly ol' Brylcreem Boys, eh? Best of everything, eh? Lap of luxury, and all that. Not like us. We have to rough it and like it. Eh, Tony, ol' boy?'

Tony was belching very quietly, with his lips tightly compressed, and appeared to be listening intently to himself. 'Eh?' he said guiltily. 'Rough it? Yes! Not half! No leave for us! Too busy! Delivering the goods!'

'Ha!' Aubrey chortled. 'Delivering the goods! You're selling tea!'

'Mmmm?' Mark was mystified.

Aubrey punched him in the ribs again. 'Wait till the penny drops, big boy! "You're selling tea!" The ol' rhyming slang — "You're telling me!" See?'

Aubrey's speech seemed to consist entirely of phrases fished up from a mental rag-bag. The two sexes were known to him as 'Geezers' and 'Dames'. Geezers were addressed in three degrees of familiarity; inferiors were called 'George,' equals 'Moosh' and intimates 'Tosh.' Similarly, the terms 'Baby,' 'Sister,' and 'Honey' expressed three degrees of relationship, remote, friendly and intimate, towards Dames. At moments of extreme enthusiasm, the title of 'Kiddo' might be bestowed on either sex. His most ecstatic expression of admiration was 'Sockaroo!' He would draw attention to himself with 'Get a load o' this,' emphasise an argument with 'Believe you me,' or 'You ain't heard nothin' yet,' and finally underline it with the exclamation, 'I got a million of 'em!' To sit down was to park one's carcase. To close the door was to put the wood in the hole. Milk was 'cow-juice', Egypt was 'Egg-wiped', and money was 'the ol' mazuma'. After each demonstration of this besotted Basic English he beamed as if he had proved himself to be a witty and original conversationalist.

'Wilf, boy,' Aubrey said, 'I got another dozen cases o' the ol' fire-water. Want a couple for the Mess? Okeydoke! Same price as the last lot. How's about some petrol for yours truly? One good turn, you know!'

Wilf looked uncomfortably at Mark. 'Got to be going,' he muttered, 'eh, Tony? Queer ol' cove, the Colonel. Raves if you're late for dinner.'

Aubrey reassured him. ''At's all right. Mark's a regular guy. Eh, Mark?'

'Oh!' said Wilf, still dubious. 'Come down to the Lodge to-night. Make it eleven o'clock. You can fill up your tanks and put the rest in the back in four-gallon cans.'

'Herh! Herh!' Aubrey gloated. 'But definitely! One for the road?' He poured more drinks.

From the depths of her armchair, Jenny extended her blood-red fingernails as if expecting them to be kissed. 'Tomorrow evening, Tony dear?' she cooed. Mark saw the muscles of Ruth's neck quiver; he looked hastily down into his whisky to avoid the bright points of light in her eyes, and suppressed the little thrust of laughter in his own throat.

When the two officers had left, with Aubrey at their heels to show them out, she sat up and spoke to Mark. 'He's a wonderful boy, my Aubrey.' It was the old Jin speaking again, her voice hard and coarse. 'Brains! I never meant him to take that farm seriously, but he put a good man in and we're making a fortune out of it. Aubrey knows where to get a good price for the stuff. And the things he's got a finger in! Dances, he organises. He made fifty-eight pounds out of a dance last Saturday. Packed to the doors with soldiers, it was. And boxing matches. And I don't know what else. Born a business-man, that boy, I always said. And popular! You ought to see' — she sounded more like an old bawd than a mother — 'how the girls go for him!'

Throughout dinner Jenny, who had apparently mastered the art of eating industriously and talking incessantly at the same time, entertained her guests with tales of Aubrey's business genius, of Moss's progress — he lived in London and came down to Torquay at weekends — and of her own social successes. Mark and Ruth concentrated on their food, exchanging an occasional hunted glance and from time to time murmuring in an embarrassed pretence of admiration. Mark wondered how Jenny had ever been able to terrorise him. She was still trying to exercise her charm on him, talking at him, casting knowing glances at him and nudging him slyly with her elbow; but he found her antics repugnant and only faintly funny. It was unappetising to face her enamelled middle age over food.

After coffee, Mark explained his business. 'It's Mother. She's looking very ill. She's practically running your shop for you, and all on her own. I wondered if Aubrey couldn't come up for a month and take over, and she could come down here for a rest with Dad.'

'Why didn't you ask Moss about it?'

'I did. He said the shop was your affair.'

Aubrey intervened. 'I'd like to, Markie, but it can't be did.' He went on to explain how busy he was, how impossible it would be for him to spend a month in London. Despite his stock phrases, he was fluent, aggressive and confident. He put point after point with sickening persuasiveness. Mark could not argue. Aubrey had the debased genius of the brilliant salesman, the ability to hypnotise. Even when he said, 'Have another cup of coffee,' it was sales talk, irresistible. 'Tell you what,' Jenny put down her cigarette. 'I'll put someone else in for a month. Cost me a lot, it will. It's no joke hiring labour these days. And they'll probably swindle me blind. Still, got to stand by your own family. You tell your Mum and Dad they can come down, and welcome.'

'They could stay at the farmhouse,' said Aubrey. 'We entertain a lot here. They wouldn't like it. Plenty to do at the farmhouse. Your Mum could make herself useful if she wanted to.'

'I'm sending her up a chicken,' said Jenny. 'I sent Mill one last week, and a five-pound note along with it. I don't forget the family, I don't.'

At ten o'clock Mark and Ruth declared themselves to be tired after their long journey and escaped to bed. Jenny accompanied them to the door of the dining-room. She took Mark's arm and said, archly, in his ear, 'Never seen you in such a hurry to get to bed before. I wonder why.' At the foot of the stairs, she said, 'Well, I won't come up. You know your rooms. On the same landing — handy, eh?' She stressed this remark with at significant movement of the eyebrows. 'No sleep-walking, mind!'

Mark followed Ruth up the stairs. He had not realised until today how much he had matured since he had joined the Air Force. Once he had been frightened of Jenny, for she had known how to play on his instability and lack of assurance. Now, a man who had hunted among the clouds, he had returned to find that she made no more impression on him than a scarecrow.

Heartened by this, he was able to look on Ruth for the first time with a feeling of mastery. Now, easy in mind, he said good night to her on the landing, kissed her softly on the mouth and watched from his bedroom door until she was in her room.

He was eager for the morning, when he would escape from this house into the keen autumn air and be alone with Ruth. He felt sure enough of himself now to speak his heart to her. He fell asleep before the taste of her kiss had gone from his mouth.

They had a late breakfast next morning, made their excuses to Jenny and drove away. They stopped on the sea front and got out of the car. Ruth slipped her arm through Mark's. 'It's early yet. We don't need to start back for a couple of hours. Let's walk for a while and make the most of the sunshine.'

'Good idea. I could do with a little fresh air.'

She laughed. 'I wanted to say that, but I didn't think I ought. I was ever so glad to get away.'

They walked for a while in silence, their shoulders touching. It was a warm, easy silence, a silence that spoke, for each was thinking of the other, and each felt able to divine the other's thoughts. How different it had been, Mark, remembered, with Paula. With her he had been terrified of silence; he had talked desperately all the time. The first time she had taken him up to her room, he had stood at the front gate, afraid either to leave her or to follow her into the house, chattering insanely, rummaging in his mind for one pointless topic of conversation after another. He had gone on talking at her back, breathless and terrified, as she led him upstairs; he had not stopped until she sat on her divan, took his two hands in hers and said, 'Well, darling?'

The memory, with Ruth's warmth against his side, was an unpleasant one. But it could not disrupt the communion that had miraculously come into being between Ruth and himself. They lolled for an hour in a park, in two deck-chairs side by side, and as they threw twigs and pebbles at each other's feet they felt that this too was a kind of speech between them, more binding than words. They gossiped, talked of things that did not matter; and every chance remark had to them its own overtones, conveying something vastly different from the empty words.

They had tea, and walked back to the car, drunkenly, bumping into each other and giggling secretly.

On the way back to London, driving through the dusk with Ruth slumped sleepily against him, Mark asked, 'Like to get married right away?'

She stirred. 'That's a bit sudden.' Her voice was drowsy, without surprise. 'You're sure it didn't just pop out, sort of, in a weak moment?'

He put his left arm round her. 'You're not being sarcastic, by any chance?'

They drove on in silence. 'Do *you* want to think it over?' Mark asked.

'Of course not, silly.' She giggled. 'Here; that reminds me. I had a postcard from my friend Dolly — Dolly French, she works with me. I've told you about her — she's just got married. I didn't like to show you it before. It was a bit naughty, and anyway, you might have thought I was hinting.' She produced a coloured postcard from her handbag, and Mark peered at it in the dim light. The picture was of a young man in slippers and pyjamas opening his street door to find a mass of milk bottles, loaves and newspapers arrayed on the doorstep. He was saying something over his shoulder to a woman, and the caption read, '*The Bridegroom* "Darling, what day was it we went to bed?"' Ruth said, between giggles, 'That's nothing. You just read what Dolly's written on the other side.' On the back of the card Mark read, 'You should have seen *our* doorstep!' There followed several exclamation marks and then, 'Oh, Ruth, pet, hurry up and get married. It's wonderful! Loveliest love, Doll.' Ruth sniggered, 'Isn't she terrible? She's just like that! She's nice, though.'

Mark laughed. 'Well, you might have answered me properly.'

'Well, you might have asked properly.'

Mark drew into the roadside and stopped the car.

'Go on,' Ruth said brightly. 'Don't be shy! There's only me, and I won't laugh at you.'

'Shut up, you little beast,' said Mark. 'Will you marry me?'

'Well,' she said, 'you asked for it, darling. Here it comes!' She put her arms about his neck and turned her face up to his.

7

'They said one o'clock, didn't they?' asked Ruth. 'It's ten-past.'

Mark looked up from his Sunday newspaper. He, too, was impatient and a little nervous. Faintly annoyed with himself, and with Ruth for sharing his mood, he answered, 'Between one and half-past, they said. There's plenty of time. Sit down, dear. You'll wear a track in the carpet walking up and down.'

They were expecting Bones and his wife, and Davy, as guests for lunch. The last two days had gone by in a breathless rush. Mark had wanted to apply for a few days' extension to his leave, so that they might marry by special licence.

'Why rush it, darling?' Ruth had replied. 'We can be married on your next leave. That'll give us time to get a few things together, and do it properly.'

Confronted by her innocence, Mark had been unable to confess the reason for his urgency; death was not a subject for conversation between them. In any case, he could apply for a marriage leave as soon as he returned to the squadron; he would not have to wait more than a few weeks.

'I'll come up and see you before then,' Ruth said. 'Every week if you like.'

There had been an interview with Ruth's parents, Mark awkward, they clumsily benevolent; a formal engagement party between the two families at Ruth's house last night, with handshakes, kisses, toasts and telegrams; Mark had telephoned to make sure that Bones and Davy would be coming to London on Sunday, and had arranged this lunch for them, to celebrate the occasion.

Joe appeared in the doorway. He was clad in singlet, trousers and slippers. His face was red with wrath and his hair, greased, brushed and then disarranged, stood up in spikes. 'Where's your mother?' he shouted. 'Call this a shirt?' He held up the crumpled garment.

Clara came out of the kitchen. 'It's not ironed yet,' she said patiently. 'Here's one I've aired for you.'

'Very nice of you,' grumbled Joe. 'What am I supposed to do when I want a clean shirt? Get a warrant from Scotland Yard to search the house? Look up my horoscope? The bedroom is the place for clean shirts, not the kitchen. In the kitchen you cook.'

'Don't talk so much,' said Clara. 'Come in here and open this tin of peaches for me. Then go upstairs and get some clothes on. It's a disgrace, hanging about all the morning and still in that state.'

'Merciful God!' Joe confronted his son with an expression of despair. 'Me, she blames! Open the tin of peaches! Sweep out the front garden! Scrub the stairs! Beat the carpet! Clean the silver! Perhaps I should go to the top of the street and play the bugle when I see the visitors?' He went into the kitchen.

They heard the familiar rumble of the coalhole lid, and the sound of footsteps on the front porch. 'Oh, my hair!' Clara gasped. 'My apron!' She began to dart about the room. Joe stampeded past, the shirt streaming behind him, and vanished up the stairs. Ruth was nervously straightening the knives and forks. 'There's nothing to get flustered about,' said Mark, with a touch of peevishness. The bell rang, and he went downstairs.

He opened the street door. Bones was standing in the porch, with a girl who hugged a big bunch of flowers.

'Hallo,' said Mark. He paused. 'Where's Davy?'

'He couldn't come.'

'Oh...' Mark stepped back. 'Come in.'

Bones shepherded the girl into the hall. 'This is Nell,' he said. The girl reached out from beneath her flowers, squeezed Mark's hand warmly, smiled and said, 'Hallo!' She was shorter than Bones, and sturdily built, with a broad, pleasant face and dark hair drawn back from her forehead.

Mark took them upstairs, where his parents were waiting like two children to be presented. There were introductions. Ruth looked expectantly at the big bunch of chrysanthemums in Nell's arms, but Nell gave them to Clara, kissed her cheek, and said, 'I hope you like the colours. I love the bronze ones,' before she turned to embrace and congratulate Ruth. Bones produced a spray of gardenias, held his cap to his breast, presented the flowers to Ruth with great solemnity and kissed her.

'Where's your other friend?' Ruth asked.

Bones frowned and smiled. 'He's terribly sorry. He was kept back.'

'Oh, I'm so disappointed,' Ruth said. 'It doesn't seem complete without the three of you. What about some drinks?'

Joe came forward, very stiff and solemn, with the tray. 'Mrs. Gascoyne?' he said primly, 'What would you prefer?'

'Sherry, please. Do call me Nell.' To Clara, who was standing with her hands clasped in front of her and a frozen smile on her face, she said, 'I've just realised that those are artificial flowers on the table. Aren't they lovely? They're nicer than my chrysanths. Where d'you get them?'

Clara blushed with pleasure. 'They're only paper. They sell them in the market? I could get you some.'

'Oh, please!'

There was a lull in the talk, and they all found themselves becalmed for a moment in a self-conscious silence.

Bones said, 'Well, we look as if we're all posing for a photograph!' Everybody laughed. Ruth said, 'Let's sit down,' and the formal group broke up in a clamour of movement and conversation. Joe rushed about refilling glasses, his diffidence broken down by the combined glow of alcohol and good humour inside him. Clara went into the kitchen, Nell followed her, asking, 'Can I help?' Clara was at ease now, happy and animated. 'No, dear. I can manage. You go back and keep an eye on those men.'

Clara served the soup. Nell uttered cries of delight and asked, 'How do you season it?' Clara sat down beside her, explaining volubly. Bones was listening to Joe, professing a breathless interest in the craft of tailoring. Mark and Ruth exchanged brief, satisfied smiles. The meal progressed; everybody was in high spirits, cheered by the warmth and the red glow of the gas fire, the taste and the steam and the smell of good food, the talk and the laughter and the drinks which Joe urged on them. Clara hovered about them, keeping their plates heaped and beaming over them as if they were all her children. Joe became more and more boisterous. 'Go on, boy,' he shouted at Bones, thumping him on the shoulder; 'take your jacket off. Don't be shy!'

Mark said to Nell, 'Every time you call your husband Kit, I look round to see who you mean. I'm not used to it.'

'Bones?' Nell said. 'I must say you found him a jolly appropriate nickname!'

Clara was indignant. 'Oh, no! You shouldn't call him that, Mark! It's not nice! And it's not true — he's not bony at all!'

'Oh, yes he is!' retorted Nell. 'He's all sharp corners and knobbly bits!'

'As a matter of fact,' Bones intervened gravely, 'my nickname isn't derived from my striking appearance. I got it at a squadron concert. I blacked my face and sang, *Waiting For the Robert E. Lee.*'

'Sing us it now,' said Nell.

Bones spread his hands, rolled his eyes, and began to bellow, 'Watch them shuffle along...'

'That's enough,' Nell said. 'It'll be kindest to forget the whole thing.'

Bones said, 'I'll eat another portion of that apple tart if it kills me.' He turned to Clara. 'I couldn't think of a more glorious death.'

Nell puffed her cheeks out and put her fork down. 'Not me! Or I'll bust! I shall have to bring Kit here more often. You'd fatten him up in no time.'

Clara was radiant. 'Oh, I know how to look after them. I've brought two of them up!' She stood up. 'Leave a little room for my cake, though. Cut it, Joe. I'll get some clean plates.'

From the kitchen she called, 'Mark dear, come and take these plates. I'm watching the coffee.'

Mark joined her in the kitchen. She gave him the plates, and whispered, 'They're lovely people, your two friends, aren't they?' She frowned and added, 'Not like the other one.'

'What do you mean?'

'Couldn't come!' she said fiercely. 'I can imagine!'

'Mother!' Mark's protest was cut short as she pushed him back into the dining-room.

They sat in armchairs round the fire, busy with coffee and cake, the women still talkative, Joe and Bones sleepy, Mark concealing beneath an air of thoughtfulness his annoyance at his mother's words.

'Mark!' There was a pressure of hands on his shoulders. He blinked, and stirred himself. He was drowsy with repletion and the fireside heat. 'Mark! I asked you a question!' Ruth was standing behind him, shaking him playfully.

'Sorry, darling. I was thinking.'

'Daydreaming, you mean. You should have seen the frown on your face. Where did you put my handbag — in your bedroom or your mother's? I want my other hankie.'

'In mine. I'll get it.'

'No; you sit still, silly, and carry on dreaming. I'll get it.'

'No.' He got up from his chair and went to the door. 'I'll be back in a moment.'

Ruth followed him out on to the landing, and slipped her arm through his. 'You can hardly keep your eyes open, poor old thing. It was cruel to wake you up. What were you thinking of?'

'Oh, nothing much.' They went up the stairs, leaning on each other.

In his bedroom, she took the handkerchief from her bag, and sat down in front of the mirror to tidy her hair. Mark sprawled on the bed.

'Like 'em?' he asked.

'Mmmm.' She brushed industriously. 'Not stuck up, are they?'

'Why should they be?'

'Well, I mean that kind of people. Well-to-do, I bet.' She turned in her chair, and said accusingly, 'Your other friend didn't come.'

Mark yawned, and stretched his arms. 'I can't help it, can I?'

'No. I wonder if *he* could, though?'

Mark sat up. 'You too! For Heaven's sake, Ruth, it's just too stupid to talk about. He was kept back. After all, there is a war on.'

She shrugged her shoulders and looked away. 'Sorry.'

Mark put his arm round her shoulder as they went downstairs, but he was disturbed and resentful. His mother was clearing the dinner table as they entered the dining-room. Ruth joined her, and Nell insisted on helping. Mark sat down and offered cigars to his father and Bones. The three men smoked, enveloping themselves in blue clouds and a satisfied silence which the clatter of crockery and the women's chatter could not penetrate.

'What time shall we start back to-night?' Bones asked. 'We'll make good time in the car, but I don't want to leave it too late.'

Mark, preoccupied, continued to stare into the fire for a few moments. 'Oh, after supper. Nine o'clock O.K.? Had any excitement while I was away?' It was the first time he had asked about the squadron since Bones had arrived.

'One or two flaps. Not much. I've been breaking the new boys in.'

Mark gave Bones an uneasy look, was about to speak, fell silent, and spoke at last. 'What kept Davy? I should have thought they'd leave him alone if he was down for a pass.'

'Oh, you know how it is. Things come up.' Bones puffed busily. 'Wizard cigar, this.'

'Pre-war,' Mark said. He was puzzled; Bones had made no attempt to explain what duties had kept Davy — the first thing Mark would have expected him to do; a seed of doubt was growing fast in Mark's mind. 'When did he know?'

'Who? Davy?' Nell had come into the room to collect some more plates, and Mark fancied that he saw a warning look pass between Bones and her. 'I don't know,' Bones said. 'Some time Friday, I suppose.'

'I 'phoned you Friday midday.'

Bones stirred uncomfortably in his chair, and pulled a cushion up behind him. 'Well, it must have been after that, then.'

Mark leaned back, closed his eyes and inhaled cigar smoke with a long, quivering breath.

Joe got up and walked heavily to the door. 'Excuse me,' he said. 'You know where I'm going.'

The door closed behind him. Mark sprawled in his chair, looking at the ceiling through the smoke haze. 'Bones' — he sat up suddenly and leaned towards his friend in a strange attitude of agonised resolution— 'I...'

'Listen,' Bones said, 'before your father comes back. Davy's in hospital.' Mark rose to his feet. 'What? Why didn't you... ?'

'He's pretty badly hurt. I didn't want to upset your people. I meant to tell you when we were going back tonight. It's not exactly the kind of news to bring to an engagement party, is it?'

'Does Nell know?'

'Yes.'

'What happened?'

Bones explained. He, Davy and another pilot had gone up to intercept a German bomber that was prowling over the Humber. The bomber — perhaps it was a decoy — was escorted by a squadron of Messerschmitts, but the three Hurricanes had attacked. Bones had tried to keep an eye on Davy's tail, as was his custom, but had found himself with his hands full. They had destroyed the bomber and scattered the fighters, and a few moments after they engaged the sky was clear. Bones was circling to find the other two Hurricanes when he saw Davy's machine heeling across the sky with a long track of smoke unrolling behind it and a little glow of red beneath the engine. Bones had dived after him, calling on the radio telephone, but receiving no reply. From fifty yards away he had seen Davy, alive, hauling back the cockpit cover and pulling himself up before rolling the machine over and dropping out with his parachute. Bones had watched in anguish as the tongue of flame flickered along the cowling, fearing that at any moment the other machine might explode into a white ball of incandescence as the fire reached the petrol tanks. Then he had seen Davy waving to him, pointing earthwards. Looking down, he had seen what Davy was indicating-the ground beneath covered for miles with a black rash of houses. Davy had settled back into his cockpit, reached for the controls and, the machine still responding, had brought his Hurricane round in a steep turn and put her down in a long dive towards open country. Bones, following, had seen the flames and smoke obscure the cockpit of the other machine; then, terrifying seconds later, Davy's Hurricane rolled over and a little black bundle dropped away from it. The parachute opened, bearing Davy gently to earth. A moment later, the Hurricane exploded and dropped like a fireball. Davy had been picked up by Home Guards and rushed to hospital, terribly burned.

'Have you been to see him yet?'

'No. They wouldn't let me. Otherwise I wouldn't have come down here. I've 'phoned several times. They think he'll pull through, but he's having a bad time.'

'Can't we ring up now and find how he's going?'

'I've promised them not to 'phone again till this evening.'

Mark wandered aimlessly round the table, fingering the edge of the tablecloth. He uttered a long sigh, and said, explosively, 'Bastard, bleeding, bloody luck!' His grief, which it was impermissible to acknowledge even inwardly, the vague feeling of guilt at having been absent and happy when the disaster occurred, the more remote echoes of fear that the news had awakened, all combined to deepen the shame with which he remembered his suspicions of a few moments before; suspicions which he loathed all the more because they were bred in a part of him which he had hoped was dead. He looked beseechingly at Bones, and began, 'Do you know what I —' But it was impossible to confess. He sat down and said, 'I'll tell Ruth. Not my parents.' He sat wretchedly with his hands clasped between his knees.

Nell came wobbling into the room in a pair of Ruth's high-heeled shoes. She asked Bones, 'How d'you like 'em, darling?'

130

'Horrible.'

She waved her arms wildly, overbalanced, flung her arms about her husband's shoulders and said, 'Then you can buy me a pair next time you come on leave.'

The rest of the day passed without further mention of Davy, and late that night Mark and Bones went back to the squadron together.

1944

1944

1

There are times in war when a great peace descends on the battlefield. The fury of an hour ago becomes remote; tomorrow's ordeal is not to be thought of. All is quiet, and the soldiers sprawl contentedly with their mess-tins and their cigarettes, listening to the song of the birds.

It was on such an evening in August, 1944, that a platoon of British infantry were squatting at a roadside in Normandy, their rifles and equipment lying by them on the grass. From the south, towards Falaise, came the rumble of an unending carnage. A surrounded German army was being annihilated. It was only a few miles away, but the noise seemed unbelievably distant. The sun was setting behind the woods, outlining the dark splendour of the tree-tops with a fiery border. From the pale evening sky there came, without cease, the noise of aircraft, now muttering faintly, now rumbling powerfully overhead, as the British Typhoons flew unchallenged to and fro between their airfields and the targets on which, with a murderous monotony, they discharged their rocket missiles.

A few of the men looked up idly as a flight of four Typhoons came unhurriedly towards them, returning from Falaise. The aircraft were still over the enemy positions, flying in line astern, travelling at an altitude of only a couple of hundred feet.

More of the men looked up as a succession of hollow popping noises came to their ears, too dully to disturb the peace of the evening. Thin, rapidly-dispersing smoke puffs leaped into the sky around the British fighters. The Typhoons flew serenely on, ignoring the anti-aircraft fire; until one smudge of smoke spread just below the leading machine, and the Typhoon dipped, sideslipped towards the ground and levelled out again.

'They've got him!' said one of the men, pausing in the act of licking a cigarette paper.

The Typhoon glided towards them. They watched anxiously until it had passed, whining shrilly, almost over their heads, its engine silent, its propeller idling. The machine was flying a straight course; it seemed to be under control.

The soldier spoke again. 'He's all right.' He went on making his cigarette.

The Typhoon disappeared beyond the tree-tops.

The job was done. Their rockets had gone rushing down on to the white ribbon of road, exploding into the jammed, crawling column of vehicles. They had left behind them wreckage and confusion, fire and a spreading pall of black smoke. Now there was only the uneventful flight back to the airstrip. Mark looked in his mirror and saw his flight following in meek procession.

To his right he could see nothing in the sun's glare. He looked to the left and saw a wisp of smoke staining the pale blue of the sky. The wisp became elongated, streamed past. There was a fragment of time in which his lazy brain struggled to absorb what his eyes had seen. The moment of reaction came too late.

He felt a stunning blow at the back of his head and fiery needles driven into his back. The daylight turned blood red. For a couple of seconds he lost consciousness; then he saw the earth tilting up in front of the sheen of the propeller arc. His brain was numbed, but his pilot's hands fought with the control column and brought the Typhoon's nose up, pointing to the skyline.

Beneath the red haze the ground rushed past; fields, woods, tiny, shattered cottages, roads and racing puffs of shell smoke.

His clothes were becoming warmly soggy in several places. The strength was draining from him. His limbs were becoming leaden and his will was deserting him. He switched off the engine and lowered the flaps, fighting to reduce flying speed.

There was a wood ahead, then a meadow, and beyond it a cornfield. A last whisper of instinct told him that he must not overshoot the meadow, that he must set the machine down before he reached its further boundary. He fish-tailed wildly on over the trees. The bottom seemed suddenly to drop out of the cockpit. A great wave of sickness, and the red haze thickened into darkness. He had already fainted when the Typhoon crashed into the corn.

2

He was buried. He was imprisoned in the darkness of the coffin. His body could not move; somehow he was aware of the tons of damp earth pressing on the coffin lid.

He heard voices. They were far away. They came to him only as a gabble. His consciousness excluded them and sought peace. Then thought began. Voices? What voices? He listened. He heard them gabbling again, quacking, high-pitched, unintelligible, ridiculous, like scrambled speech on the radio. From the noise, through the thick darkness, words filtered. 'Needle... tea... tell him... hot...' A voice came to him, sharp and angry: 'Who told you to?' Two other voices, immediately above him. 'Look, do you want your sweet rations, or don't you?' And, as he tried to understand, the reply came. 'I told you. You can have it for five fags a day.'

He was afraid to open his eyes, to see the darkness. He commanded himself: open your eyes. His eyes remained closed. Red spots were pricking the darkness under the lids. Open your eyes. Fear spread through him like a sickness and he knew at last that he was alive. He opened his eyes.

The daylight hurt: a curtain of coloured spots swirled in front of him; beyond it was a smooth brown expanse intersected by ragged seams. It was hard work trying to think. His brain was as stubborn as a cold engine. He heard scuffling footsteps, creaking, the clink of a spoon in a cup and the sound of someone drinking. The conversation close by was still going on. Beyond it the angry voice was still droning. 'What about today's admissions? How many of them have you recorded? None, I suppose.'

He tried to put the impressions together like the pieces of a jigsaw puzzle. 'This way, corporal. Put him down gently. I'll get Number Three bed ready.' There was more movement, and a gentle moaning. The pieces of the puzzle came together. He was looking up at the sagging brown ceiling of a marquee. He was in a bed. Somebody else was being put in another bed. The two men close by were orderlies. The voice from the entrance of the marquee was that of an officer. He sighed. He noticed that breathing was a labour.

Why could he not move? He fought to move his arms, his legs, his body. They were imprisoned. He wriggled his toes gratefully. He could do the same with the fingers of his left hand. Those of his right hand were immovable.

There was a pressure on them, soft until he struggled against it, then pitilessly firm. He conducted a little debate with himself before he dared to move his head. He tried, and found that he could do so. He felt the friction of bandages against the pillow-slip as he turned his head, very slowly and carefully, to the right. He pulled a face. There were no bandages on his face. A black burden of fear lifted from him; he was flooded with joy at this one discovery. He grimaced madly, revelling in the obedience of his muscles to his will.

He could see the bed on his right, and the bulk of other beds beyond it; the man in the bed, covered to his chin with blankets, his face white and waxen, his eyes closed; the brown patch of withered grass between the beds; a faded red tent-pole; the patch of daylight in the doorway, dazzling and painful; and the outline of a man stooping in the doorway.

He shut his eyes and rested for a few seconds. Speech was the next step. He swallowed. 'Hey, sonnie.' For those two words he had marshalled lungs, mind and muscles as carefully as if he were trying to shout an order across a parade-ground; yet there was only a whisper. Terror returned. He croaked. 'Orderly! Orderly!'

The orderly came and stooped over him. The boy's smile gave him a second's flash of happiness; in it there was pleasure and welcome, as if to a visitor long awaited. 'Ah,' said the boy, 'we've been waiting for you to come round.' He turned, and called to the man in the doorway. 'He's O.K., sir. Want to see him?' To Mark he said, 'Try not to fidget, sir. And don't talk. You'll be all right.'

The doctor came. 'The devil! You've taken your time. Feeling all right?'

Mark nodded. 'A bit dopey,' he whispered. 'How bad is it?'

'You kept us busy for a while. Some shell splinters; and you got knocked about in the crash. You're very weak. We shall have to be careful with you, and you'll have to help us. But you're all in one piece. That's what you wanted to know, wasn't it?' He gave some instructions to the orderly in a low voice. He spoke to Mark again. 'We've got you pretty well patched up for the moment. As soon as we can, we'll have you flown to Blighty, and then they'll really start work on you.'

A little while later they gave him a drink that looked like milk and tasted like chalk, and he fell asleep.

There followed a period in which he lost track of time. In the alternation of sleeping, waking and wallowing in the half-world between, it was impossible to retain a sense of the proportion between seconds, minutes and hours, or to distinguish clearly the sequence between day and night. Sometimes he would know that it was day when the breeze stirred the tent-flaps and the sunshine lit up a patch of worn grass; or he would awaken to full consciousness to find himself alone, everyone else asleep, a patient whining quietly in another bed, the orderly slumped in his chair with a forgotten book and a flickering hurricane lamp on the table next to him; and the night would seem interminable and full of torment.

His body was braced and bandaged so that he could not move at all. It became a prison, in which his *self* struggled vainly for movement and release. Nothing in his life had ever been as agonising as this lying motionless in an overheated cocoon of bandages and blankets. He had time to think, to fear, to imagine, to give way to the torture of boredom. Alone with his body, he discovered sickness and pain.

He was being taken from one place to another. He looked forward to these moves, though his mind was not clear enough to make sense of them. They were blessed breaks in the timeless monotony. He liked the swaying, dreamy sensation of being carried on a stretcher, and longed for the occasional glimpse which he had at these times of the sun and the blue sky. Sometimes, however, the sunshine was more than he could bear and made him sick.

He became a connoisseur of pain. There was not a corner of his body which it did not visit. He knew the throbbing, spreading pain, the dull, persistent pain, the stabbing, boring pain, the pain that was like a fire within him or a pair of hands wrenching at his entrails. He would fight the pain, breathing hard or grunting to give himself relief; then he would surrender to it and moan, like a child. He found that to cry out brought ease, and he lost his shame at giving way. He would even, like a child, moan to advertise his loneliness, to appeal for consolation or — if no one else was present — to console himself and give himself the illusion of companionship.

The orderly would come, at such times, with the needle and Mark would drift away from his body into a drugged half-sleep. He never lost consciousness completely; he would find himself withdrawn from the world, unable to intervene, yet observing it, with his senses, through curtains of red and black. It was in this state that he travelled from stage to stage of his journey home, aware only as in a nightmare of the roar of engines as he lay in the aeroplane on his way to England.

He had lucid periods in which he would take a childish pleasure in being helpless, coddled, the object of other people's attention; or in which, thinking outside himself for the first time, he would worry at the effect on his mother of the news (which must have reached her by now) that he had been wounded. There was a little cinema in his mind in which he saw the scene in his home when his parents received the news. He ran the film over and over again. At other times he began to compose the first letters that he would write to his wife and parents when he was settled in the English hospital, or the first remarks that he would make when they came to see him; and here his vanity took command, and he decided on the precise pose of patient suffering that he would adopt.

He had no idea how long he had been travelling when he heard women's voices, saw within his limited field of vision stone steps, women's skirts, felt himself being put to bed by cool, capable women's hands. He gave himself up to the cool ease of the sheets and told himself, 'I am in England.' This should have meant something to him. He repeated, 'I am in England.' There was no response. He was tired. He fell away once more into the dark stupor.

3

Now his ordeal began.

All he wanted was to be left in peace, to be kept in the drowsy borderlands from which pain and the greater agony of thought were banished. But they stripped the bandages from him, probed wounds, tapped broken bones and broke them again. They took him out of bed and wheeled him about on trolleys. They examined him, X-rayed him. There was operation after operation. There was no peace. He lay in his bandages, at bay. Doctors stood over him, talking impersonally across his body, handing to each other reports and photographs, making mysterious references to his condition which gave him fresh cause for terrified speculation when he was alone again.

When sleep came they drove it away. When he had talked himself into a brief equilibrium of mind, they upset him. When the pain faded they brought it back; until he wanted to cry, 'Leave me in peace! Let me die and be done with it!'

But — his mind seized on a new subject for debate — did he want to die? His brain said one thing, his outraged body said another; and behind the eloquent pain there crowded a host of past experiences, all the things that had awakened in him the fear of life and the despair of ever attaining his full human stature; all pleading on the side of death.

The debate raged inside him. The nurses and doctors knew nothing of it except that his temperature rose dangerously from time to time. If they had known it, the chart at the foot of his bed was the record of a battle's progress. One day, at a moment when Mark was fully conscious and lay looking up at the doctor with eyes that were clear and comprehending but uninterested, the doctor said, 'You know, old man, it's entirely up to you whether you pull through. I'll be quite frank, since you're a soldier. We can do the right kind of job on your body. You're the one who has to find the resistance to stay alive.' Mark smiled faintly at this reminder of the urgency of the debate within him. He closed his eyes so that he might listen uninterrupted to the voices inside his head. For the first time he became aware how many of his comrades had been killed. For four years — in his first squadron in 1940, flying sorties across the Channel, instructing at a school, back on active service as a Typhoon fight-commander — he had possessed the soldier's gift of ignoring the dead. He had been able to drive his feelings down beneath the threshold of consciousness. Now that he was no longer kept intact by the tension of battle, the dead of four years crowded back to haunt him.

Ruth and his parents came often to see him. Each of them in turn would sit for ten minutes by his bed. But they could not reach him. They knew it as well as he. They sat shyly by him, smiling primly, chattering with an unconvincing brightness, trying to pretend they did not notice the bandages, the splints, the pulleys, and above all his distant eyes. He felt pity for them, and embarrassment when they were with him, but he was secretly relieved when they went.

Ripples of pain spread outward from a point in his head. They followed one another with a pendulum regularity, each wave bringing a separate, stunning shock. He had the normal instinct for life, but the pain, the constant pain, reinforced his fears and made him weary of continuing the struggle. In the air, he realised, as he thought of his dead friends, he had risen above his problems, but now he had fallen back into their midst, and he might never be able to escape them again. How to solve them? He still did not know. The dead: it was always the dead he turned to. He felt a closer identity with them than with the living. They knew him; they would not betray him. But they were gone. He could not look for their comradeship when he returned to the world. The millions of people who were left, out there in the world, what did they know of him? What treatment could he expect at their hands when he went back among them?

It even came to him to envy the dead, for they were at rest, they would be eternally honoured, their problems were solved. He felt guilty at remaining alive, and frightened at the prospect of facing life again. Day after day, the phantoms trooped past, and it was with them that his real converse was held, even while his lips whispered cheerful inanities to his living visitors.

One night he awoke, screaming, 'Mickey! Mickey!' The night nurse came and found him rigid, his eyes dilated, his face covered in sweat. She wiped his face and soothed him, went to consult the sister and came back with a sedative. He resisted sleep, for it seemed shameful at this moment when a year-old grief had suddenly slipped its leash. The sedative was too strong, and he slept.

In the morning, calmed by the night's rest, he was able to think coherently about the incident and to recall Mickey's death a year ago.

He had just returned from a flight over Belgium when the news had come that his brother had been killed in action in Italy. He had been unable to absorb the fact. He had not seen Mickey for a long time; all he could do was to tell himself, without effect, that he would never see him again. Even the sight of his family's sorrow had scarcely stirred him.

Now, however, he could grieve. He lay staring up at the ceiling, remembering their lives together, sentimentalising the bonds between them, flinching as he recalled the contempt he had so often felt for Mickey in boyhood, the coolness he had frequently demonstrated towards him, the snubs he had visited upon him. He could see Mickey's face, with its shining snout, its big, protruding teeth, its happy, silly grin, idealised by memory.

He remembered the first photograph that had been taken of the two of them, himself a fat baby, still swaddled, in a push-chair, Mickey a bewildered-looking little boy in a jersey and comically short trousers standing beside the chair. He had never realised before how his mother must think of the two of them; she could always see her babies in them, beautiful and innocent. For the first time he understood her misery at Mickey's death. He remembered how she had looked, her full cheeks become flaccid, her eyes vacant beneath the ugly, swollen lids, her hair quite grey and straggling in disorder. The anaesthetic of action had worn off. A year had passed and he could feel the pain. But now, as then, tears were denied him.

Another secret visitant was Davy, who still lay in a hospital alive but mummified by fire, a plastic surgeon's patchwork quilt.

The white-clad doctors were gathering again; another operation. He was borne from his bed and placed on the trolley. He heard the squeak of castors as the trolley began to move. He fought down fear and weariness, and smiled at the woman's face that appeared above his for a moment. He watched the white ceiling of the corridor move blankly past. They stopped for a moment at the doors of the operating theatre and he stared in fascination at the light that burned, under thick, frosted glass, above his head.

He was moving again. He heard the doors swing gently into place behind him. People moved about in a purposeful pattern, like a ballet, heedful of each other but not of him. There was the sickening clink of instruments against glass.

The red rubber of the mask was descending on him, blotting out the world from his sight. The smell of the rubber made him sick. He breathed deeply.

4

He had a dream. There had been a succession of fragments of dream disturbing his sleep, each without relation to the others, each vanishing like a bubble in the night. He had awakened, feverish, and closed his eyes again.

Loudspeakers were shouting. The universe was filled with their shouting. He was running across the grass towards his Hurricane. The field extended for miles, and it was covered with men running, with bouncing strides, towards their aircraft; not the dozen pilots of a single squadron, but a horde of men, all the men he had ever seen die, swarming across the grass as far as the eye could see. He was running, running, and the loudspeakers were shouting all the time, but he came no nearer to his machine.

He was flying, climbing. The sun was his target. It came nearer and nearer, until its incandescence filled the sky. He was melting in its heat, and his clothes became a soggy burden. He opened fire at the sun, and it was a bloody face over the white, winged collar of a dress shirt. Its mouth opened, and a shout filled the vast sky. 'You wait and see!'

He was diving. The sky was dark with aircraft burning, crumbling, blowing up all round him. He was diving, diving. He wrenched the control column back towards him, but the machine would not pull out of the dive. He blacked out again and again; each sickening surge of darkness through his body was like another death.

Now he was earthbound, walking along an alley whose pavements sloped to a gutter in the middle. The first-floor windows of the houses lining the alley were open and at them sat women, some sewing, some with their hands in their laps. He was trying to fly, swimming through the air with a kind of breast-stroke. His feet were heavy and he could only rise a few feet from the ground. He swam laboriously, toiling to rise. As he came level with the first-floor windows the women closed the shutters on him. He saw the shutters closing all along the alley. One of the women turned her face towards him, a pale, peaked boy's face. He struck at it, but could not reach it. He trod air frantically and rose until he was level with the rooftops. He saw the blue sky opening above him, and he wanted to soar into the heights. He could not, and swam on. Below was a white, dusty country lane. On the left of the lane was a meadow in which people were crowded at a long table, enjoying a banquet. He was unaware of his identity, but he assumed that it would cause him to be made welcome by these people. They ignored him.

He pushed among them, seizing one by the arm, tapping another on the shoulder. One man turned to look at him, and the man's face was blank and shining like a bald head. He became desperate, full of self-pity. He was hungry, and he fought to reach the table which was piled high with foods which he could not recognise but for which he craved. Mickey was tugging at his arm, trying to hold him back. He flung his brother away and Mickey fell back, bloody and mutilated. He lunged forward to catch him and fell away into a pale vastness of space.

He was alone in a great, echoing château. He was sprawling on a bare, broad landing, firing a rifle between the marble balustrades. Through the big window to his left he could see the other wing of the château from which they were firing at him. He did not know who they were but they were familiar to him. Bullets came towards him, slowly so that he could see them. He kept changing his position to avoid them. They shrieked off the polished walls and scarred the fluted stone pillars that supported the high ceiling. The unseen enemy was closing in on him. He could not see or hear them. He fired his rifle at nothing. They were moving in the other wing. They were coming up the stairs. The courtyard below was full of them. In a moment they would have him.

He threw his rifle over the balustrade and fled, seeking his friend. There was a room with huge, bronze doors. Beautiful women were carved in the bronze; they smiled at him, but the bronze was hard and cold to his touch. He could not open the door. The enemy were coming closer. He could feel their presence on the stairs. He pushed with all his force and the doors swung slowly open. He was holding a knob, and it dragged him into the room, making him aware that the door was opening of its own will.

The friend he sought was not in the room, but Davy was coming to meet him, holding out a withered hand, smiling with his black and shrivelled face. Mark knew that he must not let Davy touch him. He had betrayed Davy. He fled from the room, feeling guilty because he was deserting Davy. Without looking round, he knew that Davy was following him. Now he knew that he had to face his enemies. But he could not find them. He hunted for them in every room of the château. The fear was becoming unbearable; fear of being trapped by them, fear of not finding them. There was no way out of the château.

He awoke, lay exhausted for some minutes until the fear had gone, and decided to die.

Now that the decision was made, he felt tranquil, and rested. He lay and watched the nurses busying themselves about him, troubled only because they were wasting their time. He endured pain, underwent operations, had his dressings changed, in a state of ironic detachment. He was pleased to have a secret; even the mental occupation provided by the necessity to plan his tug-of-war against the doctors was a blessing. He was happy and amused.

He had never before believed in another world, but now he was possessed by the conviction that he was going to enjoy the companionship of all the other dead. Death, to his fancy, had become a pleasant prospect, another kind of life. He willed his own death. He sought to weaken himself by undertaking a host of petty exertions against which the doctors had warned him. He tried to avoid taking nourishment, and gloated like a child at every spoonful of food he was able to waste.

The energy drained from him. A warm drowsiness took its place, in which time and the affairs of men were of no account.

One afternoon, during visiting hours, his uncle Moss walked in.

He wore a brown tweed overcoat with a broad check pattern and a wide-brimmed, American trilby hat. His red, double-chinned face grinned at Mark over the parcels which he clutched with both arms.

Moss stacked the parcels at the bedside, keeping hold of a huge bunch of flowers.

'Oy!' He roared to a nurse who was studying a temperature chart on the other side of the ward. 'Over 'ere, gel!'

Mark smiled. He knew the nurse. She could be professionally cheerful, but more often she displayed an icy aloofness against which the patients' chaff was of no avail. To his surprise, she neither ignored

Moss nor reprimanded him. She came hurrying across the room and, with the slightest hint of bewilderment in her smile, said, 'Hallo!'

Moss gave her the flowers. ''Ere y'are ducks. Present for a pretty girl.'

'Thanks,' she said. 'What's all that?' She pointed at the parcels.

He jerked his thumb at Mark. 'For this geezer. Cigars. Peaches. 'Ot-'ouse grapes. Oranges. Books. Chocolates. All black!' he said proudly.

'Black?' Mark spoke for the first time.

'Black Market. You're gettin' be'ind the times, boy. Two most important words in the English language, them.'

'You'll have to leave them with me,' said the nurse. 'I'm afraid he's not equal to all this lot yet.'

Moss waved a hand airily. 'All right gel. I'd trust them big blue eyes anywhere. 'Ave a dollop yourself. Share it out among the boys. As long as you let this bloke 'ere 'ave a sniff at it. 'Ere,' he said. 'I want your advice. Is this stuff any good for 'im?' He pulled a bottle of brandy from his pocket.

The nurse made a face of mock horror. 'Gracious! You'll kill him with that. As a matter of fact, you shouldn't have brought it into the hospital at all.'

'Well, I know one thing. I ain't taking it away with me. What about you? Don't tell me you don't fancy a nip now and again.'

'I'm afraid I'm not allowed to accept it.'

'Afraid!' Moss snorted. 'Afraid! Go on! Take it! Raffle it! Give it to the poor! Only I ain't takin' it away with me!'

He took the chair that was standing at Mark's bedside, turned it back to front and sat astride it, resting his folded arms on the back of the chair. 'Well,' he said roughly, 'you made a bleedin' mess of yourself, didn't you, boy?'

Mark laughed weakly. He had not laughed since the crash. Moss was the first visitor who had not sat looking at him with dumb pity. 'You're not looking so good yourself.' At first glance he had thought the expression on Moss's face to be one of brutality; then he had discerned the lines of strain.

'Ah,' Moss grunted. 'Lot of worry I get, these days. I got an ulcer.' He went on, not without pride. 'Nerves, it is. All the big business-men got ulcers. My doctor told me.'

'I'm glad to hear you're getting on in the world,' said Mark. 'They're not taxable, are they?'

'What aren't?'

'Ulcers.'

146

Moss uttered the rapid succession of grunts which passed with him for laughter. Mark realised that he was talking coherently for the first time in weeks; for the first time his mind was focused on things outside himself. In the heat of his bed he felt buoyant with pride. Emboldened to the point of insolence, he asked, 'How's business? Still making millions?'

'I should live so long,' said Moss. 'It's all outlay these days.'

'Why? What are you up to?'

'Houses. I started buyin' 'em in the Blitz, when they was goin' dirt cheap. Prices been goin' up again since, but now with these flyin' bombs nobody wants to come back to town, so there's plenty more bargains. It's all outlay, though. And a bloody big gamble, with the bombs.'

'I'm sorry for you,' Mark jeered, and was surprised to hear himself laughing.

When Moss had gone, Mark called for the nurse. It was her turn to be surprised, for he announced that he was famished, and asked for something to eat.

Mark, in truth, had all the stubborn hunger for life in him that any normal man possesses. It is only at the lowest ebb of energy that despair is able to outweigh the will to live. In Mark, the balance had been very fine, and it had only needed the incursion of Moss's rough animal vitality, momentarily startling him back from enervating dream to the living world, to tip the scales.

5

Now that the spark of life waxed brighter, Ruth, helpless before, was able to kindle it further with her visits. She had learned not to sit clasping her hands together uttering strained, silly, cheerful remarks. She talked of all the petty things which at first, for fear of worrying Mark, she had refrained from mentioning to him. Now she saw that his mind was starved of normal activity, that he seized on these things and exercised himself joyously with them.

'I had another row with the landlady about the ceiling,' she would say. After their marriage they had taken over the flat which Mickey and his wife had once occupied, and with it a long-standing dispute about the state of the ceiling.

'The cow,' Mark would rage. 'She wants shooting. Wait till I see her again.' And Ruth would sit back contentedly, laying out as she listened the fresh handkerchiefs and pyjamas she had brought for him.

Mark would say, 'I don't like you staying there on your own with all these flying bombs.' This had become one of his principal anxieties. 'Why don't you stay with your parents?'

Ruth would reply, 'Don't let's go over that again, darling. If I give up the flat now we'll never get another. Besides, you haven't seen my new wallpaper yet.'

He yawned, inattentive but satisfied, as she chattered to him about a film she had seen. With his eyes shut, he could pretend that it was Sunday morning at home. He was in bed. Ruth was sitting at the dressing-table, combing her hair and talking incessantly.

Their married life had been neither a success nor a failure. It had only consisted of a few seven-day leaves, a number of weekends and a lot of correspondence. It was in the air that he had discovered himself; his flying had remained a greater passion in his life than his marriage. With Ruth he had learned, for brief periods, to find new satisfactions in living; he had found tenderness and a new kind of human companionship. But, although he had not consciously realised it, all this had only occupied a corner of him; it had only served to sharpen his confidence and his zest for flying.

Now he looked ahead and saw in married life a completely new territory, unexplored, unconquered. The little that he had known of it made him long for it, but he could not help feeling scared at the new problems, the new dangers that would confront him, and for which he was so little equipped. However, he was impatient for the time when he could make the attempt.

Thus his mind, like an obedient machine switched into reverse, accumulated reasons for living. He went once again through all the debates which, on the borders of delirium, he had conducted within himself. This time each discussion led him to an opposite conclusion to that which he had previously reached. He would not be alone in the future, stranded between a community he had rejected and another which rejected him. His service, his wounds would surely be a passport into the living world.

A packet of letters arrived. The top letter was covered with re-addressings. It must have been following him for months. The writing of the original address was familiar. He opened it. Yes — he smiled as his recognition was confirmed — it was from Paula. 'Dear Mark,' she wrote, 'How are you? You silly boy. I often wonder whether you are still alive. So I wrote. How are you? All right? I hope you will let me know.

Love. Paula.' Under this she had written: 'PS. — I married a Major!!!' On the next line, 'PPS. — He is forty-five.' On the next line, 'PPPS. — He is in Egypt. When are you next on leave?'

Mark laughed, wrote in big letters across the bottom, 'Jealous?' and slipped it into an envelope with his latest letter to Ruth. There were several letters from pilots in the Typhoon squadron to which he had belonged. There was one from Bones, who led another squadron in the same wing. He lay back, clutching them happily. The men who had written these letters were his brothers. It seemed to him that in his hands he held his letters of credential to the future.

1948

1948

1

The leaflets appeared in the borough on a fine Saturday morning in May.

A horde of little boys invaded the streets, giving the leaflets away, pushing them under front doors, scattering handfuls of them. The heady spring breeze seized the fluttering leaflets and sent them somersaulting along the pavements, whirling up into the bushes, where, as the wind tried to tug them loose, they sought the eye of the pedestrian. They lay everywhere in the gutters, the black letters staring up from them like eyes.

The Vicar of St. Saviour's Church, which stands on the corner of Khartoum Road and a smaller side turning, was given one by an excited urchin, He stood, blinking in the bright sunlight, and read the leaflet. He asked the boy, 'Do you know what this is about?'

'No, mister.'

'Where did you get them from?'

'A man give 'em to me, mister.'

'Why are you giving them away?'

'For a lark, mister.'

The little boy ran off before the clergyman could say any more. To the children this was an exciting game, a mission with which they had been entrusted, the excuse for a thousand kinds of make-believe.

Wherever people went that day, they found the leaflets. Housewives found them in their baskets when they came home with the shopping. Postmen found them in the pillarboxes.

The centre of the community was its market. The busiest time of the week in the market was on Saturday afternoon. From two o'clock onwards, when the menfolk had had time to get home from work, wash, change, eat and rest, the shops were crowded and the stalls were surrounded by shoppers, the married couples walking arm-in-arm, the men taking pleasure in carrying the baskets for their wives, in helping them decide what to buy, in looking at the things they could not afford and making plans for the future. They bought ice-creams for themselves and toys, from aged hawkers, for the children. People bumped and pushed each other, but everybody was smiling and animated. The noise that ascended from the slowly-moving crowds was one of life and happiness.

This Saturday afternoon, however, there was something new in the market that killed its gaiety. At the top of the street, facing the crowds that came surging round the corners into the market, stood a line of young men spaced so that everybody else had to pass between them. They were big, burly young men with broad shoulders, some wearing caps and chokers and frayed clothes, others more respectably dressed. They were giving away the leaflets, and as they did so they chanted slogans denouncing the Jews and advertising a meeting that their party was to hold on this spot in a week from Sunday.

They did not shout at the tops of their voices, in competition with the brazen-lunged street-traders, but they kept up a grim, monotonous chant which drove the smiles from the faces of the people who streamed past them. The shoppers pushed on into the crowds; and in place of the usual good-natured and high-spirited chatter, there was a mutter of low-toned talk above which the shouts of the hawkers rang strangely. The passers-by looked at each other with troubled and sometimes suspicious faces. It was not only the Jews in the crowds, faced with their ancient enemy, who felt the touch of fear. The chill crept into every heart. Men and women said to each other, 'There's going to be trouble. You'll see!'

The burly young men tried to distinguish amongst the people who passed them. To some they offered leaflets; to others, insults. Sometimes, however, they made mistakes. It was particularly hard, one of them confided regretfully to another, to tell which of the women was which. Most of the housewives looked alike, with their hair covered by brightly-coloured kerchiefs and shabby coats on their backs. Their faces, too, were so alike; the war had ended three years ago, yet in the faces of these women could still be seen the strain of wartime, of danger, of scattered families, as well as the still-present burdens of queues and shortages. How to tell one from the other? It could not be helped, then, if occasionally a Jewish woman received a leaflet and a smile, or a Gentile woman was helped on her way with a violent push and a muttered, 'Out of the way, bitch! I can smell your kind a mile off!'

Some of the shoppers took leaflets. Some refused them. Some drew away from the young men. They were tired of excitement, tired of trouble. They wanted to be left alone; all of them, and in particular the Jews.

The afternoon passed in golden sunshine. The evening was glorious and serene. There was no excitement in the evening, nothing to disrupt its cool and mellow peace.

Crowded buses bore pleasure-seekers towards the West End. The High Street was thronged with strollers. Thousands queued outside the cinemas. Others flocked to the dog tracks. The public-houses were full. Children played in the streets. Elderly couples took their ease in the parks, admiring the brilliant flower-beds and the avenues of trees amid whose masses of pale-green foliage the spikes of white and pink blossom rose like candles on Christmas trees. Some sat at their front doors, smoking, gossiping, reading the sporting pages of the evening papers and ignoring the front pages. For tonight all these people had shut out the world from themselves, and they were happy.

A couple of hours after midnight the frightening clangour of fire-engines was heard in the streets. People lay in their beds listening, or padded to the windows, as the powerful vehicles came snorting one after another round street corners, gathered speed and roared away into the night. From along the streets came the sounds of windows being open and shut, of voices raised. Only the heaviest sleepers were undisturbed.

The noise died away. The excitement was forgotten. The streets were quiet again. In the distance, bombers could be heard exercising, muttering conspiracy in the dark corners of the night. The people slept.

2

Mark slipped out of bed and padded across to the window. He liked to walk about barefoot in his bedroom. The cold shock that came up through his soles with each step was invigorating. He pulled up the blind and bowed his head at the sudden dazzle of sunshine. The curtains stirred and the morning breeze came sweetly into the room after the night's heaviness. The stillness of Sunday morning was in the air; no throb and hum of factories, the murmur of traffic greatly subdued, only the sparrows and thrushes unabashed among the rooftops.

Ruth groaned, mumbled something to him, turned over in bed and pulled the blankets up to her chin.

He walked into the kitchen, put a kettle on the stove and, still barefoot, went downstairs. He pulled the folded newspaper from the letterbox. As it came free a crumpled piece of paper fluttered to the floor. He picked up the leaflet and smoothed it.

It was headed, 'Calling all Britons.' He felt a jolt of pain, like an electric shock, in the deep, ugly scar that ran down behind his right ear from the crown of his skull. The leaflet advertised the coming meeting.

He went upstairs, burned the leaflet and scattered the ashes out of the kitchen window. He did not want his wife to see it. He told himself that he was not going to let this upset him; he had too many things to worry about already. He tried to be aware of the lovely spring weather; to hear the birds; but he could not. He applied himself to the newspaper, but his consciousness would not absorb what he was reading. Every few minutes the pain darted along his scar again. A news item caught his eye.

'Ruth!' He could hear his wife moving about in the bedroom.

'What do you want?' Her voice was unfriendly. 'Is the kettle on?'

'Yes; it's nearly boiling. Remember those fire engines last night?'

She came into the kitchen. She looked unwell. Her cheeks were heavy; there was no lustre in her hair. Her waistline was thick and ungainly. She tied the cord of her dressing-gown. 'I didn't get to sleep for a long time. I had pains. You went off quickly.' There was a hint of accusation in her voice. She placed cups and saucers noisily on the table. 'What was it, then? Is there something in the paper?'

He did not want to tell her now. He regretted the panic that had made him call out to her. He answered unwillingly. 'Yes. It was the synagogue in Willoughby Row.'

'What happened?'

'They don't know. There was a lot of damage done inside, but they saved the building. It says here the police are investigating.'

'Police!' Ruth shivered. 'We don't need the police to tell us it's deliberate. It's not the first time it's happened. Oh, God!' Her hands went on calmly with the business of making tea. 'I'm sick of it all.'

Mark looked at her with pity. She was in the sixth month of pregnancy. She was nervous and lonely, and he did not know how to reach her. 'Drink your tea,' he said harshly, 'and put some clothes on. It's still chilly, even with this sunshine.'

'That's all right. I'm still wearing my woollens. Any good pictures in the West End? Look at the adverts. We could go tonight.'

'Nothing much. Anyway, we promised to go and see my parents. Got no objection, have you? Or is it too much trouble to see them once a week?'

'I haven't said anything,' she protested. 'I thought you might like a change. You look so tired.'

'Well, I'm not.' What a baby he was, he thought, as he brushed his hair in front of the mirror. Whenever he wanted to comfort her he ended by wounding her. He said, 'I'm going out for a walk. Is there anything I can get you?'

'No thank you, dear.' She spoke as if there had been no tension between them. 'Be back by one o'clock.'

He turned away in distaste from the mirror. He had changed in the last few years. The healthy tan had gone from his face. The lower parts of his cheeks were pale, with a faint blue shadow of stubble. The skin on his nose and above his cheekbones was red and rough, and on his nose it was drawn tightly over the bone structure, so that there was now a hint of a curve in it. He often looked to see if his hair was receding; in fact it was, a little, at the sides. Above his ears he still had the hair cropped close, military fashion; there were gleams of grey in it, though the thick hair above was still black and glossy. And, of course, there was the deep ugly scar at the back of his head.

He laced his shoes and put his jacket on. 'I'm off now. Ta-ta.'

Walking rapidly down the street, he tried to put himself in harmony with the mood of the morning, with the rustling, richly-clad trees, with the sunshine, with the white clouds that towered above the rooftops. He longed to be able to stop his mind from functioning, but it raced on like an uncontrollable machine, frightening him, fatiguing him, and keeping him apart from his surroundings.

It was three years since he had come home with a few souvenirs and high hopes. He still had the souvenirs — his Air Force cap, a few photographs, the Luger pistol he had won at cards, a squadron Christmas card, a row of medal ribbons — but the hopes had gone. He suffered from a double frustration. There were the difficulties and the disappointment he shared with millions of ex-Service men; this alone he could have borne. Far worse was the disillusionment he felt as a Jew who had come home thinking that the war had made possible a new relationship with his fellow men. He longed to be able to live his own life and let the world go its way; to make of his home a little refuge of warmth in which he and his wife might hide. This was his only ambition, for the centrepiece of his former life had been smashed to dust; his wounds had left him unfit ever to fly again.

However, though this loss left him with a vague emptiness of spirit, it did not hurt him. He was so weary of war, of any kind of overreaching effort, that he did not look for any new objective to give his life meaning. He no longer wanted to strive for anything, only to avoid striving. Youth, and the desire to achieve, were over. Now he would be content with a warm, lifelong hibernation, shared with his wife; to make a living, and to be left alone.

But it was impossible to shut the world out. It was in their minds. It came through the letter-box every morning with the newspapers. It entered with every worried visitor. It shouted from the radio. It lay in wait whenever he went out to work or Ruth to her shopping.

They had been sitting at home one evening a week ago, resting at the close of a hot, oppressive day. Suddenly, from the sky above them had come an ear-splitting explosion like the crack of doom that set the windows rattling, followed by a series of rumbling echoes. Ruth cried out and ran down the stairs to the street door. Startled by the noise and mystified by her action, he followed.

They stood on the doorstep watching the downpour of rain and enjoying the cool air.

Ruth sighed, and said weakly, 'Thank God!'

'What's the matter?' Mark asked. 'It was only thunder.' A woman had come out on to the porch of the next house. She said to them, 'Oh, my Gawd. I thought it was the atom bomb. Didn't you?'

Mark was about to indulge in polite derision when Ruth spoke again; 'So did I.'

'It made my stomach turn over, it did,' said the woman.

'I shan't be able to face my supper tonight.'

'But who would drop an atom bomb on us?' asked Mark.

'You never know these days,' said the neighbour.

And Ruth added fearfully, 'They're all mad.'

Mark had the feeling of mysterious forces gathering; in this borough circumstances had focused them as through a burning-glass.

The district lay between the Ghetto area of the East End and the great industrial areas of north-east London. The bombing of the East End during the war had sent thousands of homeless Jews surging outwards in wave after wave. They had penetrated to every corner of Hackney. There were no demarcation lines. They lived in the same streets, often in the same houses, as Gentiles. They scrambled for the same buses, crowded in the same cinemas, jostled in the same queues in shops and markets.

Now that there was a shortage of everything — of housing, of transport, of food and goods in the shops — Jew and Gentile saw each other as rivals. The Jews were still sick with the memory of their six million kin murdered by Gentiles in Europe. Their neighbours were inflamed by the knowledge that in Palestine, in the last year, Englishmen had been killed by Jews.

Mark remembered seeing two elderly women shrilling at each other in a trolley-bus. They looked very much alike, they were both tired and burdened with shopping bags. They were probably both grandmothers, each gentle and beloved in her own home, with the children gathered about her. They must both have lived the same hard life and both sat in their kitchens beneath the bombs. Perhaps they had both sent sons to one war and grandsons to the next. But, watching them screeching at each other, their wrinkled faces twitching with hatred, Mark had realised that they could not see each other. They were both blinded by fear. Each saw before her not another woman, but a monster created in her own mind.

On another occasion, a bus conductor lurched accidentally against a Jewish woman. He began to utter a good-natured apology and stopped in surprise as she shouted abuse at him. 'Who do you think you are? You think you can push us about whenever you like? You'd like to trample on us, wouldn't you? Call yourselves civilised? Beasts you are, wild beasts!' The conductor looked at her with bewilderment, then with hatred and disgust.

A Jewess walked up to a greengrocer's stall. Before taking her place in the queue, she stepped forward to see whether the vegetables she wanted were in stock. A woman screamed from the queue. 'Take your place in the queue. You bleed'n' people — push to the front everywhere.' She turned at bay and cursed back. Other women joined in and she hurried away, her face scarlet and streaked with tears.

3

'You sit by the window,' said Ruth. 'I've moved the armchair over there. I'll get you a cup of tea.' She rose and began to put the plates together.

Mark had enjoyed his lunch; and he was eager to show his wife that he, too, wanted to forget the morning's quarrel. 'That's all right. You have a rest for a change. I'll look after the tea and the washing up.'

'Oh, no! I'm not going to let you smash any more plates. They're too hard to get.'

He was too sleepy to insist. He moved over to the armchair and made himself comfortable by the open window, enjoying the sunshine and the light breeze. He read for a while. His eyes smarted and he let the paper drop. His head sank back and, lulled by the splash of water and the clatter of crockery from the kitchen, he drifted into a half-sleep.

A noise probed at his consciousness. He tried to exclude it. He heard it again; the street door bell. Ruth called from the kitchen, 'Go down, darling. My hands are wet.'

His legs wobbled under him for a moment as he rose, still tired and dizzy; but he hurried downstairs, for the sound of an unexpected caller always aroused in him a vague sense of alarm. He saw two shadows through the frosted glass panels of the front door and paused for a moment, his heart thumping with suspense. He opened the door.

'Mr. Strong?' The speaker was a stocky young man of Jewish appearance with a war disablement badge in his lapel. With him was a tall, elderly man with a yellow beard and an old-fashioned bowler hat.

'Yes.'

'One of the neighbours recommended us to call here. We're from the Willoughby Row Synagogue.'

'Oh.' Mark was annoyed. He thought of his broken sleep and yawned slightly.

'Did you see the morning paper?'

Mark made a stupid noise of interrogation. Then he realised what the young man was talking about. 'About the fire, you mean?' He felt surreptitiously among the coins in his pocket, trying to decide how much to subscribe if this was a collection.

'Yes. What paper did you see it in?'

He told them.

'There wasn't much in that one,' said the young man. 'Here's what happened. Somebody climbed over the back wall and forced a door to get in. They stacked a lot of old newspapers and a can of paraffin under the altar hangings and set fire to them. It was lucky a policeman saw the glow through the front windows, otherwise the whole place would have gone up.'

The older man said, 'There have been many such attempts lately.'

'All over the place,' the ex-soldier went on. 'And with all this excitement this week, and the meeting next Sunday, they may try again. Anyway, we're getting up a list of Jewish ex-Servicemen to mount a guard over the place every night till things get quieter. The more people we get the less often each one will have to take a turn. Can we put your name down?'

160

Mark flushed. 'I really haven't got the time,' he said. 'My wife isn't well. I can't leave her alone at nights.' He uttered the excuses desperately, as they came to him. 'Can't they hire a watchman to do it?'

'They've got a watchman. He was on duty last night. The fire brigade had to wake him up to get the keys.'

'What about the police?' He was determined not to have anything to do with this business. He remembered with a pang of shame the last time he had entered a synagogue. It was a couple of months after his return from the Air Force; he had been roaming about London for days, lonely and despairing, obsessed by the feeling of exclusion from this strange, post-war world, returning more and more in his thoughts to his war memories, longing to be able to go back into the past, to meet again the irrevocable dead; and at last, eager for a refuge, fired for a moment by the hope of finding some fold into which he might enter, he had walked into a synagogue. He had stayed for an hour, watching the old men nodding and mumbling and bearing their sacred scrolls before them, and had fled; it all seemed as barbaric and alien to him as it had when he was a child. He looked back on this episode as a moment of weakness; he did not want to be reminded of it.

'The police!' said the young man bitterly.

'Well, I certainly think you ought to go to your own members first.'

'This doesn't only concern our members.' The ex-soldier was becoming angry. 'You let them burn synagogues and they'll be burning your houses next.'

'Come,' the old man interrupted. 'If the gentleman is not eager we should not press him.'

Mark mumbled again, 'It's only fair to try your own members first.'

'Don't worry.' The young man turned away. 'We won't bother you again.'

Glad to get rid of them, but eager to justify himself, Mark said as he began to close the door, 'Let me know if you can't get enough of your own members.'

The old man raised his hat. 'Good day. I am sorry if we disturbed you.'

Mark stood in the hall for a moment, then went back to his armchair. Ruth was folding the tablecloth. She asked, 'Who was it?'

'Oh, no one.' He wanted to spare her any more worry. He opened the Sunday newspaper.

Ruth went on folding the cloth with quick, violent movements. She took it out to the kitchen and came back. 'Shall I cut you a pear?' she asked. Mark made an affirmative noise, still avoiding her look. She stood at the sideboard and peeled a pear wastefully. She knew that everything between them depended on her patience, and fought to restrain herself. But it was as if she were inhabited by an angry stranger. 'No one?' she said suddenly, 'I suppose you were talking to no one in the hall? I suppose that was no one I heard going down the front steps and shutting the gate behind them?' She offered him the pear on a plate.

He would not look up from the newspaper. His hand groped and took the plate. He said, 'Thanks!' and went on staring at the print. He, too, was fighting his anger. Since the interview with the two men he had been possessed by strange and disturbing feelings with which he wanted to wrestle without interruption from anyone.

Ruth sat in the chair facing him, leaning forward with her fists clenched in her lap as if there were a pain in her body. 'Mark!' She could not help it: the terrible desire to nag was fed by the need to wound him into taking notice of her, by her fear of letting him fight alone against the mysterious anxieties and obsessions that were besetting him, and by her alarm — magnified by her imagination — lest the visitors had brought some bad news. 'Mark! Who was it? Is anything wrong?'

'Oh, leave me alone.'

'Mark!' She snatched the newspaper from his hands. 'Pay attention to me! I'm talking to you. Who was it? I'm not a baby. You can tell me.'

The newspaper tore as Mark tried to take it back from her. 'Now look what you've done.' Part of him wanted to strike her; part of him wanted to embrace and comfort her, receiving comfort in return. 'Who do you think it was? Prince Monolulu come to tell me the Derby winner?'

Ruth burst into tears. Mark was shocked and a little frightened. It had never come to this point before. But there was a sick rage inside him that could only find its outlet in cruelty. 'Well,' he said savagely, 'what have I done now? I've hardly said a word. I'd still be reading my paper in peace if you hadn't started nagging. God knows how I've put up with it all this time. I'm just about fed-up with it!'

She raised her face, and he could hardly recognise her, so ugly did she look with the tears rolling down her cheeks. Her voice, too, was unfamiliar, thick and high-pitched, unbearably strained. '*You're* fed-up? You've had enough? What about me? I'm the one who's having the baby. I'm the one who has to stay at home all day in a poky, smelly little flat. I'm the one who's had to smile and be patient all the time. I don't know what's the matter with you. You never seem to be more than half interested in anything — me, your parents, your job. Oh' — she sniffed horribly — 'I've seen it.' She dried her eyes. 'For two years I've felt as if I was married to a ghost.'

'Perhaps I am!' shouted Mark. 'I wish to God I'd been killed in the war. So what?' He marched into the bedroom and slammed the door behind him.

He lay on the bed with his legs apart and his arms under his head, trying to understand that last remark which had come unbidden to his lips. 'I wish to God I'd been killed in the war.' He wondered what could have led him to say such a silly thing.

Yet it awoke echoes that still vibrated within him, as faint, disturbing and elusive as the overtones that linger in the ear after a note of music has been struck. It brought back to him the feeling of desolation with which he had wrestled in those first weeks — so many years ago, it now seemed — in hospital. More strongly still it reminded him of the day when he had come home, a civilian at last.

He had hurried from the train, trying to arouse within himself the feelings which, through six years of war, he had expected to enjoy on this day; the eagerness, the thankfulness, the longing for his wife. But, standing on the platform at Waterloo with his bags and boxes around him, he had experienced only a dull, pervasive terror that weighted his limbs and made him reluctant to move. The station gates opened out on to a strange and complex world in which he had forgotten his way about; his wife and family were shadows flitting across the foreground of his consciousness, disturbing him but arousing no emotions. He did not want to go forward; he wanted to turn round and go back. Where to? To the Air Force? No, to the past; and this, he told himself dismally, was impossible. He wanted someone to talk to, someone in whom to seek strength, before he went on. He called a roll inside his mind, and to name after name he answered, 'Dead.' Then he remembered Bones. It was months since they had exchanged letters, but Bones must still be about somewhere. He had — he groped in his pockets for his notebook — a telephone number. In the telephone box he dialled the number and suddenly, as he listened to the bell ringing at the other end, he realised that he had forgotten Bones' surname. It was ridiculous, and a little frightening.

A woman's voice answered. He groped for the name. 'Is Mr... ah' — he remembered — 'Gascoyne there?'

'No' — the voice was that of a well-trained housemaid — 'you've got the wrong number. His daughter-in-law lives here. I'll get you Mr. Gascoyne's number.'

Mark said, 'Thanks.' Then it came to him that there was something wrong. 'Daughter-in-law? Here, I say, miss. I want Christopher Gascoyne.'

There was dismay in the voice that answered, 'Oh! I thought you wanted the old Mr. Gascoyne. Mr. Christopher was killed in the war. He was in the Air Force.'

Mark heard himself say, 'I know.'

The maid asked, 'Would you like to speak to Mrs. Gascoyne?'

Mark knew that he ought to; it was the thing to do. But he did not know what to say to Nell. She was one of the shadows. 'No, thank you. It's all right.' He hung up the receiver and left the booth. He was on his own now.

The war was always there; but when he turned towards it as a refuge from the present, it was beyond his reach. After a snub, or a failure, or a disappointment, he would submerge himself in the memory of the great days, roaming the streets for hours as he re-enacted mentally some episode from the past. Then he could say to himself, after some glib buyer had outsmarted him or some official had humiliated him, 'That was *me* in nineteen-forty! I wonder where *he* was.' But the more consoling the dream, the harsher the awakening.

Why was it that, to relieve his own feelings, he had to try Ruth so persistently, to strain her patience? It was as if he were testing her loyalty unceasingly, exploring fearfully to find where lay the limits of her love. Yet he knew that if he pressed her too hard he would discover those limits and drive her beyond them. He dreaded this, for he could not bear the thought of life without her; and he was convinced (except in those moments when his confidence deserted him altogether) that she had equal need of him. It was this longing to cement their imperilled marriage that had prompted their decision to have a child. But, now that the first flush of excited tenderness had worn off, he found himself apathetic, sometimes slightly disgusted at the change in Ruth's appearance, and — when he allowed himself to think of it — apprehensive about their future and that of the child in a bewildering world. As for Ruth, pregnancy had brought her new anxieties, and had left her too ill and nervous to help Mark as she had before.

His thoughts were interrupted by the sound of the door opening stealthily. Ruth came in. She asked softly, 'Are you asleep?'

'No.'

They both looked at each other with the same expression, at once defiant and contrite, each waiting for a sign in the other's face.

She went to the dressing-table and sat facing the mirror. 'I just came in to do my nails,' she said. She saw his reflection in the mirror. 'Take your shoes off. You'll dirty the quilt.' She watched the mirror intently for an angry movement, and listened for an angry reply. She relaxed as he sat up on the bed and unlaced his shoes obediently. 'Do you want to sleep?' The tension was melting from her voice. 'I'll lower the blind.'

'Please.'

She lowered the blind, came back to the bed, slipped her shoes off and lay by his side on the blue coverlet. 'I'm tired, too,' she said. 'It's funny. I haven't done a thing today and I feel worn out. My head hurts. It feels as if it's stuffed with thoughts. I don't know how they all got there.'

They lay still and silent in the gloom. Then Mark began to talk. He told her of the two callers and their errand. She listened contentedly. Later she would think about what he had told her, and anxiety would creep back. Now she was happy, for he was telling her everything.

4

They went in the evening to visit Mark's parents, who now had Mickey's widow, Mill, and her seven-year-old daughter living with them. Mill went out to work every day and Clara, who no longer helped in the fish-shop, stayed at home to keep house and look after the child.

Mill reported on a recent visit to old Jacob, who, at the age of seventy-seven, was still hale and still living on his own in the old house. 'It ain't right,' she said. 'He squats there over his old frying-pan, he does, sniffing at his sausages and bristling his whiskers at you like an old tramp on the road. I bet it's months since he had a bath. All them piles of junk round him, dust on everything, all the windows shut tight and so dirty the room's half dark. I was ashamed to take the child, I was.'

They told Mark, too, of their money troubles. Joe's asthma was now so bad that he could only work at irregular intervals. Moss had often helped them, but now the doctor had ordered Joe to go away to the South Coast for a while, and without more money to pay his expenses and keep the home going in his absence, this was impossible.

Joe was savagely opposed to asking for more help from Moss. The more abject his defeat in life became, the more it shamed him to confess his failure to his rich brother. He declared, coughing, that he would rather go into the hospital than beg more money from Moss.

Clara listened to him without protest, but when it was time for Mark and Ruth to leave she went with them to the street door and asked Mark to see Moss and get the money from him.

Mark agreed, and the next morning he set out earlier than usual so that he could visit Moss before starting his own day's round.

As he strode down the street he whistled loudly, partly to reassure Ruth, partly to dispel his own feeling of depression.

He arrived at the garage where he kept the decrepit old car with which his employers had provided him. He unlocked the car door and made himself comfortable in the driver's seat. There was an unpleasant smell of stale leather. He opened the bottom of the windscreen; the breeze as he drove would be refreshing. He switched on the engine and tugged at the starter. The car panted and shuddered and whined like a sick dog. He tried again and again; the starter would not work. He got out and used the crank. He abandoned the attempt to achieve a good humour and felt better. He drove off, whistling, softly this time, and without self-consciousness.

His present job was the latest, and most humiliating, of a series that he had tried since the war. On his return from hospital he had called at Badgett and Dogg's. He had guessed in advance what his reception would be — many other men had told him their stories; his presentiment had been fulfilled.

'So glad to see you back, old man. Are you feeling all right? Fine, that's fine. Must have shaken you up quite a bit, eh? Yes, yes, we'll be glad to have you back with us. Of course' — and then it had come — 'we can't promise much of an opening at the moment. Man of your calibre, you know. Mean to say, we've had a pretty good team with us right through the war. There's your old job, though. What were you getting? Four pounds a week? Well, well, that would never do, would it, old man? We could make it five. For the time being, of course.' The speaker had been Venner — a new Venner, hearty, relaxed, talking as if there were no shadow of the past between them. Mark had asked about Sanders. 'Sanders? No, he didn't come back from the war, poor chap. In the Navy. He went down on an Arctic convoy.' ('Of course,' Mark thought; 'everybody!') 'Well, think it over, old man' — a gentle pressure of the hand on Mark's back, ushering him towards the door — 'no hurry, is there? By the way, did I tell you?' Venner had to control his voice as if he were boasting of an achievement, 'I'm married now — two kiddies. Have to meet the wife some day, eh? Well, give us a ring when you've decided.' Mark had gone away thinking, as he often did on such occasions, of Davy, imprisoned for years in a hospital, his face rebuilt into a hideous, puffy mask, his hands shrivelled and useless. Walking out of the office, with Venner's patronising hand on his shoulder, Mark had been oppressed by a familiar sense of the unfairness of existence. He had never rung.

He had tried to get work with the airlines. If he could no longer fly, the next best thing was to be near aeroplanes. 'We're terribly sorry. There's nothing at all. We have thousands like you coming to see us.' He had called a number of times at the centre which the Government had set up to help ex-officers to find work. 'Do you know, Mr. Strong, you really will have to accommodate yourself to present conditions.' Applying for several jobs, he had been recognised and snubbed as a Jew. He had been offered a job by Moss. He had refused; sometimes he regretted his fastidiousness. His Uncle Sid was working for Moss; the hideous little man was flourishing, with a house, a gleaming Buick and a luxurious wife.

Then there had been the Leviathan Press. The venture had begun when he met Rod, an ex-Army man who knew a dozen ways of making a fortune. Rod inspired confidence, with his ruddy, pleasantly porcine face, his military moustache and his everlasting talk about 'the good old Seventh Armoured'. He had everything lined up. All that was needed was a little capital, a printer, a binder and some paper, and you were in the publishing business. Mark was impressed. His hopes soared. He put up as capital the last of his gratuity. Rod found a backer who put in another few hundred pounds, and talked a back-street printer into giving them six months' credit. It was only at this stage that they began to discuss what to publish. Again Rod had the idea. 'A volume of Early Elizabethan novels. Nobody's ever read 'em. Go like hot cakes.' While the volume was being printed Rod went from one firm of binders to another. It was no use. None of them would take on the job. Finally, they placed the sheets with a firm which could not guarantee delivery in less than a year. There was very little money left and no more credit. Rod hit on the idea of using the remaining money to make a little profit on the side. He cultivated a large circle of dubious acquaintances in night clubs and bars, ran up a formidable expenses account out of the Leviathan Press's funds, and bought a large consignment of paper on the Black Market, only to discover that it was of a quality which no publisher wanted. The bales of paper remained for months in a basement, growing yellower and soggier at each inspection. That was the end of the Leviathan Press. Rod grinned happily, said, 'Well, it just goes to show. Sorry, old boy,' and went to Rhodesia.

Later, after a further series of disappointments, Mark had — on the strength of the experience he claimed as 'a managing director' of the Leviathan Press — been taken on as a traveller in the London area by a firm which published a range of crude, fly-by-night coloured comic papers, film magazines full of pictures of bathing beauties, and sixpenny novelettes. He had to go to hundreds of little tobacconists and newsagents and talk them into buying stocks of this rubbish. He hated the work. It was vulgar and pointless and every visit humiliated him, but despair had made him bold, and he had developed a good line of patter which brought him about eight pounds a week in wages and commission. Sometimes he was scared at the thought that he was thirty years old and trapped in a blind-alley job; he had made as little headway as a boy who had just left school. He studied the employment columns of the newspapers every day and wrote scores of applications for jobs, without result. To Ruth he was always painfully optimistic. 'It's only till I find something better.' Or, 'It's all experience, dear.' And she would answer mildly, 'As long as it's for your future, darling...' But sometimes Mark wondered whether she saw through his talk, whether she was inwardly as frightened as he was, whether, even, she nourished a secret disappointment in him.

He drove easily, without attention, through the morning traffic. He was able to feel when driving a pleasure that was a faint reminder of the old joy of flying; his hands were able to regain some of their instinctive skill.

He pulled up outside a white, tall office building off Oxford Street and took the lift up to the third floor. He opened a door on whose frosted-glass window was the name *United Kingdom Sporting Agency* and walked into a room that looked like a combination of thieves' kitchen and telephone exchange. More than a dozen girls sat at a long switchboard that covered three walls, their fingers busy with plugs and cables, their voices a subdued babble mingling with an endless clicking and buzzing. As for the men who filled the rest of the room, Mark found it hard to decide which kind looked the most vicious — those with well-cut brown suits and gorgeous ties, their fat, purple cheeks shining with prosperity and face cream; those with broken noses and broad shoulders; or those with dark, sunken eyes and thin, grey faces. Some leaned against the wall by the door, some sat on chairs or the edges of tables, others stood in groups or moved from one group to another. They argued, in harsh or high-pitched voices; they studied racing newspapers and manuals of form; around them swirled blue smoke.

Beyond the glass partition which formed the fourth wall of the room, an inner office could be seen, furnished expensively, with a thick carpet covering most of its polished floor and, in the centre of the carpet, a broad table covered with telephones. Pacing up and down in this office, alone, like a captain walking his bridge, was Moss.

Mark gave his name to a girl, who told him that Moss could not be disturbed. 'Mr. Strong will be another ten minutes yet. We dare not interrupt him.' Mark, who had been here before, knew what was happening. Thousands of pounds' worth of bets were coming in, and Moss, alone in his soundproofed room, had to work out without delay his policy for the day; which bets he would accept, which he would pass on, which he would cover by placing bets himself. Swiftly and accurately he would make complicated mental calculations involving huge sums of money. He would take his decisions boldly and without hesitation. Uneducated, almost illiterate though he was, his life in the jungle in which he prowled had developed monstrously those faculties which he needed in order to survive; and every morning he was mathematician and general in one.

A quarter of an hour later Mark was admitted to the inner office. Moss blinked at him like a tired man, put an aspirin on his tongue and washed it down with a glass of water. ''Allo, boy. Siddown. 'Ow's the folks?' His voice had thickened; he had to force his words through a filter of phlegm.

They exchanged family talk for a few minutes. Mark delivered his mother's plea for help.

'All right, boy,' Moss grunted. 'No sooner said than done. You know me. Nothing's too good for my family. You can pick the money up yourself, and slip it to your Ma. All right?'

Girls were coming in every few seconds with slips of paper for Moss. The telephones on the desk were continually claiming his attention. He swallowed another aspirin. 'I live on the bloody things,' he said. 'One long headache my life is. No joke, this game. One slip in here' — he tapped his head — 'an' I'm done for.' He was a general who had to fight the decisive battle of his life all over again every morning. 'In here,' he repeated, 'goin' all the time, like an engine. Gives me no rest.'

'I'm sorry for you,' said Mark.

Moss turned his bloodshot eyes on Mark and smiled grimly. 'You can laugh. What's it all for? I sit here and make money. This' — he touched his forehead again — 'makes money. It won't stop. It gives my dear wife a house in Twickenham and a flat in Park Lane. She's got two cars to choose from, a mink coat to wear at the Palladium and a Pekinese to carry under 'er arm in the Park. It gives 'er enough money in 'er bag to lose a bloody fortune every night at faro. She's mad, she is, gamblin' mad. It gives my son everything 'e wants and pensions to 'alf my family. What does it give me? A bloomin' 'eadache.' His tongue flicked out quickly, like a lizard's, and carried another aspirin back into his mouth.

He slumped in his chair and looked malignantly at the silent gesticulations of his henchmen beyond the glass partition. He was on show to them all the time; but this was as he wished; for his presence impressed them and gave them confidence. He could speak his doubts and anxieties; he could groan with weariness; they would not hear. Through the glass window he remained the red-faced, ruthless, back-slapping Boss.

'There's going to be trouble up our way,' said Mark. He told Moss about the leaflets. He was grateful for the chance to talk; this thing was eating at him. 'Sometimes I think we ought to move to another district. I mean, with a baby on the way —'

'Be your age, boy,' Moss grunted. 'Learn the lesson. There's only one thing that'll put you where they can't hurt you — money. With money you can laugh at 'em. They slam a door on you — money opens it. It'll get you all the things in life that other people got.'

'Except respect.'

Moss laughed harshly. 'Listen, boy. When I open my wallet I get respect. The bigger they are the broader they smile.' He cleared his throat. 'Grow a thick skin. Don't care for nobody. Have pity for nobody. Nobody's got none for you. It's a dirty world. Play it their way. Play dirty. When you want to enjoy yourself, enjoy yourself. — the lot of 'em. That's the way to be happy.'

'Are you happy?'

'Why shouldn't I be? I got everything I want.'

'You've got a headache,' Mark said. He rose, and looked down at Moss. 'Uncle Moss, I think you hate your life as much as I hate mine. You're wearing yourself out. You make money, but you can't enjoy it. Every day the worries pile up instead of getting less. From where I am, you don't look a man to be envied.'

'Go away, boy. I love it. It's the breath of life. That's how you tell a strong man from a weak one in this rotten world. I'm a strong one, see? I make my way.'

'Till you get a stroke and drop in your tracks.'

'All right, so I'll go down punching. I still love it. You're the boy that wanted to see life. I'm the one that's seeing it. You're selling comics.'

'Yes.' Mark turned towards the door. 'That's about the way of it. And now I suppose I'd better go and sell a few more.'

Moss waggled his hand in dismissal. A girl pushed past Mark with a telegram in her hand. Moss reached for the telephones, pressed buttons, snarled at a dictaphone. He had plunged into his battle again.

5

The week passed like a sick dream.

On Wednesday morning the weather was dull. Bulging grey clouds pressed upon the roofs and made the sky seem small. A damp, insistent wind pried at street doors and whirled eddies of grit at people's faces, roaring from time to time into sudden gales.

Mark had come out of a shop and was just about to step into his car when he heard, through the mutter of the wind and the noise of traffic, the sound of aero-engines. It was as if his body had heard before his mind, for he stopped with one foot on the running-board and wondered what it was that had caught his attention. He looked up as the sound grew louder. A Dakota — a twin-engined transport machine — appeared out of the grey mist and moved slowly across the space between the tall buildings, swaying as it fought the wind. He stood listening for some time after it had vanished. In imagination he was in the pilot's cabin of the Dakota, peering through the blurred windows, feeling the machine bucketing beneath him and the controls wrestling under his strong hands; the clouds pressing down from above and glimpses beneath of factory chimneys and glistening roofs.

The moment of glory was gone. He was standing foolishly by his car, watched suspiciously by a policeman, with a briefcase full of comic papers under his right arm. For a few seconds his soul had been born again in him, the spirit that had sustained him in the days when he had been able to say to himself: *I belong*. Now it had flown out of him again and faded into the mist with the engine's roar, leaving so great a sense of loss that this time he felt it was gone for ever. The scar at the back of his head throbbed, a reminder of his injuries, a warning that however obscure the road into the future might be, the way back to the past was closed.

It was cold and showery all day. He went on his rounds depressed by the morning's incident and by the change in the weather. On his way home in the evening he saw slogans chalked and whitewashed on walls, and printed on sticky-backed little labels that had appeared everywhere — on lamp-posts, fences, shop-windows, telephone booths. He was frightened of slogans. They were like evil whispers. Arguments could be answered but slogans — any slogans — lurked beyond the grasp of reason. They entered into the consciousness as imperceptibly as germs into the blood stream. Whether they sold tooth-paste, baking powder, social reform or hatred, they were a poison among men.

He did not stay indoors long. The rooms in the flat seemed tiny, imprisoning, overheated. Ruth's presence, as she moved silently and stealthily about, always afraid to offend, was a burden. He felt the same embarrassment with her as he did with a stranger when conversation lagged. He was afraid to tell her about his day's work or to discuss the news, the affairs of the world with her, for any innocent remark might plant in her imagination the seed from which, in the course of some lonely day, might spring the most unforeseen and monstrous worries.

They spoke little at supper. There was a constraint between them, a kind of truce; as if, unable to find the way to draw closer together, they remained aloof from each other for fear of quarrelling again. Nevertheless, he was excessively attentive to her before he left the house. He found an attractive programme for her on the radio, arranged the cushions in the armchair, set within her reach on an occasional table a bowl of fruit, her knitting and the newspapers. She did not question him; she had become used to his leaving her without explanation and returning, silent and worn out, after roaming the streets for hours. As he went out he saw her looking after him as if she were trying to remember who he was.

A cold, penetrating rain was falling, but he would not go back indoors. He forced his aching legs into an automatic, sleep-walking rhythm and let the confusion of thought rush in on him. He became only half-aware of his surroundings, so that, when from time to time he bumped into someone or pulled up in the roadway as a lorry roared by, there flooded into his consciousness, in the train of the first muscular shock of fright, a sudden din of street noises as if a loudspeaker had been suddenly turned up, and he perceived all at once the bright hues of dresses, pillar-boxes, delivery vans flaring like coloured fire through the grey rain, and the reflections of traffic lights flashing swords of ruby and green against the dark, wet sheen of the pavements.

The awareness of time and of fatigue receded from him. Dusk filtered dismally into the rain-mist and thickened into darkness. High overhead, suspended street lamps came to life like brilliant pearls in the gloom. Drops of rain crawled icily on his skin. He tried to wipe them away, but they left a tickling sensation, and his hand, when he put it back in his pocket, was wet. More raindrops stung his face. His coat was heavy with rain and his sodden trousers chilled his legs; yet within his clothes his body was damp with an unbearable fever heat. Discomfort dragged him back into the world, and he hated the world. He felt lost in the street, and in time, and in life. He was in Bishopsgate, and he was too tired to go on. Down-and-outs skulked against the walls, bundles of hair and rags and lice stirring in the darkness; he hated and feared them. A couple of workmen waited, stamping their feet, in a bus shelter. They looked drab and downtrodden, but he hated them because they stamped on the earth as if they owned it while he stole through the darkness like a shadow, as much an outcast as the aged wrecks scratching themselves against the walls.

He boarded a trolley-bus and took a seat near the rear platform. He sat with his head turned away from the other passengers, staring at the dark streets that rushed past the rain-jewelled window, his forehead touching the cold glass, his body settled inertly in the upholstery like a wet sack, his hands in the pockets of his raincoat. From the upper deck he heard drunken voices raised in a rowdy and discordant song. It seemed to release a current of fellowship among the other passengers who exchanged smiles and chatter and a twitter of laughter. He shut himself off from the cheerful noise behind a wall of disgust and self-pity. His consciousness seized on the rushing sound of the bus wheels on the wet roadway, magnifying it inside his head, letting it act as a narcotic. He uttered a loud, harsh sigh and relaxed into a pretence of sleep, his head lolling back and his legs stretched across the gangway.

His body lurched across the seat as the vehicle came to a stop. There was a clatter of footsteps and shadows darkened the red glare beneath his closed eyelids. The bus was at a halt; he realised that people were trying to pass him. He felt someone stumble against his foot. He fought the instinct that would have made him draw his legs back and lay unmoving, barring the way, quivering with anger inside his clothes.

''Ere, mind your legs, chum.'

He did not move.

'Leave 'im alone, Bert.' It was a woman's tolerant voice. ''E's 'appy. I wish I was.'

They stepped over him and as they left the bus he heard the man's voice, remotely, from the street, 'Can't 'old their beer, these youngsters. A sniff o' the barmaid's apron and they're on the floor. No wonder the country's goin' to the dogs.'

The bus was moving again. A woman's voice was coming from the platform. He opened his eyes. An elderly working woman, brawny and big-bosomed, with a red, merry face, was standing at the centre of a pyramid of bags and parcels. She stowed most of them on the platform and grasped the last two, puffing and grunting as she tried to heave them into the compartment in front of her. Mark sat up, wanting to help her. Then he imagined her as one of his enemies and thought, 'To hell with her!' Shame overcame him, and he was about to take the bags from her when the conductor came clattering down the stairs, swooped nimbly past her, and seized the bags. ''Ere y'are, Ma. Service with a smile.'

The woman came and sat next to Mark, breathing heavily. 'Thanks, boy.' She wiped her forehead with a handkerchief. 'Phew! I must o' been barmy tryin' to drag this lot 'ome on a night like this.'

The conductor, a young lad, was leaning against the doorway of the compartment checking his tickets.

'On late turn, boy?' she asked him.

'Too true. Be glad when I get my shoes off tonight.'

'Ah,' she said, 'My boy's on the buses, too. Rotten job. Not worth the money, it ain't.'

'Oh, I dunno. It'll do me. Better than the job I had for the last few years.'

'Wha's 'at, boy?'

'Soldiering.'

'Ah, my boy, too. Well, aircrew 'e was. Ain't you ever thought of goin' in for driving?'

Despite himself, Mark found himself listening to their conversation, envying their capacity to enter into easy, friendly talk, hating them for ignoring his presence.

'Yes,' the conductor was saying, 'I'd like to have a go at that.'

'Or you could be an inspector,' said the woman. 'That's all right. That's cushy, that is.'

'Nah. Not me. Reportin' blokes! I saw enough o' that in the war. Give the other bloke a chance, that's me!'

Yes, jeered Mark silently, give the other bloke a chance! That's a laugh!

The woman was speaking again. 'I dunno, mate. My boy's like that, too. But I tell 'im, that's all very well, you got to think o' yourself in this world, never mind the other feller.'

As if convinced by her own words that it was time to make herself comfortable, she leaned expansively back in her seat, edging up and pushing against Mark. He moved, out of habit, then — fiercely and with anger — resisted her, sitting tight and jamming his elbow against her side. Not this time, he thought. She turned towards him. Now, he thought, now the hate will pour from her. He flinched physically as she began to speak; the second before the whip falls is the worst.

'Lord love us,' she said, 'you aren' 'alf wet, mate. Catch your death, you will. Your feet must be soaked.' Mark sagged away from her, stripped of his self-pity, inarticulate.

'You give yourself a rub down when you get 'ome,' she went on, ''Ave a good 'ot drink. Nasty weather, this. Can't be too careful, you can't. I keep telling my boy. Don't you try and be clever, I say to 'im, just because it says May in the calendar. You look after yourself.'

She went on talking, spreading her warmth about Mark and the conductor as if they were both her sons. Mark could think of little to say when it fell to him to speak. He was too numbed mentally to think. He grinned shyly at her. He had seen his own mother, on many occasions, rush fiercely out of the house to chase away some small boy who was playing on her doorstep; she would end by chatting amiably with the boy and offering him an apple, or a cake, or some cherries; and the boy would grin shyly at her, as if he could not summon the courage either to speak to her or to run away. That was how he felt now.

The bus slowed down: another stop.

'Well,' the woman heaved herself to her feet. 'Good night, mate,' she said to Mark. 'Good night,' to the conductor.

Mark watched her lower herself toilsomely to the pavement and stand in the rain while the conductor passed her bags to her one by one.

The bus was starting off again when Mark, on a sudden impulse, darted past the conductor and jumped off. 'Here,' he said. She was still standing in the drizzle, as if daunted by her burden. 'Let me help.' He took the two heaviest bags from her, leaving her with only some small parcels to carry. 'There, that's better. Which way do we go?'

'Did you get off specially to 'elp me?' she asked wonderingly. 'You shouldn' a done that, boy.'

'That's all right,' Mark lied. 'I was getting off next stop, anyway.'

They trudged through a maze of back streets, while she told him of her daughter's approaching wedding — the reason for all the parcels — her son's adventures on the buses, the ages and fortunes of her other children, her husband's state of health, her opinion of present-day food prices; with the same directness she asked him if he was married, whether he had any children, and a host of other questions. 'I'm glad my girl's getting settled,' she said. 'She's a good girl, but she's full of spirits — got too much love in 'er to be single and safe. She'll be all right now she's got a decent feller. I was the same,' she confided. 'When I was eighteen, I had to be in by ten every night, and my old man come out looking for me if I wasn't. Lucky for me 'e did, too, many a time.' She sighed, 'I was a good-looker in those days, I was.' She went on to talk with the same frankness of her married life, her early difficulties with her husband, the hardships she had endured. Mark listened in fascination; it made him happy to be bound to another human being by such confidences. If only — he thought — if only he could unlock his tongue and pour out all his own troubles as easily. He felt complete trust in this stranger; it seemed to him, in her presence, that confession would ease him and bring clarity of mind. But he could not persuade himself to speak.

They came to a bombed site. To right and left tall houses loomed like black cliffs in the gloom, and behind, the rounded end of a block of flats towered, in a faint glow of light, like the prow of a liner at moorings. The edges of the open ground looked like a yesterday's battlefield: craters, puddles, fluttering paper, heaps of rubble and a litter of rusty iron; but in the middle, a group of prefabricated dwellings stood, neat and white, all of them mute except one from whose yellow-lit windows leaked dance music.

The woman paused at the gate of one of these houses. 'Here we are,' she said. The rain had stopped, and the air was sweet with the scent of flowers. Mark peered at the little garden in front of the house. White irises glimmered in the pale darkness; and in the centre of a smooth, rain-glittering lawn, a mass of scarlet tulips reared, sleek and proud, in a diamond-shaped bed. The garden was like a little monument to the patience, persistence and instinct for beauty of the human race.

The woman stood with her hand on the wet gate. 'It's nice, ain't it?'

Mark murmured, 'It's beautiful.'

'Considering we 'ad to start all over again after the war.' She looked at the pathetic little hutch of asbestos and sheet metal, with its spotlessly-curtained windows. 'It's not what we're used to. Everything went in the war. Thirty years it took us to get a home together, and it all went in a night. Still, you don't want much, do you, to be happy? This' — she indicated the house — 'and this' — she pointed to the garden — 'and you're all right. So long as they leave you alone.'

On her doorstep, she urged him to come in. 'Don't be shy, boy. There's only the old man inside. Let me make you a cup o' tea. Warm you up, it will.' Mark hesitated for a moment; he wanted to accept, to talk more with her; there was something in this house that he was seeking. But his shyness overcame him. He mumbled a refusal, bade her good night and left.

He was cold and wet, and his legs were stiff with fatigue. He had to find his way back to the main road through dark and narrow streets, and after that there was still a mile to walk in the intermittent rain. He was not depressed, however; the encounter had cheered him, although he suspected that somehow he might have missed the chance of deliverance. A strange feeling of confusion and wonderment had fallen upon him and as he walked, trying to fathom it, his step was brisk and cheerful.

6

At eleven o'clock on Friday morning Ruth was sprawled on the settee in the front room trying in vain to rest for an hour. She had a lunch appointment with her old friend, Dolly Chancellor. The occasion, the first break in the monotonous round which had governed her life for months, had aroused in her a tremulous excitement, a sensation of enchantment which she had not felt since, as a child, she had looked forward each year to her summer holiday. She was determined not to set out too early, but it was an agony to wait. A tickle of impatience ran between her shoulder blades, and although she shut her eyes and tried to relax among the cushions, her breathing was laboured and self-conscious, and she could hear her heart thudding inside her breast as if it were frantically measuring off the seconds for her.

How triumphantly she had said goodbye, a few months before, to the girls at the office — frightened but joyful, knowing herself to be envied. And what a grey, drear disillusionment her life since then had been; every day the shopping and the housework, the worry of having to make do on what Mark alone earned, without her wages to help any more, the long hours during which she was left alone with sickness, depression and her own frightening fantasies, the visits — recently begun — to the pre-natal clinic. For relaxation? An occasional book, when she was not too tired to trudge to the Public Library, visits from her mother and her mother-in-law or afternoons spent visiting them, an occasional telephone call to Dolly or to one of her other old workmates, a visit to the cinema with one of the younger women among her neighbours.

There were few of the women in the street whose company she was able to enjoy; not because she was snobbish (although, when she looked at the grimy, miserable little houses and her drab, defeated neighbours, she remembered with longing the freedom and comparative comfort of her girlhood and felt that she had suffered a come-down), but because, looking at these big, cowlike women dragging their laden shopping bags past her window, she would wonder with a flash of terror whether she was not looking upon her own future.

She forced herself to believe that Mark would prosper. But what if he did not? A year slipped by, and another, and another, and he was still saying, 'All I need is a start.' Each time he explained another venture to her she wrung from herself a fierce, pathetic faith in him; but in the lonely days that followed, there would come disappointment, sometimes bitterness. Would there be another year wasted, and another, and another, and still no start? Would hope and ambition fade until even disappointment died and there was only lethargic acceptance, a work-broken middle age, a train of defeated years to live out until it was time to die? That was the future she saw in the faces of these women, each of whom spoke, when she was in conversation with them, with the same weary pride of the vanished glories of their youth — the holidays, the fine clothes, the jobs, the ambitions, the suitors — and with the same resignation of their present burdens.

They were kindly enough, except when weariness and exasperation provoked them to screeching quarrels. A dozen of them would cluster round a pram on the pavement, each woman crowing and beaming as if the child were her own. Ruth, as an expectant mother, was greeted by every woman who met her with embarrassing solicitude and eager advice; and she was often visited by women whom she hardly knew, with gifts of eggs or lard or bottles of milk — 'I had it to spare, ducks, and I said to my hubby, well, Mrs. Strong across the road could do with it.' But their interests were so pitifully narrow! They could only speak of children, of prices, of which grocer or which butcher they preferred. The world beyond their doorsteps was a vast darkness in which moved terrifying shadows; of all the world-wide traffic of human affairs only muffled and distorted echoes reached them, rousing in them wild hopes, and ludicrous fears which were reflected in the lunatic rumours that circulated among them.

"This here infantile paralysis,' one woman would fret. 'They say it's all these Displaced Persons are the cause, bringing over their dirty ways.'

Or: 'They reckon the Russians are gonna come over an' bomb us. Eh? When? I dunno. It says so in the papers. It breaks your 'eart, don' it? Did you 'ear them planes goin' over last night? I stayed awake for hours — I didn't know what to expect! You don't know, do you, these days?'

Now they were all talking about what might happen on Sunday. Not only were the organisers of the meeting active everywhere, but a rival party had appeared in the borough to organise a counter-demonstration. The walls were smothered with the clamant posters of both sides. There was no relief for the eye anywhere: even on the ground, sprawled in huge letters of chalk or whitewash beneath the feet of the shopping crowds and the wheels of the day's traffic, were the rival slogans, all beginning with the same: 'Clear out...' 'Smash...' 'Fight...' 'Unite against...' — words that hurt like barbs in the minds of tired people. There was no refuge even in the home, for loudspeaker vans toured the streets all day, setting up a racket that echoed from wall to wall and penetrated clamorously into every room. Ruth could hear one now, quacking ominously somewhere in the distance, a constant, nerve-racking background to her thoughts.

After a week of suspense, Ruth was as overwrought as any of them. Indeed, the helplessness and ignorance that she saw among the other women scared her all the more because she felt the same blight taking hold of her. After a few months at home she seemed, despite all her efforts to pull herself together, to be perpetually bemused, unable to grapple with any problem that demanded clear thinking, abandoned more and more to the sway of her emotions, alternating between hysteria and tired indifference. Often, when she tried to discipline herself into reading an intelligent novel, she would fall asleep. At the cinema she sought only to be drugged for an hour or two by visions of wealth and beauty. She found it impossible to concentrate when she looked at the newspapers and sometimes lay on the settee for hours doing nothing but stare at the travel advertisements, evoking with pain and delight her old girlhood dreams of blue seas, golden beaches, white-topped, blue mountain ranges rising from the clouds, crying gulls and the reedy music of flutes.

She lay with her eyes closed, but there was no rest for her this morning. The impatience seethed inside her, and from the street the living world flung jagged splinters of noise to tear holes in the walls of her solitude. Two women went by, excitedly exchanging gossip, each trying to outshriek the other. From the front garden of a house opposite she heard the screams of a child, frantic, lacerating, persisting with an incredible vigour; and the mother's voice, coarse and unhappy: 'Go in! Go in! Go in!' The woman kept repeating the same words, over and over again, in the same monotonous voice, wanting to tame the child like an animal instead of striking it or dragging it into the house. 'Go in! Go in! Get inside!' — endlessly, until Ruth wanted to open her eyes and stand up and hammer at the window, herself shrieking to the woman to stop. Further along the street another child could be heard, giving voice to a ceaseless and obstinate moaning, like a cat in the night. She wanted her own child to be the embodiment of love and beauty. She would finger the fluffy, spotless baby clothes, the garments whose silky, gleaming softness seemed to radiate joy and purity, and would feel in her breast a warmth and tranquillity as real as if the baby were already in her arms. But the distant howling that rang in her ears seemed to her to be charged with a misery and violence that no child should experience, and she shivered with panic at the thought that she might grow into the likeness of these mothers who could not help venting their own unhappiness upon their children. Fear, insecurity, strain were everywhere; were in the air that her child would breathe from the moment of its first feeble cry. She checked herself. This was one subject on which she was determined not to be despondent. Once let herself become heartsick, and the remainder of her pregnancy, as well as its climax, would become an ordeal almost beyond bearing instead of a source of hope. Her child was the clue to the future. It seemed to her (as if millions of other babies had not been coming into the world through all the years of wrath and terror) that the addition of this one tiny, helpless being to the human race must surely induce the God whom she quietly and privately worshipped to bestow on the earth the mercy He had for so long withheld. Life must become better — nothing else would bear thinking of.

And perhaps, when her child was born, the days of her loneliness would come to an end and Mark would be drawn to her again, out of his isolation. Perhaps he would become once more the Mark she had married, youthful and brave, not the man who had been cast down from the heights to which he had soared. He had come back to her with a burden of bitterness, the nature of which she could only dimly comprehend, and which therefore frightened her. Even worse was her awareness that she was unable to help. Each time she looked at Mark, her love and anguish for him grew; but her impatience with him also grew. How long could she bear this conflict within her? How could she preserve their marriage? She thought passionately of their child as the answer.

Into her soliloquy there intruded the scent of lilac. She became conscious again of the external world, of the sunlight, of the birds richly shrilling, of the trees whose foliage was a filigree of green leaves, golden light and black shadow. It was nearly midday. She could slip the leash of duty at last, and escape from this imprisoning room. Filled with joy and excitement, she washed, tidied her hair, rummaged in her handbag — yes, she had plenty of small change, and the five pound notes so painfully saved and waiting to be banked might at least be used to impress her friend with her prosperity — made sure that she had a clean handkerchief and the front door key, closed the front door with a bang that set her heart racing exultantly, and hurried up the street.

She arrived punctually at one o'clock at the restaurant in Frith Street which Dolly had suggested. One of the reasons for the immense admiration in which she held Dolly was her friend's impressive acquaintance with a host of 'little places' at which to eat and shops at which to get the best bargains. Mark and Ruth never ventured beyond the Corner House, a sham Chinese restaurant and an equally counterfeit Spanish restaurant; they were afraid of 'getting caught'.

She saw Dolly sitting at a table and felt a hot surge of delight at the eager and unsimulated smile of pleasure with which her friend greeted her. Dolly was small and slim, with fair hair and smooth pink cheeks; she looked a schoolgirl, although she was two years older than Ruth. She rose and came forward with quick and excited movements, a tennis-playing hoyden.

'Darling.' She pressed Ruth's hand. 'How are you? Fattening up nicely? You don't show it, do you? It's your coat — clever girl! Isn't it a wonderful day? Radiant. I felt as if I could sing in the street. You're a bit pale, you know. I've sent the waiter man for some sherry. That'll put some colour into your cheeks. What a lovely handbag! Now *do* sit down, and I'll shut up and let *you* get a word in edgeways.' She flopped into a chair. 'Phew! Can I talk!'

Ruth giggled gleefully. 'Oh, Dolly, you don't change a bit. I'm fine. You shouldn't have ordered that sherry. I don't think I ought to. Not in my condition.'

Dolly mimicked her. 'Not in *my* condition. Oh, dear, you are a pet. All you needed then was a Victorian blush. My dear, my own two brats are the most beautiful creatures in the world, and I've never said "No" to a drink in my life. I went to a party only two months before I had Brenda, and Roy said that after seeing how I carried on he wouldn't be surprised if I gave birth to a bottle.'

'How are Roy and the children?'

'Oh, everyone's grand. Roy's still with the firm, of course. They've given him a department now — Trade Deliveries — you know, where that dirty old man Walker used to creep about. We've put Brian to school — he's nearly seven — it's a lovely place, beautiful surroundings and *ever* so progressive, and we bring him home every week-end. Brenda's two and a half — she's not at all feminine — her chief occupation seems to be tearing the house apart. She's lovely. Roy says she has the most hellish right hook he's ever encountered in a long career of amateur boxing.'

The waiter arrived with the sherry. Ruth looked at the glasses in dismay. She had not imagined they would be so large.

'You must come down one weekend,' said Dolly. 'Try and squeeze it in before you pop the little papoose. There's a very good train service to North Dorking — we'll meet you there with the car. Well' — she raised her glass and beamed lovingly at Ruth — 'what do you want, dear, a boy or a girl?'

Ruth said shyly, 'A girl.'

'Ah, well, here's to pink ribbons.'

Ruth felt the warmth of the sherry spread through her, increasing the tingling sensation of freedom and happiness that made it difficult for her to sit still.

'How's Mark, dear? I suppose he's got over that awful time he had in hospital. Time heals, dear, doesn't it? It all seems like a bad dream now, those days.' Dolly broke off, turned to the hovering waiter and ordered expertly. 'It wasn't too bad for Roy. He didn't have a lot of it. The Petroleum Board tried to keep him out. Important man, my old Roy. I don't know who bullied him more to stay, me or his chief. I didn't half get bitchy. It was no use, though, off he went and became a sailor and grew a lovely beard. I can still feel the tickle. I used to get the wind up, though, while he was away. Do you know, I haven't seen Mark since the war. I can still remember him in that uniform of his. You and your handsome pilot!'

Ruth felt a flash of relief that Dolly could not see Mark as he was now, sallow and civilian; then pain, at the memory suddenly revived of the man he had been; and a slow flush of shame at the treachery of her first reaction. 'He's in publishing,' she said doggedly. 'He's doing quite well. Well' — she lost courage suddenly and became a little incoherent — 'as well as can — you know — these days. We're still living in the same place. It's not a very good district, but you have to hang on to what you've got nowadays. Anyway, we couldn't think of moving till the baby's born.'

'Yes,' murmured Dolly. With her head on one side, she looked at Ruth with a kindly, searching anxiety. Then she smiled brightly. 'Dig into that soup, old pet; it gets cold quickly. Do you want to see a flick this afternoon, or sit in a park and jaw, or do you feel up to doing a bit of shopping with me?'

They decided to shop. When they had finished their lunch Dolly paid the bill, skilfully overcoming Ruth's protests. As they walked out into the sunlit street Ruth experienced a moment's dizziness. The sherry, the excitement, above all the subtle intoxicant of laughter, were having their effect in the afternoon heat.

They had a wonderful afternoon. They walked the length of Regent Street and explored Oxford Street. Ruth did not feel in the least tired. She loved the crowds. 'Where do they all come from?' she murmured, as if she had never seen them before. She rejoiced in the bustle, the chatter, the fragments of conversation overheard, the street cries, the cacophony of traffic. There were barrows laden with fruit at every corner, hawkers with dancing dolls, and a whole pageant of people, funny, exotic, frightening, glamorous, at whom to stare. She seized Dolly's arm and squealed like a delighted child when they passed an Indian clad in a jacket of bright yellow silk, white silken tights and a huge white turban, with a furry white beard framing his dark face from ear to ear. Dolly's comments, always gay, sometimes scandalous, kept her laughing till she ached inside.

The huge stores were like temples and palaces, with their frontages of white stone or immaculate, polished bronze, their flowered canopies and their stately but deferential commissionaires. Their windows offered glimpses of a dozen new worlds of enchantment. Behind the gleaming glass could be seen elegantly furnished rooms, beautiful carpets, visions of what life might be. In one shop window blue seas lapped a beach on which sprawled waxen beauties, hypnotic in their immobility, haunting their gay sun-suits, sheltered by huge rainbow parasols from the white glare of arc lights. In another, a single hat was enthroned in isolation on a classical pedestal, amid draped fabrics. In another, crystal bottles of scent were cunningly arranged. There were smart costumes, flowered, light dresses that breathed coolness and refinement, jewellery in nests of velvet, and sleek furs.

Dolly bought lavishly, stocking her bag with books, toys, bath salts, plastic crockery, as triumphantly as if she had won them at a fair. In Selfridge's she bought Ruth a pair of cream coral ear-rings. 'Your colour exactly, dear. They just set off that glossy black hair of yours. Stephens' Blue-Black I always call it.' Looking at herself in a mirror, Ruth felt magically transformed by the ear-rings. This was how she wanted Mark to see her. Her cheeks were flushed and she was young again, frantic with energy, beside herself with pleasure. She scurried to another counter and bought a lipstick for Dolly.

They had tea and pastries in an old-fashioned restaurant that was like an enormous museum of gentility, with red carpet, gilt-framed mirrors, fragile white chairs and whispering old ladies. Ruth sat in solemn silence, abashed by the murmuring quietness of the place. She wondered why everything seemed so remote from her, why there was such a soft, mad feeling inside her, why the chair seemed so strangely buoyant and the floor beneath her feet as insubstantial as a cloud. Even Dolly's voice — dear, sweet Dolly's voice — came echoing from far away. A waitress was looming over her, as disapproving and severely clad as a governess. She stared at the chalky-white face that swayed above hers and fumbled pointlessly in her handbag. She puzzled to think what her fingers were doing, then realised that she was looking for money to pay the bill. There was a cold little shock: all her small change was gone. Guiltily, but not without pride, she took one of the notes that lay between the pages of her Savings Bank book and put it on the plate.

They were standing on the pavement rapt in worship of a hat in a shop window. It was an entrancing hat, a straw boater adorned with flowers and a frothy veil. Ruth stood in a daze of fascination, held not only by the hat but by the reflections which flitted in the window's sheen, above all by the shadowy image of Dolly's face which hovered there. She was tiring; her legs ached already. A feeling of sadness, a desire to find easement by confessing all her troubles to Dolly, warred with the blissful silliness to which the afternoon's excitements had reduced her and which still provoked, in another part of her being, a contrary desire to boast to Dolly, to lie childishly about her life with Mark.

'It would just do you, wouldn't it?' said Dolly.

'Me? Don't be silly. I've got nothing to go with it.'

'You can lengthen a dress. You know, you won't always be pregnant.'

'It wouldn't suit me.' Ruth blushed. 'I'm not slim enough.'

'Oh, tommy rot. You come in and try it on, pet. You don't have to buy.'

'Me?' protested Ruth. 'I wouldn't dare walk out of the shop without buying.'

'Leave it to me, old pussy cat. I've got enough cheek for two.'

Facing the tall mirror inside the shop, with the assistant at her elbow, Ruth saw herself — hat, dark hair, oval, creamy face — with a thrill of approval. If only Mark could see her! Fuddled by the electric lights, which seemed to move and multiply before her eyes, she groped behind her for a chair and sat down heavily. How sleepy she felt! Perhaps this was what she needed — to become glamorous again in Mark's eyes. The women's magazines were always full of homilies to wives, particularly to expectant mothers: 'Don't Let Yourself Go.'

'How much is it?'

Instead of being appalled, she was filled with a reckless determination when the assistant replied, 'Three pounds fifteen, madam.'

Astonished, she heard herself whispering to Dolly, 'I'm going to get it', and then, terrified by the sound of her own voice, but unable to check herself. 'Mark gave me some money to buy myself a present. He's like that. He's a dear.'

As if in a dream, she paid the money over, faintly aware of the numbness in her finger-tips as she counted out the notes and of the frightened obstinacy that possessed her. The air she breathed was like ice in her throat.

'What's done is done,' she told herself as she left the shop. Her legs were trembling. Dolly was suggesting another drink before they parted. She was too dazed and terrified to refuse. In the chromium-glittering bar she mumbled something about, 'Nothing strong for me,' and dumbly swallowed the gin-and-orange that Dolly bought her. It came to her vaguely that she might be expected to reciprocate and she ordered another round of drinks, ignoring Dolly's protests. She raised her second glass and said, 'All my love, Dolly, darling!' She felt as if there were a pebble in her mouth when she spoke. She began to laugh, quietly and intensely, with tears glistening in her eyes, her whole body shaking.

'Oh, I say,' said Dolly as they came out into the street again. 'You're tiddly.' She put her arm round Ruth's waist. 'Shall we get you a taxi?' Ruth felt a final pang of fear at the thought of spending her last few shillings, but she was too shy and confused to demur. 'I do feel guilty,' Dolly chattered on. 'You tell Mark it's all old Dolly Chancellor's fault. Tell him I'm a boozy old slut, and a hag, and a harridan, and it was me who led you into evil ways. Pile it on for all you're worth. I won't mind a bit. But for heaven's sake bring him down to see me soon, or he'll go round thinking that for the rest of his life!' Ruth was still laughing.

With miraculous speed, Dolly extracted a cab from the traffic stream and brought it in to the kerb. Ruth climbed in and sprawled across the back seat. Her hat was pushed to one side and her hair disordered. 'Oh, Dolly, Dolly, Dolly,' she said, still gasping with laughter, 'we've had such a wonderful day. Wonderful!'

Dolly, stooping in the doorway of the cab, squeezed her hand. Ruth stopped laughing suddenly. Tears began to stream silently down her face. She cried, 'Dolly, I can't face it any more.'

Dolly came into the cab and put her arms round Ruth. 'Boozer's gloom, darling. You'll soon get over it. Ah, there,' she said as Ruth, sobs shuddering in her breath, shook her head. 'I was only joking. It's this.' She patted Ruth's belly. 'You get so depressed sometimes when you're preg. You just want to cry and cry and cry your miserable heart out, and it's all the worse because you've no idea why. I know all about it, my pet. I've had a basinful.'

'It's not that,' Ruth murmured in a child's voice. 'It's everything. Oh, you don't understand. I haven't told you a thing.'

'Take it easy, old girl.' The taxi-driver was looking back at them questioningly. Dolly said to him, 'Don't you worry, old sport. It's all ticking up on your meter. We won't keep you long. Now, now,' she said to Ruth. 'What is it, pet? Come along. Tell your silly old Dolly.'

Ruth sat up and touched her eyes with her handkerchief. 'I had such a nice time today, Dolly. It took me right out of myself. It was like being a little girl again. I wish I didn't have to go back.'

'Back to what?'

'Back to everything. Everything's all wrong — everything! Everything since the war.'

'I know, dear. I know what you mean.'

'Oh, I thought it would be all right when it was all over. We'd earned a bit of peace and quiet, hadn't we? All that Mark went through, and me living without him all that time. And look what it's like! It's like — oh, it's all like one long miserable night, and never a gleam of daylight. When the war finished, I thought, well, thank heavens for that, we couldn't have stood it much longer. And we're having to go on standing it, and we haven't got any nerves left to face it with. And now they're starting to talk about another one. And everyone seems to be bickering and making it worse for each other. Dolly, I've reached the point where I can't stand another minute of it.'

'I'll tell you a secret,' Dolly whispered, as if comforting a child. 'I feel like that every morning. Not another day, I say to myself. But what the hell, here I am, smiling.'

'Oh, but Mark; You haven't seen Mark. He's changed so much.' She wailed, 'You wouldn't *know* him, Dolly. He goes about eating himself up, and he never says a word to me. I'm out of it. I'm right out of it. I keep calm when I'm at home, and I smile, and I act as if it's all nonsense to worry. I've always thought it was the best thing to do. And I can see him looking at me as if he thinks I haven't a care in the world. Oh, Dolly, he must hate me for it! He must think I've got no sense. He must think I haven't got a feeling in me.'

'They always do. They haven't got much sense themselves.'

'But I don't know how to talk to him. That's the horror. If only I could talk to him! And then I open my mouth, and I say, "Change the electric bulb in the bedroom," or "Let's go to the pictures." And he gives me such a tired look, and I feel absolutely beaten.'

'Darling, it's not just you; it's everyone.'

'But we're different.' After a hesitation, she added: 'We've got all your troubles and a bit more.'

'You — oh, yes, there is that.' Dolly pondered. 'I can't cheer you up with brave words about that. It would be too beastly of me. But look here, Ruth. Make quite sure in your mind how much of what you feel is due to the mess that everyone's in, and how much of it is due to your own troubles. I don't know, dear, but I'm sure it's important. I'm sure that's got something to do with it.'

Ruth replied with a half-convinced nod. 'Yes, but —' She broke out, 'Why don't they leave us alone?'

'*They* don't leave anyone alone. No, really,' Dolly went on before Ruth could speak her resentment. 'I'm not just playing with words. I'm trying to say something serious. I wish I was clever enough to say it. It's just that everyone feels that we're pretty well up against the end of everything. No one knows where the blows are coming from. It's all in the dark. I suppose some feel they must put it all on to someone else. Oh, I wish Roy was here. He talks all about these things. I listen to him for hours.' She puffed out her cheeks and pulled a comical face. 'I shall start boo-hooing myself in a minute. Listen, my lamb. Don't let it get you down. Keep smiling if it kills you.' Tears gleamed for a moment in her eyes. 'Let the rotten, beastly old world go its own way, and you go yours. Many's the time I take the old newspaper out of Roy's hands, when I see that frown on his face, and dump myself on his lap instead.'

Ruth smiled back at her.

'That's better, my love,' Dolly said. 'You take my tip. Two of you can be the whole world if you want to, and slam the door on the rest. And if you've got a kiddie — well, there's nothing else you need to think about, you take it from me. You wait till you've got your own little bundle of trouble. You'll see!' She pressed Ruth to her. 'I love you, old darling. Come soon!'

She spoke to the driver and stepped out of the cab. The door slammed. Dolly, waving, moved slowly backward and was lost in the crowd as the cab slid away from the pavement.

Alone, Ruth sank back into the upholstery and let the alcohol fumes waft her into a state of giddy remoteness from the world. With the release of confession, all the tension had ebbed out of her, and her slack limbs trembled. She laughed continuously, quietly but with little squeaking noises that seemed to be wrenched from her. All the time, tears ran down her cheeks. 'Laughing till I cried,' was her description of this state. It made her feel weak, happy and free.

She sniffled, and mopped the tears across her flushed cheek with her handkerchief as she thought of Dolly's last words to her. She cherished them as if she had been entrusted with a great and dazzling secret. Why not, indeed? Why not shut out the vast and cruel world from Mark's life and her own? They had only to will it. Each could become the other's defence and refuge. Everything within themselves was pure. The poison came from outside. She had only to tell Mark, and alcohol had given her the courage to do that. And so she laughed and cried.

Mark arrived home early from work. The flat was empty. His dinner was on the stove; the kettle had been filled, but the gas was not lit. Never mind! Ruth had told him that she was spending the afternoon with a friend, and he felt virtuous as he lit the gas and put the knives and forks out.

He was looking forward to her return. He had good news for her. His wages and commission this week had totalled ten pounds. To earn this much had cost him many exertions and humiliations, but he was happy. Their living expenses came to six pounds a week; they would have four pounds to put in the bank. With the five pounds he had already left with Ruth to be banked, it augmented comfortingly the sum they had accumulated to meet the costs of her confinement.

A half-hour passed. He switched on the radio, heard the six o'clock time signal, but paid no attention to the news that followed. He put his meal out on the table and tried to eat, but his appetite had deserted him. Anxiety was crawling in his stomach. He chewed stubbornly, but the meat remained an undiminished lump in his mouth. He tried to swallow, and was sickened. He looked at the clock. It was ten-past six. Only ten minutes since the time signal? It seemed longer than that. He became aware of the radio announcer's voice in the room, and he switched off angrily, as if the announcer had been deliberately trying to harass him. This was getting beyond a joke! She must have been caught in the evening rush hour. What right had she, in her condition, to allow that to happen? Had she no consideration for him, leaving him to get his own dinner after a hard day's work?

He tried to read the evening newspaper, but the print before his eyes was less vivid to him than the images, born of fear and anger, that took shape in his mind. He imagined her mangled in a street accident, or taken ill and rushed to the maternity hospital ahead of her time.

He thought of telephoning the hospital, of going to his parents to see if Ruth was with them, of asking the police to look for her. It was nearly seven o'clock. He walked about the room. He wanted to batter at the walls. How could she treat him like this? What harm could have come to her?

There was the sound of a car drawing up at the gate. He rushed to the window and saw a taxi. Oh, God! What had happened? He was about to run to the street door when Ruth stepped out of the cab. He felt an emptiness of relief for a moment, then resentment flooded into him like air into a vacuum, and astonishment at her appearance. She wore a fantastic hat that had slid over to one side of her head. Her coat was hanging open. Her face was flushed and smudged. He waited, paralysed by a stifling sensation of unbelief. The door opened and she stood before him.

There was a silence. She spoke, in a small voice. 'Hallo.'

He stared at her. The anxiety and the rage that had been fermenting inside him choked him, then forced an exclamation thickly from him: 'Where the hell have you been?'

She teased him with a secret smile. '*You* know!'

She came into the room, walking steadily, but with a faint air of wonderment, as if this were an unexpected achievement. 'Aaaah!' she sighed, putting her head on one side and offering him a loving but fatuous smile. 'I had a lovely day.'

'I bet you did,' he cried, still too astonished to do anything more than stare at her.

She reached the armchair, sat down with a bump and smirked at him. 'I *am* a bit tiddly.' A little giggle escaped from her, on a shrill, rising note. It was cut short as she looked at him wide-eyed, with a dismay that somehow did not seem quite sincere. 'I *am*!' she breathed, in a tone of discovery.

'That — bloody — what's that bloody contraption doing on your head?'

'It's not a contraption. It's a hat.'

'Hat? That?'

'C-A-T — cat; H-A-T — hat. Like it?'

'Where'd you get it?'

She looked guilty. 'I bought it,' she muttered.

A suspicion came to Mark. 'Where's the money?' He turned on her violently. 'Where's the money for the Savings Bank?'

Ruth assumed an expression of comic and exaggerated pensiveness. At length she replied, in an incredulous squeak. 'I spent it.'

A chair went over with a crash. 'Spent it?' Mark shouted. 'Oh, dear God Almighty! I work myself stupid. I lick the boots of every rotten little shopkeeper in London. I bloody well scrimp and save.' He raged about the room. The words burst from him, breathlessly, in little squirts of speech. 'Where are we going to get the money for the hospital bill? And the pram? And the clothes?' He kicked the kitchen door shut as he passed it. 'Why do I waste my bloody breath? What do you care? Spend the money! Rush about! Get drunk! Ruin your health! A lot you care for the baby!' He choked. 'You're not fit to have a baby. My wife!' He swung round and came at her in a great stride, as if to strike her. She had relaxed in the armchair, in an attitude of unconcern. Now she looked at him dolefully, without comprehension, and closed her eyes.

He stood over her, arrested by her utter inaccessibility. For once he could not wound her with his own pain. She opened her eyes, squirmed upright in the chair and said imperiously, 'Come here.' Fascinated, he moved a step closer. She reached up, put her arms about his neck, kissed him slackly on the cheek and mumbled, 'My lovely Mark! Go away.' She lolled back, and a second later was asleep.

He watched her for a few moments, then resumed his pacing about the room. After a while he took a chair and set it down softly in front of Ruth's. His movements were slow and absent-minded. All the time he was staring at Ruth. He sat facing her for a half hour, leaning forward with his hands clasped between his knees. From time to time a shudder of rage leapt up through him and he fought down the urge to shout once more, to seize and shake her. A paroxysm died within him and he knew it was the last. Ruth snored faintly; it was the first time he had ever heard her snore. Her face, which so often recently had appeared slack and ugly in sleep, was placid and innocent. He rose from his chair, perplexed, and went into the kitchen to make tea.

When he came back her eyes were open. She gazed at him like a baby staring at a stranger. 'Oooh,' she said. 'I do feel giddy.'

'I've got a cup of tea for you,' said Mark.

She shivered.

'Go on,' Mark urged. 'I've made it strong.'

She sipped the tea, looking all the time at Mark with a wan and enquiring smile.

'Still cross?'

'No.' He hesitated for a moment. 'Did you have a good time?'

She pouted. 'Looks like it, doesn't it?' She smiled more brightly. 'It was beautiful. I felt so free. Dolly's a dear. Oh, she's so nice. She made me feel so good. We only had a couple of drinks, but I was laughing and talking and walking about in the sun — it must have gone to my head.'

Mark began to say something, but she interrupted him to add, 'Anyway, you were drunk the first time we met. Remember?'

He laughed. 'You weren't drunk today. Don't kid yourself.'

'No,' she said. She thought for a moment. 'I was' — she laid a clenched fist on her breast — 'all bottled up. Something hurt in here.'

Mark looked away. 'I know,' he muttered.

'Is that how you feel?' she whispered.

He nodded. They sat in silence, not looking at each other.

'Mark,' she said, 'we could be happy.'

'Could we?' He faced her with a wry smile. 'How do we start? The two of us get drunk together?'

'Don't mock,' she said obstinately. 'We could make each other happy.'

'How can anyone be happy — nowadays?'

'Of course we can.' Solemnly, like a child repeating a lesson, she told him what Dolly had said to her. 'She's such a lovely girl, Dolly. She looks such a scatterbrain and yet she knows so much. She doesn't have to think about things; she just knows. It's just sort of — courage— that it comes from. She talked about the baby. She said you don't have to worry about the world when you've got your own baby to think about. You can forget all the others and just be happy in your own home. Mark, darling, even if the world was going to come to an end, it wouldn't do to worry. We'd just be wasting the days we had left to us. There's an end to everything, but if you want to be happy, you don't think of it; you ignore it.' She sighed, almost in tears again. 'Listen to me talking!'

Mark squeezed her hand. 'Life's too short for chess, eh?'

'That sounds terribly clever, dear. I bet you got it from a book.'

A memory buzzed and eluded, like a mosquito in his mind. 'I don't know. Maybe.' He sat humbly at her side. 'I wish that was all there was to it. I'm in such a whirl!'

Ruth smiled sidelong at him. She felt a new wisdom quivering in her blood. She put her arms loosely about Mark's neck, and made him comfortable against her shoulder, feeling him relax to the warmth and rhythm of her.

'There,' she breathed. 'That's all there is to it.'

Once again, Sunday: the unaccustomed stillness over the city, the unaccustomed clarity of the sunlight. Lunch was finished. Mark and Ruth were resting before paying their weekly visit to Mark's parents.

'What a lovely day it's been,' Ruth said. 'Breakfast in bed! You weren't even as considerate as that on our honeymoon.'

'I was too shy. Especially in the mornings.'

She laughed. 'Not as I remember it. Tired?'

'No. Why?'

'I thought you might want to stay in and have a sleep this afternoon. It was so late when we went to bed last night. I haven't stayed up talking so long since I was a schoolgirl. Didn't we jaw? It must have been two o'clock by the time we turned the light off.'

'It was nearly three. I heard three o'clock strike a little while after.'

'Did you stay awake? I fell asleep as soon as I shut my eyes.'

'For a little while.' Mark remembered contentedly the mood in which he had lain awake for nearly an hour, dizzy with sleeplessness, the darkness swirling with coloured lights; happy because his wife lay near to him, radiating her warmth and in his care.

'I'll write to Dolly today,' Ruth said. They had agreed last night to visit Dolly the weekend after next. They had also wasted an ecstatically silly hour planning a holiday which they told each other they could manage before the baby came, but which they both knew they would not be able to afford. They had enjoyed the discussion all the more because it was sheer, delicious fantasy. After hours of this, Mark had switched on the light and asked, 'Shall I make a cup of tea?' Ruth had answered, 'Silly, it's the middle of the night.' Mark had turned the light off again and at last, laughing and murmuring 'Good night,' Ruth had fallen asleep.

'It was nice in the park yesterday,' she said. They had spent the afternoon and evening in the park, boating on the lake, strolling among the flower-beds and listening in deck-chairs to the military band. 'I thought it was about the nicest day we'd ever had together. There you were buying ices, and holding my arm, and hovering over me, and putting your coat round me whenever it blew up breezy, even though it was blazing sunshine. I didn't half laugh at you on the quiet, the way you were dancing round me.'

'You shouldn't tell me that. You're puncturing my vanity.'

'I don't care. It'll do you good. Isn't it funny? When you're married, the more you get used to each other the more apart you seem to get. You can only really wake up if you make yourself feel it's starting all over again.'

'That's a profound truth. And now, if you're ready, we'll step out.'

'Are we going to walk there?'

'Through the back streets? No fear! We'll ride down to the Junction and get another bus up from there.'

'Why don't we walk? I'm not an invalid, you know.'

He frowned slightly. 'Never mind why. We'll ride.'

As they walked down the street Ruth sang to herself, smiling blissfully at people who turned to stare at her. Bay windows were open to the sun, each offering a morsel of life to the passer-by: a clatter of tea-cups, a man's voice saying, 'That 'orse wouldn't win if yer put 'im on bleed'n' roller-skates,' a child's shriek of joy and, heard from back gardens, the snapping of shears and the whisper of sprays. Birds quarrelled madly in the ivy. The pale leaves of lime trees stirred in a million changing patterns of light and shadow. Ruth and Mark were both in the mood to be delighted by all the beautiful banalities of a spring afternoon.

On the bus Ruth smiled at the conductor as he clipped the tickets. Everybody was her friend today. The conductor was carrying on a conversation with his only other passenger, an old man with a dirty beard, wearing a thick scarf and a huge mouldy-green ulster overcoat, and carrying a haversack stuffed with newspapers of some kind. 'I ain't a-kiddin' you,' the conductor was saying, 'I've 'eard Sargent. I've 'eard Beecham. But I tell you, there ain't one of 'em to touch this Sabata bloke. It's a treat, the way that man keeps a 'old on 'is orchestra. Talk about a bloody sergeant-major! Tell the difference right away, I can, moment I switch the wireless on.'

'Ah!' said the old man profoundly. He sought for revelation among the tickets that littered the floor. ''Ypnotism.'

'Eh?'

''Ypnotism. 'E 'ypnotises the band. Eyetalian, ain't 'e? They're the ones for that kind o' thing. It's like the evil eye. They can do that, too. This other one, Tosca-something — they reckon 'e can do it, too. Article about it, there is, 'ere.' He pulled out one of his newspapers. '*Psychodynamic Gazette* — that's the paper for an intelligent man. Don' 'alf tell yer some things. Pleasure to sell it, I tell yer.'

'I'll 'ave one o' them,' said the conductor. 'Not that I follow that kind o' thing much. Music's my line. Beethoven. Tchaikovsky. Verdi. They're all the same to me. It's a real pleasure of an evening, to listen-in to a good concert.'

'Ah!' the old man pondered. '*The Messiah*. I like that one.' He turned to Ruth hopefully and offered her a newspaper. ''Ere y'are, lady. The way to banish all yer worries. Telemental Transference. True sympathy between 'uman beings. Look each other in the eye and see each other's problems. We've sent full details to old Stalin and President Truman. Only 'ope for the world. Twopence.'

Ruth said, 'No, thank you,' joyfully.

'There's a concert tonight,' said the conductor, pursuing his own line of thought. 'Mozart's *Jupiter Symphony*. One of old Beethoven's piano concertos. Old Adrian Boult, 'e's conducting. 'E's the bald one. Seven o'clock it is.' He looked at his pocket watch. 'Don't know yet whether I'll get off work in time. We lost five minutes on the last run gettin' through all them crowds in the 'Igh Street.'

'What crowds?' asked the old man.

'That meeting. You know, ol' What's-'is-name an' 'is party. Been in all the papers, it 'as. You should 'ave 'eard the noise when we come by. It looked like trouble all right.'

His words only half-penetrated Ruth's complacent musings. How odd, she thought, that in the last two days she had completely forgotten this thing that had worried her all the week. She looked at Mark, and knew that he had not forgotten it.

'That's why we didn't walk,' he said. 'It's best to keep off the streets on a day like this. As a matter of fact, I wondered before we came out if we oughtn't stay indoors altogether. Still, it's safe enough just going past in a bus.'

'Of course it is!' Ruth was indignant. 'It's only one street corner, isn't it? If a couple of gangs of people want to stand and yell at each other, I don't see why everyone else shouldn't be able to go about their own business. What are the police for, I'd like to know?'

'It's a waste o' time,' said the old man. 'Yer won't settle the world's troubles by bashing each other up. Telemental Transference, that's the only way.'

'You want to look out, though,' the conductor said. 'I been past there already. What with them that's for 'em, and them that's agin 'em, and all the bloody fools that's just gone to 'ave a look, and 'alf the bloody coppers in London, it's a bit of a crush.' The bus drew up at Dalston Junction, and the conductor handed Ruth ceremoniously down on to the pavement. 'Look arter yourself, lady,' he called as she took Mark's arm.

Mark had to hold Ruth close as he escorted her across the road junction into the High Street. There were many more people out than he had expected to see, and their black figures, all hurrying in the same direction, dotted the roadway. Policemen were trying to keep the way clear for wheeled traffic, but their efforts were in vain, and a block was already forming.

They boarded a bus going northwards, glad to be out of the crush. It was only half a mile to Khartoum Road, and the meeting-place lay halfway along their route; but they realised already that it would take more than the usual couple of minutes for them to be safely past it. The bus moved slowly for a few yards, then came to a standstill behind a line of other vehicles. Ahead of them, the throng of people thickened into the fringes of a crowd into whose depths the traffic was immovably wedged. Mounted policemen rode ahead, the crowd parted and the bus moved on a little, only to stop again.

By now the bus was in the thick of the crowd. The passengers looked out through the windows, impatient and nervous, yet feeling safely detached by their elevation and by their isolation behind sheets of glass. There was no coherence about the scene they saw framed in the windows. The meeting was out of sight, and might well have been out of mind as far as all these crowds were concerned, for there was no sign of any purpose in the currents of movement that surged among them and no signs of partisanship — or of any enthusiasm or passion whatever — in their behaviour. Thousands of faces were vacant except for a vague, greedy curiosity. Deeper into the crowd eddies of confusion were visible as those who had pressed their way in, their faces already uplifted in alarm as if they felt themselves being sucked into a gigantic funnel, met those who had passed the point of panic and were trying to push their way out.

Whatever inclinations or prejudices had brought these people together (and from the vapid excitement of those still on the fringes of the crowd it could be sensed that the majority had been attracted by nothing more than the desire to have their nerves stimulated by the sight of crisis and violence) were being pressed out of them as, losing control of their own movements, they were crushed closer and closer together. Hundreds of people who obviously wanted only to get past and go their different ways were pushing vigorously along, keeping close to the boarded-up shop-fronts and exchanging abuse with those who barred their way. Even inside the bus, behind the shield of glass which muted all the noises of the crowd into a vague, general babble, it could be felt that the mob was on the boil, with nerves fraying, tempers rising and the undercurrent of panic growing more powerful. The red, sweating faces of policemen, which could be seen here and there, betrayed — in place of their customary calm — a black, scared anger of this great beast of a crowd that had to be kept under control. The tall buildings that rose on both sides added to the impression of confinement, as if the people who rolled on in a compressed mass, all unwilling, but all carrying each other forward, were beasts pouring between stockade walls into an abattoir. The brilliant sunlight dazed them and made the whole scene more frightening and unreal. The heat turned them into itchy, sweating, maddened animals shoving and shouting at each other. The noise beat at their ears and dulled their minds. None of them knew what was going on.

In fits and starts, the bus crept through the crowds. At last it was level with the street-corner on which the meeting was being held. Here, at the core of the crowds, were gathered the few hundred partisans of rival causes whose animosities had attracted the curious multitude to this place. There was shouting and counter-shouting going on among them, and some of them were fighting. The crowd around shrank back from them, leaving a space in which a confused movement of policemen went on. Those behind the front ranks of the spectators were loud with interrogative clamour. Groups formed everywhere to exchange and debate rumours.

The voice of the speaker could be heard now, through amplifiers, a deafening, quacking noise that reverberated from one high wall to another. The words were indistinguishable, but words were not needed in this atmosphere. People had not come to hear words. The bull's bellow of defiance that came from the loudspeakers, the shrieks and shouts of the crowd: these, the language of modern politics, acted directly on the nerves.

The babble of shouting grew in competition with the tireless voice. Groups of people were chanting slogans, each inaudible except as a tom-tom rhythm. It was not the words but the rhythms with which the slogan-shouters were exciting themselves and others. From one quarter of the crowd a song welled up, unexpectedly loud and harmonious; a few demonstrators had begun to sing a parody of a popular song and the spectators, innocently and absurdly, had taken up the tune and were singing the original instead of the parody, as cheerfully as if they were whiling away the time before a football match. The song rose up and died away among the dizzying confluence of noises.

There was more fighting at the heart of the crowd. The foremost spectators were trying to keep clear of it, and their fear sent blind shudders of movement rippling back through the crowd. The bus was at a standstill again, and Mark, faintly alarmed by the situation and repelled by the stupid and beastly spectacle, put his arm round Ruth's shoulders. As he did so he saw a surge of movement by the crowd, not a deliberate pressure, but a blind wave of curiosity and panic, break up the line of policemen that held it back, and the policemen were swept apart. They struggled with the groups of people that mobbed them, no longer the organised masters of the crowd, but frightened individuals hitting out in self-defence at all around them.

Individual shouts and screams began to break out of the uniform din. Pulse-beats of savagery and fear seemed to be radiating outwards through all the thousands of tightly-pressed bodies. The figures of mounted police could be seen bobbing among the sea of heads, and those fleeing from them, trying to thrust a way to safety, made the crush and confusion worse.

A man, in flight from two others, leapt up on to the rear platform of the bus. Ruth cried, 'Oh, Mark!' The pursuers pulled their quarry down, and the three disappeared in a struggling heap behind the bus. The mounted police, in an extended line, were drawing nearer. Their batons were still sheathed, but the tossing heads of their horses seemed to scatter fear among the crowds. In the midst of the panic, little fights were going on everywhere. Who the combatants were, why they were fighting, how foe recognised foe, no one could tell. A young man stood at bay in a shop doorway, his legs braced wide apart, dark hair rumpled, blood streaming from his nose. Three other young men circled him warily, crouching like wolves, their eyes on the leather belt he kept wrapped round one clenched fist with the sun gleaming on its silver buckle. Another man stood over a prostrate body, kicking it with vindictive regularity, ignoring the crowd that streamed past him and the approaching police. These mysterious combats, in which it seemed that the participants were not fighting for or against anything, but merely for something to hit out at, added to the dreamlike fascination which the whole scene had for those on the bus.

The mounted police were now only about fifty yards from the bus. The crowd, recoiling before them, seemed to surge up and break over the stationary vehicle like a great wave. People swept past in a torrential blur of faces, their shouts and screams pouring out in a cataract of noise. Some, seeking refuge, jumped on to the bus, hastily finding seats or running up to the top deck. In a few moments the bus was crammed full. The heat in the compartment, and the smell of crowding, terrified people, were unbearable. A woman came running from the police, arms upflung, mouth wide open in a scream. Her face seemed all mouth. She stumbled and disappeared in the onrush. Ruth screamed. Mark, trying to fend off the press of people in the gangway, said, 'It's all right, dear. We'll soon be out of it,' but he was desperately afraid for her. They were trapped on the bus. They dared not descend. The horses were so near that the passengers on the bus could see their eyes, bulging and panic-stricken, seeming to mirror all the gathered fear of the swarming crowds.

The bus was full, and the conductor was trying to keep more people from clambering on. He was swept out of the way. The passengers shouted at the newcomers and tried to repel them. Mark held on with both hands to the steel gangway posts and forced his body forward to prevent the weight of struggling people from pressing against Ruth. 'My wife,' he was shouting. 'For God's sake don't push; you'll hurt my wife!' He cried to Ruth to keep close against the window. In the street missiles were flying. From the rear of the compartment came the crash of breaking glass and the hysterical screaming of a woman. Two men crushed together in the gangway were cursing each other and exchanging blows, each of them shouting the same, 'Stop pushing,' and 'Leave us alone!' Fighting was breeding fighting among people who had no reason to fight, the beginnings of it all forgotten somewhere at the core of these scattering crowds. Ruth, whitefaced, was shaking violently and murmuring, 'Oh, God! Oh, God!'

Two mounted police managed to take up positions in front of the bus, turned their horses' heads to clear a path and parted the crowd before them. The driver, one window of his compartment broken, hunched over his controls and the bus moved forward at last. It bore with it a clinging cluster of people hanging on to the rear platform, some of them being dragged along the ground. The conductor was striking with his metal ticket-punch at clinging hands, toppling the intruders off the bus. The vehicle was crawling forward steadily now. Mark gasped to Ruth,

'We're nearly out of it!' In response to the conductor's appeals, a policeman jumped aboard and began to clear people off the rear platform. A man resisted and the policeman, beyond patience, smashed his rolled cape across the man's face, then flung him down into the roadway, where other policemen picked him up and threw him like a sack into the back of a prison van. The struggle on the platform sent a last heave of panic along the gangway and Mark, forced under by the weight upon him, was crushed back upon Ruth. He shouted incoherently and at last pushed the other people off.

At last the gangway was clear. The seated passengers, trembling and dishevelled, were chattering and gesticulating at each other, uttering broken, childish complaints. Handfuls of people still came running past the bus, but the thick of the crowd was left behind, and the escorting policemen turned and rode off. Ruth lay huddled against the window, moaning, her eyes shut. Mark tried to raise her up. She whimpered, 'Leave me alone! Oh, God, oh, God, oh, God!'

He said, helplessly, 'Ruth, what's the matter?'

Without opening her eyes she muttered through clenched teeth, 'Quick, quick, quick!'

Mark shouted, 'Stop the bus! For God's sake, stop the bus. Get an ambulance!'

Nobody understood until a woman, leaning forward from the seat behind, called the conductor urgently. Ambulances were racing to and fro in the street, their bells clanging. In a few moments the conductor had stopped one of them and Ruth was lifted into it.

8

'I should go home now, if I were you, Mr. Strong, and get some rest yourself,' the Matron said. 'Your wife is sleeping comfortably now, and she is not to be disturbed. Come back in the morning. It'll be outside visiting hours, but as soon as the doctor's seen her, and unless he rules it out, we shall let you have a few minutes with her.' She had a firm, clear voice and she looked at Mark levelly to show that, although she felt sympathetic, she could not be budged.

Her voice, to Mark, sounded muffled and remote. A strange chaos of vague thoughts and unbidden memories was alive inside him, protected from intrusion by an insulating wall of incomprehension. It was hard for words to penetrate.

'Your wife is quite comfortable,' the Matron repeated. 'There is no danger at all, and there's nothing for you to worry about. You heard the doctor — there was no internal injury. It was only shock that brought on the miscarriage.'

He heard her without feeling, for he was empty, after the hours of waiting, the first incredulous bewilderment, the slow torments of impatience, the bouts of rage, the spells of dizzy physical weakness. The Matron, her voice kindly but insistent as a drill, was hammering words through the wall of numbness. He felt anger against her and resisted it. He reminded himself of how kind she had been to him. Had she not brought him a cup of tea while he was waiting to see the doctor? But he wanted to be left alone. He wanted to shout at her, 'Oh, shut up!'

He had taken the baby for granted. He had thought of it less as a living entity than as an embodied hope, for himself and Ruth to share. And now that it was gone...

'You really must get some rest yourself,' the Matron was saying. He stared at the cosily-covered desk-lamp and the cosily-curtained windows. It was dark outside. How many hours had passed since he had walked, in a dream, up the hospital steps behind the stretcher? The darkness, seen through the window, sprinkled with tiny bright lights, was vast and inviting. He wanted to escape into it, away from everything human. Everything human was hateful.

'You've had a trying time, too. You must look after yourself.' The doctor had also told him that, the little man standing in the corridor brusquely lecturing him about his wife's condition. 'Shock... no haemorrhage... very lucky... soon get over it... might happen to any woman... often does.... We've put her to sleep for the night... you can see her tomorrow... the main thing is to help her over the shock of it... she'll be mortally frightened of trying again... yes, of course she'll be able to have children... that's the main thing, to try again very soon... mustn't give her time to dwell on it... give her another one to think about instead.... You'll have to convince her... you must....' The doctor had hurried away, for ambulances were arriving all the time and the casualty ward was full of injured people.

Talk, talk, talk! How they were battering at him with talk! Some kind of unformulated protest, against what he did not know, was gathering force within him. He wanted to be left alone, so that his feelings might grow and break free and give him peace. 'Mr. Strong' — the Matron spoke more sharply — 'do please try to listen.' There was a prickling, painful feeling at the back of his eyes. There were tears there: for the child, for Ruth or for himself? He did not know. The Matron's words awoke him, and he felt the first complete realisation of loss, a wrench of pain like the touch of a steel blade against exposed nerves.

'Mr. Strong,' she said gently, 'Will you do me a favour?'

Mark raised his eyes stupidly.

She had put a couple of white tablets into an envelope. 'Take these before you go to bed tonight. They'll make you sleep.'

He muttered his thanks.

The Matron opened the door to show him out, and as they stepped into the corridor the policeman who had been waiting on the bench outside, his helmet on his knees, rose and smiled timidly at Mark. He asked, 'Can I get you a cab, or anything?' Mark thanked him and said that he would like to walk. The sound of their feet, echoing from the stone floor of the corridor, and the glare from the electric bulbs, made him giddy. They came to glass doors. The Matron opened the door, squeezed his hand, smiled compassionately and said, 'Rest. You must rest.' The swing doors *whoof*-ed behind him with finality, and he walked down the steps into the darkness of the street, the policeman at his side.

The policeman said, 'It's a fine night.'

Mark answered, 'Yes,' and suddenly he was grateful for the trivial token of human solidarity.

'Shall I walk with you?'

Mark explained that he would rather like to be alone for a while.

'Sure you'll be all right?' The policeman waited for a moment, received Mark's silence without offence and said good night. He walked away, his footsteps still expressing disquiet.

Mark, too, began to walk. He sank into an apathy which was as welcome as sleep. Walking, he could escape from both thought and feeling. There was the movement to drain off the suspense that had gathered for hours past. There was the cool breeze to comfort and to whisper, like a woman, among the trees. There was the hypnotic effect of rhythmic limbs, of shoes smacking on the pavement, and of the traffic lights winking gaily and pointlessly in the empty streets. There was the murmur of distant aero-engines.

It was too soon that habit led him to his own front door. He wanted to walk on past the gate: to reject all the terrors, all the burden of future living that waited to crowd in upon him in the stuffy darkness of his flat; to walk quietly away through the cool night, into nothingness. If only this street might go on and on, an empty path through the darkness leading to an end, a clear, unanswerable end of everything, from which he could step off into the chasms of space, or vanish into dark, gleaming waters! But the streets were a maze, cruel and insoluble, walled in by tall and indifferent houses from whose blank, black walls an occasional lighted window gleamed like the eye of a sleeper opened sardonically. Let him walk and walk, the streets would bring him back to this gate. A great burden of fatigue weighed upon his shoulders. The noises of the night withdrew and the door in front of him went out of focus. He braced his legs and checked the giddiness. His throat was parched; it felt as if it were full of a hot, congealing grit. He longed for cool water, to drink and to pour over his burning face. He longed to topple into cushions, shut his eyes and let himself go limp. It was hard to put the key in the lock; his fingers were as unresponsive to his will as muscleless rubber. He entered the house.

The dark hall was full of shadows, vague patches of intensity that moved about him in the gloom like spectres intent on dissolving his mind into dizziness again. A crack of yellow light showed along the edge of a door at the rear of the hall, and he heard the voices of the couple who lived in the downstairs flat. He was puzzled by something. He swayed, and leaned back against the street door as he tried to steady his brain and find what it was. Then he realised: it was the cheerfulness of the voices, their unawareness that the world had stopped spinning. There was a first little flare of rage inside him. What was the matter with them? Didn't they know that — that —? A church clock began to strike and the even, echoing notes of the bell came stealing across the moonlit housetops, into the dark hallway. But there was someone else who didn't know; or why would the clock be striking as if nothing had happened? He counted the strokes of the bell, until the thick silence rushed in again behind the eleventh. A door slammed at the rear of the house next door. He jerked forward as if it had collided with his body. A key squeaked rustily and clicked in its lock. People were going to bed.

He climbed the stairs slowly, pulling himself up by the banisters. His heart fluttered madly, as if he were climbing a mountain. It was hard to breathe steadily. His throat closed. He felt sick. He hurriedly let himself into the flat and switched on the electric light. The sudden yellow dazzle in his eyes finished him. Everything in the room broke up in front of his eyes, the moving fragments melted, and a long billow seemed to roll along the floor like a wave moving silently to the shore. He lurched into

203

the kitchen and retched over the sink. The spasms tore fierily at his throat, but only saliva dripped from his slack lips. The vain effort brought tears streaming from his eyes. He saw himself, with disgust, in the mirror above the sink. How stupid, ugly and inadequate his grief was! What an insult to its object! He drank some cold water, but the taste in his mouth befouled it, and he was sick again. He drank once more, and sluiced water over his face.

The back of his head began to hurt, and he went into the bedroom to escape from the sickening electric light. He lay down. It was hot and close, and he sweated. He closed his eyes, but his clenched, tingling muscles would not relax; the heat pressed down on him, the pillow became damp and irritated him in turn with its clamminess. He allowed himself to imagine that it was still last night, that Ruth lay near him, that today had not happened. It was not a hallucination, but a conscious device to lull the thoughts and emotions that were fighting inside him. Without turning his head or opening his eyes, he groped over the bed with his hand and gently took hold of the cool, smooth edge of the quilt; he persuaded himself that it was a hand clasped in his own.

Loud voices trampled the hot, velvet silence of the night. Gross laughter sounded in the street. A car door slammed and an engine started up. He sat up, expelling his breath in a harsh animal noise of anger and despair. What childishness! What self-deception! To be clutching a piece of silk in his sweating hand as he tried to drown in dream! He jumped to his feet, unbuttoned his shirt to the waist and flung the window open. The city was not asleep. It was awake, alive, mocking him. From out of the soft, continuous roar that had passed for silence in his accustomed ears, he now disentangled a hundred different noises: a cataract of distant laughter, a discord of drunken singing from some back street, the rush and rattle of a train, the murmur of lovers in a porch across the road, the clatter of a dustbin lid, a voice raised far away in anger, the beckoning, lingering boom of ships' sirens from the river. Out there were the swarming, separate lives that had flowed together into a mob and unknowingly murdered his child. They — his mind took hold of the word and repeated it rhythmically, monotonously, in time with the beats of pain that surged along his scar — they did not know; they did not care; they could converge into sweating, heaving crowds; they could inflict on others the same catastrophe that each of them feared, and scatter again, unpunished, into this protecting darkness. Who were they? Where were they — the guilty ones who did not know their guilt? Out there. They were mocking him from out there!

A voice began to bray from the darkness, *Mister What-you-call-it, what you doin' to-night?* — a nervous twitch translated into music. He flung away from the window, but the wireless waves went on radiating through the hot darkness and the muffled, relentless voice continued to invade the room with the same stupid words and the same spasmodic refrain, *Mister-what-you-call-it, what you doin' to-night? Mister What-you-call-it, what you doin' to-night?* Aaah! He struck at his own body with clenched fists. The world was laughing at him and he could not hit back.

He roamed from room to room, wiping the sweat from his face with his bare hand. At every step he found something to pull him up with a stab of memory. Here was Ruth's apron flung across the back of a chair. She must have been in a hurry, not to have folded it as she usually did. Here was her silly, beautiful new hat, nestling on the dressing-table beneath its veil and its heaped, vivid flowers. Pinned over the mantelpiece was a piece of paper with the telephone number of the maternity hospital at which they had booked a bed for Ruth. 'You never know,' he had said. 'We ought to keep it handy.' And she had laughed — he could hear her laughing—and answered, 'Silly, there's heaps of time yet.'

It was unbearable.

There was no outlet; that was the horror of it; no way in which he could unburden himself of the conflicting emotions that struggled within him; nothing but thunderous pain in his old wound.

He groaned aloud at the pain in his head. He wondered, fleetingly, why the wound had come to life after all these years. He tried to think clearly, but all that his mind could do was to present to him in mockery all the dreams that he and Ruth had shared, the dreams that today had killed. The child would have vanquished the sense of defeat that had oppressed him. The child would have dispelled the tensions, the despair, that had filled him since the war. The child would miraculously have ended the dull, drifting separateness which he and Ruth had not known how to bridge. The child was to have been the future. The future was dead. The future had been snatched away from before his eyes. There was no future. Until now the fantasies he had built up around his child, extravagant though they were, had been pleasant, gentle, a dreamed escape from his problems. Tonight they were monstrous, obsessive, goading him to the final nervous breaking-point towards which all the years had been slowly pressing him.

'Aaah!' This time, in the soft, protracted groan, there gleamed an edge of ferocity. He was torn by two opposing desires; the one, to seek for himself a relief from all the unanswerable questions, all the insoluble problems that piled themselves mountain-high before him as he contemplated them, to find repose in self-obliteration; the other, to hit back at the besieging world, to destroy the destroyers, to find consolation for his own suffering by heaping suffering on others. It was not so much outright revenge he wanted as to tower over some other human being, no matter whom, and to strike, and strike, and strike, shouting, 'Now cringe! Now grieve! Now cry! Now feel as I feel!' until his knotted muscles relaxed, and his mind and body were sated.

He shrank back from the edge of madness, appalled by what he had glimpsed. He relaxed into despair. There was no hope. A doom hung over the human race. Beneath its shadow men stampeded, lashed out blindly to protect themselves, and in doing so destroyed each other. They were doomed to destroy each other. And Ruth, and he, and his kind, they were marked out as the first, the universal sacrifice. 'Whoever else escapes,' he thought, 'we shall not.'

There was no hope. In the wake of despair, a great rage stormed through him, a convulsion of fury such as he had never known in his life; he was tortured physically by the effort to contain it. Pain rained its blows upon his head and goaded his body, so that he felt as if his own self had become a beast that he had snared, wrestling against the control of his reason. He shook from head to foot.

He went into the bedroom and knelt in front of the dressing-table. With numbed, fumbling fingers he opened a drawer and took out a small, cheap suitcase. His hair was glistening with sweat and the moisture ran in beads down his face, but he made no effort to wipe it away. He opened the case. He laid aside his Air Force tunic, with its row of coloured ribbons. For a moment he thought of putting it on and looking at himself in the mirror, to delight once more in the smooth blue cloth sitting sleekly on his shoulders. Savagely he thrust the childishness aside. He shuffled through some photographs. He knelt for a long time looking at one, of himself and Bones sprawling on the grass in front of a Hurricane, with a Sealyham terrier begging to Bones on its hind legs. That was — he let himself remember — that was in August, 1940. A gentler mood of nostalgia invaded him, and he felt once more the summer heat of those remote, dreamlike days, heard the rumble of engines, smelt the hot grass and the exhaust fumes. For a moment, as he felt the hot moisture in the corner of his eyes, he thought that he was going to weep. Then his mood changed. He was filled with the conviction that somewhere, on some other plane of existence, Bones was alive and waiting for him: Bones, yes, and his child, and all the others who had faded one after another and left him unarmed to face the world. It was not the other world of the clergymen that he believed in at this moment; rather it seemed that they lived somewhere in a real world, and he was stranded in a limbo of unreality; they were awake while he dreamed; they had escaped, he had still to find the way to follow.

Now he found what he was looking for; the Luger — the sleek and deadly automatic pistol. He picked it up, and the chill of the steel in his hot hand at once calmed and elated him. The unexpected weight of it made him steady his muscles. His grip closed round the butt and as the hand assumed a position that had once been familiar to it, the once-familiar impulses flowed back along the nerves, and a host of habits, movements, reflexes that had commanded his body in the days when his life had depended on their speed and precision, awoke in him once more. The mind was drugged, but the body functioned with a new steadiness; it had a gun in its hand.

He had one clip of cartridges. He slammed it into the pistol, taking satisfaction in the resistance of the spring and its yielding beneath the strength of his fingers. He had not done this for years, yet his movements were more sure than when, an hour earlier, he had fumbled to put the key in the lock. The rubbery weakness had gone from his hands; he could feel the blood throbbing in every one of his fingertips.

He rose and slipped on his raincoat — it was the same coat that he had brought back from the Air Force. He dropped the pistol into a pocket and felt the drag of its weight. He started for the door, then paused, paralysed by a sudden indecision. His intelligence reared up in a last attempt to assert itself. Where are you going? it asked. Who are you going to destroy? Yourself or your destroyers? Are you going to escape or are you going to fight?

The breath rattled in his throat. Whatever the answer, he had to escape from this flat. He went out, feeling no pang, thinking no farewell, although he was convinced that — go where he might, and whatever might become of him — he would never return.

He ran down into the street. The movement and the fresh air brought a superficial calm that belied the inner turmoil. Reason lay stunned and bound, but his madness — like a rebel army that improvises its own command and its lines of communication — had established its own processes of thought.

The dilemma that had faced him was solved. The two alternatives had become a single course of action. He would seek out his enemies and challenge them, and in so doing would accomplish his own destruction. This resolve did not appear, coherently, in his mind; but it had invaded his deeper consciousness and taken command of his being. He was like the soldier who, weary beyond endurance of fighting, rises up from his trench and goes stumbling out towards the enemy, shouting murder, yearning to vent his misery upon others, but longing, equally, for their bullets to come and put an end to his despair; a man in a trance of hatred.

But who — he paused, his hand grasping the butt of the gun in his pocket — who were his enemies? Where were they? How was he to seek them out?

9

He set off on his search.

Surely, tonight, he would find *them*. *They* were always about him. From the earliest days of childhood when he had first been able to have his own dealings with the world around him, the invisible siege had surrounded him. He had not known the whip, the Ghetto, the boycott, the gas chamber; but there had always been the hardening glance, the knowing and derisive look, the smile of contempt quickly suppressed, the embarrassed silence hastily broken, the child's insult, the adult's innuendo, the unspoken exclusion; for him, and for those before him for two thousand years, so that he roamed tonight, gun in hand, a creature all brain and emotion inflamed, one great raw wound on legs.

Who were *they*? Where were *they*? They had always been present. How could *they* elude him tonight? But the streets lay silent and deserted, the shadows gathering between the houses in a deeper darkness than that which lay, star-sprinkled and milkily luminous, upon the rooftops. Only the street lamps, here and there, cast blurred patches of pallor upon the dark walls and pavements.

They were hiding from him. *Their* laughter lurked behind brick walls and drawn blinds. The heat, the darkness, the silence itself seemed to be thick with mockery.

God help them! he thought. God help the first one that laughs, the first one that so much as bumps into me! But he walked alone, outcast in the empty streets.

Laughter roused him like the flick of a whip. Giggling, excited voices and the tramping of feet were flung in mingling echoes from wall to wall in the darkness. A gang of boys and girls came into sight, walking arm-in-arm across the pavement from wall to kerb. The girls wore long evening gowns. They were coming home from a dance. As they approached he caught the note of pleasure in the babble of their voices, and saw the lights of innocence and happiness that gleamed, even in the darkness, in the girls' eyes. There was no room to pass on the pavement. He put his head down and walked straight at the middle of them. The pistol butt was not cold in his hand any longer; it was wet with sweat. His finger was on the trigger, feeling its tension already. They swooped towards him, laughing and unaware. They were in the mood to joke with him, to encircle the stranger and dance round him, arms linked. In his pocket, the muzzle of the gun came up at stomach level. He plunged straight on at them. His eyes were smarting, full of sweat. He could not see them as human beings. They were blurred, leaping shadows barring his way. The nearer they came the less distinct they were, thickening black shadows, white faces, gleaming eyes. The pain in his head was as rhythmic as a bass drum. He was close to them now — four feet, three feet — his muscles were clenched and ready. They parted and swirled aside. He went straight on, head down, through their midst. There was empty pavement in front of him and his finger relaxed on the trigger. None of them made any remark. None of them even cast a curious glance back at the wild and haggard young man who strode away along the street with his head down and his hands deep in the pockets of his Air Force raincoat, leaning forward as if he were butting against a gale. They were all too absorbed in their own happiness.

He would make his mark: this was his obsession. He would stop *their* laughter, make *them* fear him, respect him. Respect! There was the secret of his lost hope. He compared himself with the blinded Samson, crouching between the pillars in Gaza, another man besieged by darkness and a clamour of mocking noises, another man whose muscles had contracted in angry strength, bringing the temple crashing down about him, ending the torment, destroying the tormenters: a man who had made his mark upon the world for evermore. Now, at last, he understood the men of whose deeds he had read in the past two years, during the Palestine struggles, with loathing and repudiation, the tailors and the pedlars and the mild Talmudic students who, tormented into terrorism, had prowled like beasts among the dark alleys of Jerusalem.

A shadow separated itself from the darkness of a doorway and ponderous footsteps resounded in the night. A policeman was crossing the road towards him. To halt him? To ask his business? To see what he gripped in his pocket? The policeman lumbered past with a nod and a friendly 'Good night.'

Mark did not know how long he wandered, or where, in the murmurous night. His clothes were sticking to him. His trousers chafed his hot, wet legs and maddened him. What unconscious volition guided his feet he did not know, or by what route it made them take him; but at length he found himself standing, with a vague sensation of surprise and yet a flickering suspicion that this was fated, before a gateway in a quiet side street, with a big ugly building of red brick looming in front of him. A host of memories and associations invaded his numbed mind. New and conflicting emotions assailed him. The old repulsion fought with a strange sense of sanctuary. This was the place from which, twice in his life, he had fled: the Willoughby Row Synagogue.

Someone was speaking to him. He only half-heard the voice. He turned and saw, standing in the shrubbery by the gateway, a young man of medium height. He stared at the pudgy, glistening face and the rimless spectacles. Of course... memory revived and the mind began to function... the sentry. This was the task he had refused to share. The young man, a very worthy and respectable-looking young man, carried a club — as if he was afraid of it, Mark thought contemptuously.

He went in. The sound of the gravel crunching under his shoes brought pictures flashing into his mind: himself, a child, picking up pebbles and putting them into his pocket (there was something big and hard and heavy in his pocket now: a gun, yes, a gun). He had run out again, terrified, into the street.

He was surprised to hear himself talking, in what seemed normal tones, with the young man. Snatches of meaning seeped into his mind as the other man yattered at him in a eunuch's voice. 'Good of you... short-handed... would like to go home for an hour.... Will you watch? … Get you a relief.... Mat'a-fac', coupla chaps due now....' Emptily, Mark

210

heard himself answering, 'Yes... yes... of course.... That's all right... I understand....'

The young man talked incessantly. He insisted on explaining all the details. Impatience crawled over Mark's skin. That was the porter's lodge? Right. He could rest in there? Right. He could see the gate from there? Right. He flinched as the young man made some feeble joke about 'jus' like the war... jolly ol' guardroom, eh?' Squeaky laughter from the young man. Gas ring in there? Right. 'Have a nice cuppa tea, later on, eh?' Squeak-squeak. Right. Any trouble, raise the alarm. Yes. Telephone police. No violence, mind. We don't want violence. Call the police. All right, all right!

What a strange, feeble creature, Mark thought contemptuously. How fat and yet how curiously insubstantial! Without confidence or integrity, and therefore without solid being. What would he do if he saw the gun? Faint? Screech? Titter hysterically? Call the police? Call an ambulance? No violence, mind. No violence, remember. We don't want violence. He noticed for the first time that the creature was wearing plus fours, and for the first time in twelve hours he laughed aloud. The fat white face stared. Its mouth was wide open. Mark ignored it; he was groping for the vanished moment of relief that the laughter had brought. Too late! Nor could he make himself laugh again.

At last he was alone, standing in the gateway, watching the young man scuttle away down the street.

He felt now the weight of his own reluctance, which had been struggling in the background of his consciousness to find expression; but it was too late now; he was committed; he was on his own. He looked up at the red brick building with hostility. What on earth was he doing here? Perhaps some obscure instinct, the need to seek a fold, had brought him here. If so, he was not aware of it. His presence in this place awoke in him, as it always had, a sense of embarrassment amounting to physical discomfort. What kept him here was the hope that here he might make a rendezvous with his enemies. They had been here before: he prayed that they might come again. He leaned against the red brick gatepost. The partial relief brought a first ache of fatigue to his body. He wanted to rest his feet. He let his head droop forward and a comforting lethargy pervaded him. The frenzy began to ebb from him. The tickle of urgency had gone from his muscles. The pain in his head was subdued; only a steady throb remained, like a pulse of purpose, along his scar. Thus he waited, resting like a soldier with the tired mind asleep but the senses alert like sentinels. He sought no longer, but let the night and its noises flow past him; and when a breeze stirred out of the humid darkness, to touch his cheeks with cool and timid fingers, he was passively grateful.

The yellow stare of headlamps roused him. The car whirred past. He watched the red tail-light dully until it was gone. He sank back into his torpor. Footsteps echoed and faded from another street. Somebody had a fit of coughing. The beat of aero-engines grew louder; the bomber squadrons were manoeuvring every night now. A church clock struck one. The night flowed on, lulling him with its heat into a drowsy disregard of time, soothing him with an occasional puff of breeze. Again he heard footsteps: the heavy clattering of hobnailed boots. They grew louder. He forced his eyelids open and stretched his muscles inside his clothes. Two men were coming down the street, bobbing up and down as they walked, out of step. They looked strangely black and bulky in the distance. They came nearer. One of them was swinging something at his side; some kind of heavy implement. Mark's body was alert, his imagination in a panic. His heart thumped with alarm. He moved back into the shelter of the laurel bushes, his hand once more on the butt of the pistol. There was uncertainty in the men's footsteps, as if they were looking for something. Their pace slowed. He saw their faces now, beneath black, peaked caps. They stopped at the gate and he held his breath.

One of the men spoke. 'This is it.'

The other man turned a broad, bulldog face towards the building. 'Don't look much like a church.'

'With their bloody money,' said the first man, lifting a thin pale face to examine the building again, 'you'd think they'd do better than this. Look at some of them old chapels, though. Like bloody tool-sheds, they are.' He pointed up at a signboard. 'This is it, all right. Look at that bloody writing up there.'

His companion studied the Hebrew text. 'Looks more like bloody birds' footprints to me,' he declared.

Mark waited, trembling. They walked in through the gates. He gripped the gun, but irresolutely. A moment ago he had thought he was face to face with *them* at last. Now a faint bewilderment was stirring within him. He could not understand their relaxed bearing, their curiosity, their loud and careless conversation. They had not the air of conspirators.

He challenged them, forcing the words harshly from his throat with an effort. 'What d'you want?' He stepped out of the bushes.

'Whew!' exclaimed the thin man. 'Ol' jack-in-the-box!'

'This is the Jews' church?' asked the burly man. His voice matched his face; it was like a growl gathering in the chest of a bulldog.

Mark held the gun ready in his pocket. 'What d'you want?' He saw now what had given them their bulky appearance; their old-fashioned, square-cut suits of thick navy serge. They wore soft, narrow caps with shiny black peaks. His mind, trying frantically to function normally, gave him the answer: railwaymen.

'Eh?' said the thin man. His voice, in contrast to that of his companion, was like the thin yelp of an impudent mongrel. 'You know! This sentry lark! This is the place, ain' it?'

'What's that?' Mark pointed at the object that the thin man held.

'This? The ol' jack-handle. Orf the ol' van. Don't compare with a rifle-butt. Still, it'll do to put the baby to bed with.' He swung it suggestively.

'Are you —?' Mark became inarticulate as a new confusion seized him. 'Do you —?'

'Weren't you expectin' us? Our union secretary said 'e'd sent all the names down. Some of our chaps was down 'ere last night.'

Mark struggled to shape words. None came. Then he asked, violently. 'What are you doing this for?'

'Eh?' The question seemed to have startled the thin railwayman. 'Well,' his countenance brightened, 'well, I mean — why not?'

'Do you mean to say you're doing this for people — for people you —?'

'Got nothin' agen 'em,' said the thin man defensively.

'Got no love for 'em, neither,' growled the burly man.

'I tell yer,' said the thin man; 'do it for anyone. I mean to say. All this business. People going daft. Setting fire to other people's churches. All these people getting knocked about in the streets. 'Ospital's full of 'em. It's in the papers. Thirty or forty of 'em. Never 'ad nothing to do with it, most of 'em, I'll bet you anything. Coming to something, ain' it, eh? Can't walk out on a Sunday afternoon without getting bashed up. Talk about law and order! The world's getting more like a bloody madhouse every day. What I reckon is, if the likes of us don't step in with a bit of our kind of law and order, the whole blooming world'll be fighting before you know where you are, and it'll be all U.P. with everyone. So here we are. I mean to say —' He stopped suddenly, as if he had said too much.

His companion had been gathering himself for a fresh effort. At last he delivered his verdict, with the ponderous certainty of a whole jury rolled into one. 'Fair's fair,' he rumbled, 'ain' it, mate?'

There was an embarrassed silence.

The thin man had been looking in through the door of the porter's lodge. ''Ere,' he said violently. 'You got a kettle an' a gas ring in there. You go in an' make some char. We'll take over on the gate for a bit.'

'Go on,' urged the railwayman. 'You can do with it. You don' 'alf look done in. Look as if you seen a brace of bleed'n' ghosts, you do.'

The burly man fumbled in his pockets, and his bulk lessened as he brought out two parcels. ''Ere y'are. Tea. Sugar. Tin o' milk. Char's the stuff. Eh, mate?'

Mark's hands were numb. He could not feel the parcels as he grasped them. Beads of sweat were crawling into the corners of his eyes, blurring his vision again. He wanted to be alone for a while, to still the chaos in his mind.

'Thanks,' he mumbled.

'You get that tea on, nob,' said the thin man. He pushed his cap back and wiped a lock of straggling, black hair under the peak.

Mark went into the porter's lodge. Inside the little room the heat was intolerable. He could not fix his attention on any single object. He stood over the gas ring, trying to think clearly. He thought, again and again, of the words which the railwaymen had spoken to him; trivial and fragmentary sentences, yet with overtones which stirred strange depths in him and rippled down into hitherto undisturbed layers of memory. What was it that was coming back to him from far away, muffled, struggling to pierce the mists?

In the night he heard the bombers crawling nearer. The pistol dragged at his pocket, insistently. Longing to be rid of it, planning to drop it down some open drain, he remembered how he had come by it. It was his share of a legacy. The war against violence had stopped, but the violence lived on in the survivors. He knew now whose voice he had heard tonight, through these two workmen. What was it that Bones had said? 'What they don't understand they fear, and fear generates hatred.'

The whole world was ill with fear. The blind surge of the crowd against his wife's body was only a tiny swirl within the vast blind storm whose terrible energies were already stirring across the continents. His child had not been killed by men, but by the fears of men. Ruth had been borne under in a collision of frightened people. It came to him that he

214

and his people, much though they suffered, were not alone in their suffering, but were only one family among the threatened multitudes who inhabited the earth.

He was glad now that he had come back to stand here, defending a shrine of his own people. It had been foolish of him to hate them for the distortions that persecution had worked in their character; short-sighted of him not to see that everyone else was warped, too, in differing ways, by the world's evils; faithless of him not to have known that, freed from deforming pressures, his people could grow to a full human stature, as some of them, who had set up in a land of their own, farmers and fishermen and desert pioneers, were already doing; cowardly of him to try to edge away from them and forget what he was. It had not made him any the more an Englishman, but the less a man.

But if he belonged with his own people, there were others, too, among whom he must claim his place; for Dolly had been wrong about 'shutting the door on the rest.' 'There are plenty of people who aren't frightened,' Bones had said. 'They're the ones I put my money on.'

There were all those whose stoic calm in the face of life's cruelties, whose guardianship of human dignity in their differing ways, kept alive man's hopes of graduating from the animal kingdom: Bones, Davy staying in his blazing Hurricane, the woman at her garden gate, the two working men who were standing outside now. He had met so many of them in his lifetime and he had failed to truly see them. All his life he had wanted to belong. To belong with them was to belong wherever he lived.

He had not shed his despair; but its quality had changed. It was no longer frenzied and befogging, but the resolute despair of the soldier at bay.

His mind was bright and clear, strangely released. For himself, with the vast explosion of human folly gathering in the air, he had no more hope; and with hope, fear had fallen away, leaving him free. But this new feeling — this iron despair — was in itself a kind of hope, for it was strength, the strength that can bar the way to fate.

Face to face with a black universal doom, Mark was able to discern in others, and new in himself, the courage, the unselfishness and the will to live that could redeem — perhaps not until after his own passing, on the other side of a long and terrible night — the human future.

Here he was, then, at a point of commencement, when he had thought all the purposeful impetus of his life to he spent.

The aircraft were passing overhead. Their engines shouted down from the night. Answering them, he busied himself with his duties. Now that his mind was clear, he was able to think of the doctor's words, to prepare himself for his meeting with Ruth. She would be frightened; he must give her strength; and helping her would give him strength. 'Try again,' the doctor had said. Well, it was the only thing to do, always.